Change of Heart

Grace Reed

Change of Heart

Book 1 of CHAMPION

Production copyright FurPlanet Productions © 2024

Text Copyright © Grace Reed 2024
Tune-Up © Bibi Heartsglow 2024 used with permission

Cover Artwork © Shapeless Ink 2024

The Korps Universe © Karen King 2024, and used with permission

Published by FurPlanet Productions
Dallas, Texas
www.FurPlanet.com

Print ISBN 978-1-61450-651-5
Electronic ISBN 978-1-61450-652-2

Table of Contents

This book contains depictions of: Transphobia, homophobia, ableism, and various other bigotries, comic book violence, stalking, drug and alcohol use, sex, BDSM dynamics, spousal abuse, child abuse, and gender-based violence.

This book would never have been possible without the support of my partners, friends and readers. Many, many thanks to Karen "Kraken" King especially for creating the Korps setting and being an utter joy to collaborate with, as well as to my dearest friends and found family, the gaggle of gay animals who comprise the Monsterfucker Book Club: Syntax Takes, Bibi Heartsglow, Eight-Stroke, Mabel Ramona, Runa Fjord, and Lexi Reynolds.

Love you all, nerds.

Foreword

By Karen King

Nearly seven thousand years ago, an event shook the world. An arrival of something ancient: the merging of humanity with the world of the beast, the eruption of superpowers, and the proliferation of the supernatural. In modern day, this world appears much like our own, but for the pantheon of species that occupy it, and for the extensive presence of superheroes and supervillains alike. While many states have their own super-powered forces, a vast variety of independent actors exist.

Among the most prominent independent supervillain groups is an organization known as the Korps. As far as most are aware, the Korps is an organization dedicated to world domination, led (in theory) by the shadowy Overlord, a being who has repeatedly shown up since the beginning of recorded history to try and wrap their vicious claws around the neck of the planet.

The truth, of course, is significantly more complex.

Led by high-value superpowered beings, the Korps sees itself as less of a state and more of a governance method, seeking to disintegrate repressive state-based hierarchies, and install systems of governance much more capable at effectively distributing resources to those in need. It sees state actors – "Heroes," police, paramilitaries – mete punishment out on innocents and go unpunished in turn, and knows, for all the cartoonish pretensions of the supering world, that this is the true evil, and it cannot go unchallenged.

Operating a number of satellite companies, most under-the-radar, the Korps is extremely well-equipped technologically and medically, allowing its members to essentially build the body they need from scratch, and permitting this capacity at scale. The Korps knows that inherently top-down monocultures become stagnant without personal expression, which it encourages in its members – a reality at odds with the widespread public perception that its members are simply brainwashed.

13

A notable tool at their disposal are the RCGs, or Rose-Coloured Glasses, a high-capacity HUD, communications tool, and computer-brain interface, so powerful they can be used directly as a VR headset. They can function as an assistive device or therapy tool – but the nature of the technology means they have the power to more directly alter one's thoughts. Alternately viewed with relief, mistrust, or fear by varying parts of the supering world, it is known that wherever they are worn, the Korps is not far behind.

Having emerged in the wake of the Second World War, the Korps has gradually spread its influence, eventually emerging more into the public consciousness in the 1990s, and with increased visibility, and increased emphasis on immediate action, comes more entanglements…

<hr>

The Korps began as a big pile of superhero and supervillain tropes that I'd built up a love of through various types of media, like the James Bond movies. While I originally just threw it together as an action playset of stock characters, over time, it began to morph into something very different. Using pop culture's stock antagonists to take swings at the injustices unfolding around me began to carry more and more emotional weight.

In an era when information became more and more readily available, we were able, at any time of day, to pull out our phones and view some kind of great injustice unfolding, live in front of the world – to see police forces with the budgets and supplies of small national armies crushing peaceful protestors, to watch the deceptions of nations exposed constantly and slip by unpunished, to see the suffering of those in need on our feeds 24/7…

It became increasingly clear to me, and to many, that the status quo is not a state of normalcy, but something imposed by force. Equally, to many, the concept of rallying the villains - those who challenged the status quo - and giving us a context in which we can, in some sense, strike back against it all… It struck a chord among those of my generation. In a world where fighting back seems so hard, an entity like the Korps is something compelling.

I am now sitting here writing the foreword to an actual, published work about it, and my mind is reeling. Giving the Korps as a set of narrative tools to the wider community feels like it's uncorked a flood – a need to right wrongs, a need to highlight injustices, a need to tell intimately personal stories, stories of love, stories of redemption, rushing out onto countless pages from countless perspectives.

All I have ever wanted to do is to help give people a community, and the tools they need to create, and to build the stories they need, and it is an honour and a privilege to introduce this one to you – one of love, one of *breaking free*, one of deep wounds beginning to heal...

– Karen King

CHANGE OF HEART

CHAPTER I

October 4, 2022

The sheep-bear took a sip of her chai latte and checked her reflection in the nearby wall mirror, self-consciously smiling wide and smoothing out a wrinkle in her costume's dusty rose scarf before she clicked to answer the incoming call from the reporter. A video window opened on her laptop's screen to show a petite snowy owl wearing a black tank top, sitting in a cluttered home office.

"Hi there! Glad we could finally connect," the owl said airily. "Call me Frost, they/them. Professional name aside, it's Madison, right?"

"Hi, Frost! I prefer Maddy, actually, and it's she/they for me. Happy to chat! I was so thrilled when your editor got in touch; this'll be my first interview with an actual queer outlet. The TV and the papers always ask the same questions, you know? 'How did you end up following in your father's footsteps?' 'What's it like to be Toronto's first trans superhero?' How am I supposed to answer that? Heck, I don't know, I'm just out here doing the professional Hero thing and living my life." She giggled in what she hoped was an endearing way, but worried might have come off as vapid.

Frost tilted their head sharply, smirking. "Okay! We can start there, sure! I'm sure you've been getting that question a lot, but I have to ask *something*; you get it, right? Your dad was Roger 'Heartwood' Oakes, 'The Pride of Grande Prairie,' a local independent Hero from 1991 until 1998, and then a member of the government-backed Provincial Heroes' League with the Prairie League until his unfortunate passing in 2005. How *do* you think he would feel about where you're at right now in your life? Would he be proud of your career as 'Heartforce'?"

It was a slightly different angle than most interviewers had taken, and Maddy turned the question over in her mind, heart sinking just a bit. She considered, also, the value of being more honest than her usual answers to the cishet interviewers who saw her as a mild curiosity — or a spectacle. They took a deep breath.

"That's… a good question, Frost. I'm sure he'd at least be proud of me for stepping up and wanting to do something good, once I started getting my powers. I don't know how he would have taken the gender stuff, honestly? He was a guy from small-town Alberta. My mom took some time to come around, but now she's a really dedicated ally. So, I'd like to think he could have learned, and grown, and been supportive in his own way too, hopefully?"

"Of course," the owl smiled. "By the way, you know you're not the first trans Hero in town, right?"

The sheep-bear grimaced. "I mean, yes, Sunrise, *technically* she was briefly out before defecting to the Korps…"

"Well, sure, there's her," Frost said. "But that's not even considering folks who were stealth, for all intents and purposes. I did some digging! Not a shock the morning shows didn't, but I am a little bit disappointed the *Star* or the *Globe and Mail* couldn't be bothered. Anyway, I found that there was a street-level superhero who went by 'Roncy Red' operating in the mid-to-late 60s, Polish-Canadian fox guy, minor speedster. He was found dead in a Country Style Donuts bathroom in 1970, of a heart attack." They paused, gesturing vaguely with their hands and looking off into the distance while composing their next words. "…And of course it can always be a little bit problematic to use modern terminology for historical figures, but it turned out he was AFAB and had had top surgery — the reporting in the *Telegram* was *super* gross about it, actually; I'll spare you the details, but I'm sure you can imagine — and definitely lived as a man. Since his name and civilian identity were never known, I don't feel bad about claiming him as transmasc, and the earliest trans Hero in Toronto?"

The Hero perked up. "That's cool? I didn't realize; Ontario's Heroes *told* me I was the first, not counting Sunrise, but I guess they might not have been counting unregistered capes either."

The owl nodded. "Or they might not have a great grasp on queer history generally," they said with a raised eyebrow. "Although given the way they treated Sunrise and distanced themselves from her, that's not surprising. Or consider their *own* history, I mean; when the first Barrage died a few years ago, did you see that it turned out he was a police detective in his secret civilian identity? He even took part in Operation Soap — the bathhouse raids."

Maddy wrinkled their black ursine nose. "That's terrible. I'm glad that's not happening anymore, at least; I mean, I would never want to be on a team that's still *targeting* the community like that."

Frost looked slightly askance at them. "Mmmm. Now, speaking of police and Ontario's Heroes — are you aware of Pride Toronto's decision last week to ban Heroes from attending their events in costume?"

Maddy's heart sank again. "...Wait, what?"

The owl looked to a handwritten notebook at their side and shuffled through some printed pages before finding the right one. "Okay, one sec... here we go. The Annual General Meeting was last week. 85% of members voted to extend the ban on police attendance to include professional Heroes, on the basis that most operate as extensions of the police. Which is true, of course! As an active member of the OH roster, you're legally a provincially-delegated peace officer, and have the same powers as cops to investigate and arrest criminal suspects, in addition to your, uh, talents."

Their eye twitched, and the sheep-bear hoped their outrage wasn't obvious; the Hero took a deep breath before replying. "I... well, that's interesting, and that's the board's call, I suppose? I just think it's *disappointing* to be painted with the same brush as bad cops, just because I'm trying to help people in my own way."

It wasn't as if she was actually a cop herself, she fumed silently, even if she *happened* to be allowed to arrest and detain suspects, under certain circumstances. Or because she had the legal powers to seize evidence, or commandeer civilian property, or... well, she was *better* than the cops, anyway. She'd never cause the harms they did, she was certain.

"Not the board, the membership," Frost corrected, still looking down at the page. "The executive director and several board members spoke against the motion, actually, but the vote was 116-55 in favour."

Maddy grimaced briefly before rallying with a forced smile. "I guess that just means I've got work to do, then! I'm a nonbinary trans lesbian, and I want to show everyone that there's a place at the table for us serving the community. Superpowered queer and trans folks should be able to feel included as Heroes, just like everyone else — if we did, maybe the bad guys would have a harder time recruiting."

"Is it just about recruiting, do you think? Last poll I saw, trust in and support for Heroes, registered superheroes, was still hovering around 30% among all self-identified LGBTQ2+ respondents. The other 70% clearly aren't *all* anarchists and supervillain fans, right? It's a role where you're at least working in parallel with traditional law enforcement, a lot of the time."

"I think," they said, gathering their thoughts and suppressing the urge to huff with irritation, "that Heroes have historically not done a great job protecting *everyone*, and that has an effect on our reputations from those who've been ignored or excluded. That's part of why I'm with OH; like I said, I want to *change* those attitudes."

Frost nodded. "Speaking of which, Ontario's Heroes recently announced that you're their first 'LGBTQ2+ Champion.' Is that a position you wanted? Is that something that's compatible with the other expectations of your job?"

"It wasn't something that I expected, I'll be honest! But I'll tell you the same thing I told Director Hagen when he approached me about it — I'm honoured to be the first in that role and hope I can be a resource for mutual education and respect between OH and the community."

The two chatted on for another half-hour in much the same vein, touching on the Hero's favourite pop culture touchstones (*The Hunger Games* and *American Chopper*); costuming thoughts (the OH tailors had suggested the bold reds and whites of her father's gear, while she'd insisted on subtler shades of maroon and cerise, a concession grudgingly made to her ongoing desire to distance her Heroic persona from Dad's); family (her homemaker/part-time dental clerk mom, varsity athlete little sister, and the grandfather and aunts and uncles and cousins she'd seen much less of in the years since moving to Ontario); and even some teasingly semi-scandalous inquiries about her taste in women (ideally smart, soft, and *forward*). Eventually, the questioning trailed off around the time she finished her latte.

"I think I have what I need for my piece," Frost noted brightly as their eyes scanned up and down their screen. "Is there anything else you'd like to talk about?"

Maddy shook their head with an easy smile. "No, I'm good! It was great chatting with you; really just a breath of fresh air compared to some other outlets," they chuckled.

The owl nodded. "Hey, happy to! I can give you a heads up when it's all ready to post — mind if our social team tags you? It should be up in a week or two, hopefully, once my editor gets through with it."

The sheep-bear enthusiastically agreed, said goodbye, and beamed to herself as she clicked off the video call. *That went well*, she thought, before pondering what to order for dinner.

October 17, 2022

On a Monday morning two weeks after the interview, Maddy stood near the centre of a cavernous hall deep beneath the Mississauga waterfront. Bright lights and corrugated steel panels alternated in a rough dome shape from the walls to the ceiling; the harsh glare concealed which of the clay target throwers and beam emitter cannons embedded in the walls were primed to fire at any given second.

The interview had gone live on the *Xtra* website on Friday. Her initial satisfaction had soured somewhat when it first became the target of the usual right-wing haters, but then, also, bitter criticism from within the queer community for her alleged naïveté and craven centrism; this was a deep, disappointed anger of a type that the previous puff pieces somehow hadn't managed to incite. Unnerved, the Hero had locked down her social media accounts by Saturday morning, which at least spared her *some* degree of dogpiling when the pundits — Canadian and otherwise — began disingenuously parsing her words to write their fiery weekend columns. (There'd also been a handful of vilely transphobic rants about her from British newspapers on Sunday, which made her feel sick to even scan the headlines.) She'd spent the past twenty-four hours trying not to think about it, but repeatedly succumbing to the compulsion to read the comments and check her mentions.

At least while Maddy was only on-call — their standard duty shifts on Mondays and Thursdays — the sheep-bear could distract themself and vent their frustrations by taking advantage of the gym and training facilities in the regional OH command base. Listening to the whirring in the machinery, they gently reached out with tendril-like fields of telekinetic force, probing for the telltale shifts in air pressure that would telegraph—

The program started. She'd cranked the difficulty, and immediately faced a barrage of orange discs hurled at her from a dozen different randomized angles. The sheep-bear flexed her fingers and swept her arms in great arcs behind her, mentally flicking away one projectile after another in a loose motion she always imagined as something like the inverse of fanning an old-fashioned revolver, while focusing her attention on finer detail work to a series of the targets approaching her face. For those, she mentally grasped one in mid-air with a careful, tai chi-like swoop — rolling to dodge the mock beam weapon blasts from the secondary targeting system, just then coming online — and used its own momentum to sling it around her like a discus, smashing it straight through a file of four others.

They panted, beginning to get winded, as they dove backwards. Another fan of beams lightly singed the shards scattered across the polished concrete floor; to evade them, Maddy telekinetically pushed up and back against the ground, bounding up several meters. With a final flourish, they reached out, froze several more of the clay targets in mid-air, evened out their respective altitudes, and let them fall to shatter in unison. The clock ran out, and a buzzer sounded. *"Hostile evasion rate: 100%; target accuracy: 100%,"* droned the scoring audio.

They landed on both feet, hunched in a defensive crouch, closing their eyes and grinning at the hot streak; this was the sixth perfect run of the morning. Suddenly they heard a scuffle behind them and whipped their head around just in time to see a long-tailed brown blur pass by. The next thing they knew, Maddy's knees gave out from underneath them, and they were flat on the floor, laying across a sprinkling of crumbled clay bits.

"Hey, *kid*," the rat said in his faint Maritimer accent, looming over the sheep-bear's prone form despite his slight, slender build. "Gotta watch your six better! You never know who might be sneaking up," he joylessly smirked as he chattered away. "You're stronger than you let on. Why do you stick to an evasive pattern that's all reflexes, no *muscle*? Lemme guess: don't want to look *too* butch, eh? Respect, respect. Anyway, I come bearing news! Bossman wants to see you. Like, *now*."

It was Neal Salton, her team's snickering twerp of an infiltration and stealth specialist, who operated under the callsign "Slider." He irritated

Maddy, not least because he insisted on *always* using they/them pronouns for the sheep-bear, and had lately been calling her things like *buddy* and *friendo* and *pal*, as if he was auditioning for the role of a greasy, second-rate goon in a direct-to-streaming gangster film. She closed her eyes and flexed her wrists slightly, concentrating for just a second until—

Slider yelped angrily as a wave of force exploded several rivets outward with a series of popping noises, pushing a ballistic resin-cast floor plate up from beneath him. It launched him backwards into the rear wall with a faint *thud*. The delicacy of his impact wasn't due to any gentleness in the sheep-bear's flex of their telekinetic powers, but simply as a factor of his ascetically lean build, and the practiced roll they *knew* he'd execute, to bleed off the momentum of what could have otherwise been a bone-shattering impact. "Jesus *fuck*," he snarled into the floor, seething.

Maddy cocked an eyebrow as she picked herself up and ran a hand through her dark hair to shake out the debris. "Yeah, Dad was a heavy; *I'm* not," she snapped, patting off the orange dust streaking her white leather field jacket. As she opened the door to head off for the executive wing, she looked back at the still-groaning rat and scowled. "Thanks for the advice, *Neal*, it was great sparring with you. Next time there's one of those team-building retreats up in North Bay, let's be sure to buddy up for the trust fall thing, huh?"

Ten minutes later, Maddy stood awkwardly in the office of Caleb Hagen — formerly the nigh-bulletproof Hero known as Canadian Shield, and since his retirement from the field years prior, the Queen's Park-appointed head of Ontario's Heroes. The Director was most frequently known amongst his subordinates for his episodes of unhinged rage against OH's perceived nemeses: not just criminals or *organized* supervillains like the Korps, but also Aurora Squadron and Minister Simonds, protestors and activists, civil rights lawyers, and indeed any rival authority figures he felt intruded on *his* turf or bogged down "getting the job done" with rules and regulations.

Maddy didn't care for Hagen, but had to admit that (unlike Slider, for one) he'd at least been… coolly *polite* to them, for the most part, and he said *some* of the right things about having an "inclusive team that truly represents Ontario." Sometimes. Usually when he was on camera at a press conference with his boss, the Solicitor General of Ontario, or with

Lawrence Rockwell, head of the Provincial Heroes' League, or PHL. Like the press event the previous summer, where Maddy had been introduced as a new prospect on the developmental team, or the time earlier that year, when they'd been announced as a fully-fledged Hero with an OH callsign. In private, however, was another story.

It was for that reason that Maddy tried to avoid being alone with the Director. The anger in his eyes — to say nothing of the way he physically dominated spaces with his volatile energy — made the sheep-bear nervous. Being called on the carpet had their heart racing, even before Hagen spoke a word. It was necessary to restrain the impulse to take a defensive stance and begin telekinetically bracing for attacks, despite how fundamentally *absurd* she knew that possibility to be.

The wolverine glared at his subordinate, eyes narrowed. His voice was steely with fury, his claws crabbed around a pencil held to his temple, and he seemed on the verge of exploding before the sheep-bear could say a word. "Heartforce, what in the *fuck* did you think you were doing, taking an interview like that without running it by Comms first?"

Maddy shrank into herself but managed to squeak out a reply. "You — Comms — you and Martha told me I could talk to the media on my own now! We had that meeting last month…"

Hagen squeezed the pencil in his grip, snapping it in half. "The media, yes. Softballs from *Breakfast Television* or *Chatelaine* for Scarborough soccer moms, not…" he enunciated very carefully through gritted teeth, "… *political* shit from *your community's* gossip rags."

"I mean, it's the only real serious queer media outlet left in Canada, I wouldn't call it a gossip rag—"

"I don't care what you call it, Madison. I'm disappointed," he muttered darkly. "Martha's people are doing what they can to head off the more pointed inquiries, and we can probably have this blow over without a press conference, but you're clearly not ready to be off the leash. I refuse to entertain another bloody Sunrise boondoggle; the last time was all I needed, *thank you very fucking much*. We've got to get ahead of this, get you some more face time in action, interviews with the friendly outlets; really *ram* you down the public's throats. Plus, starting Monday, you're leading GTA Team B in operations until I tell you otherwise."

She didn't understand. It might not have been the Guardians of Ontario, the prestigious and historic unit known internally as "Team A," but Task Force TO was still a respected Hero group; being given more responsibility didn't *sound* like a punishment. "…Sir? What about Lightbox? Where's he going?"

"Nowhere." He raised a sullen eyebrow, realizing Maddy's confusion, and sneered with cruel delight. "Oh, did you think this was a promotion? Not a goddamned chance, Oakes. Lightbox will still be giving the orders, *and* keeping an eye on you, from base. We're just going to put on a little show and play-act for the cameras that you're good for something other than the 'diversity' piece. Do you understand me?"

Her eyes watered with shame and embarrassment. "Yes, sir. Whatever you say, sir."

"Good. In the meantime, you have an assignment," he sneered, handing the Hero a standard-issue ruggedized tablet showing a street map. There was a marker downtown, not far from the curving towers of Toronto City Hall. "All the details are there. Break-in at a high-profile biotech firm, police couldn't investigate. Find out what happened, and if there's a risk any dangerous information might have fallen into the wrong hands. This one ought to be *perfect* for you." With that, the Director turned back to his computer, pointedly ignoring his subordinate.

Receiving Hagen's silent message loud and clear, the sheep-bear tightly grasped the device and nodded hesitantly; she hustled out of the office, jaw clenched. It was only once she reached the elevator that Maddy realized the tempered glass tablet screen had splintered and cracked under her hoof-nailed fingers.

Chapter 2

October 17, 2022

The floor number on the elevator's display panel ticked upwards as Maddy ascended the downtown office tower, but they didn't watch it. They were too preoccupied by their phone, again reading comments and replies to the interview. There was a sizeable contingent who believed they'd really stuck it to OH, somehow, and an even larger group who were having fun thinking up ever-more-elaborate synonyms for "pick-me bootlicker."

The Hero grunted, irritated, before stowing the device in her belt pouch. She stepped out to the 21st floor and approached the front desk, where a red squirrel with an undercut sat in front of an improbably large flatscreen display. The receptionist raised a cautious eyebrow and sniffed impatiently.

"Good morning…? Can I help you?"

Maddy recoiled a little, put off by the standoffishness; they smiled nervously and raised a hand to chest level to give a small wave. "Um, hello? I'm Heartforce, with Ontario's Heroes. We heard there was a break-in, and wanted to offer assistance?"

The receptionist squinted, typing something without breaking eye contact with the superhero standing awkwardly in the lobby — or indeed making any kind of facial expression whatsoever. "Someone will be with you shortly."

"Ah! Thank you," Maddy mumbled. "I'll just, uh… I'll sit down, then?"

The squirrel shrugged wordlessly and sipped a can of coconut La Croix in a vaguely intimidating way. Or, at least, Maddy *felt* vaguely intimidated as they sat down on the nearby bright violet leather settee. It was extremely uncomfortable, and they wondered if that part was *also* supposed to be vaguely intimidating.

The sheep-bear waited. She wanted to look at her phone again but restrained herself. She continued restraining herself for another forty-five minutes before she started to fish it out of her belt pouch — at which point she was startled by a ping to her earpiece, and promptly fumbled the phone to the ground. She sighed. "Go for Heartforce."

Caleb Hagen's voice growled into her ear. "Status report, Heartforce."

"Nothing to report, sir! Still waiting to meet with someone—"

He made a noise of uninterested displeasure, and the signal cut out. Maddy picked up the phone, rolling their eyes.

A few seconds later, a door to her side opened and two figures walked through with purpose. The first was a thin, ageless-looking blue anole in a square-shouldered tangerine pantsuit that hung fashionably loosely from their lanky frame; from reading the mission brief, Maddy assumed it must be Rin Gorgoni, the CEO of five years. They were accompanied by a compactly full-figured fallow deer femme in an understated pastel skirt and cardigan ensemble.

The sheep-bear stood up to offer her hand for shaking and did a double-take when the CEO continued walking past her, directly into an elevator. They briefly made eye contact with the Hero as the doors closed, coolly staring daggers at her without saying a word.

The deer, who had stopped near Maddy, tapped her on the shoulder. "Hi there," she said in a polite but oddly short tone, peering skeptically through cateye-framed glasses. "Grace Dunlop, she/her. I'm afraid Mx. Gorgoni and the rest of the board are *very* busy, but my schedule has an opening, so I can discuss the incident with you right now, if you like. Come along this way, please."

The doe swiped something to a sensor — Maddy didn't see what but assumed a concealed employee badge — and the door unlocked with a heavy click. Holding it open behind her, she motioned for the sheep-bear to follow down the broad glass-walled corridor. After a few moments making their way through a field of mauve-walled cubicles and what appeared to be a particularly lavish boardroom, the two came to a door signed LEGAL. Inside was what did, in fact, appear to be a legal department, as well as a large corner office with G.E. DUNLOP, CHIEF COUNSEL on the nearby nameplate. She urged Maddy to sit and closed the office door.

Maddy sat bolt-upright in the Scandinavian Modern guest seat. The lawyer, for her part, slid comfortably into a high-backed executive chair and leaned forward. "Can I offer you anything to drink? Coffee, tea, soft drink? Please, feel free," she said, gesturing to a glass-fronted minifridge and nearby Keurig machine.

"Um. Water would be nice?"

The older woman nodded at them and, again, gestured to the minifridge. Maddy sheepishly rose to her feet, briefly perused the selection to find a green glass bottle of Perrier and opened it before sitting back down.

"So," the deer began, with an inquisitive mien. "Why are you here?"

Maddy sipped at her Perrier and hoped she was sufficiently charming. "Thank you for seeing me, Ms. Dunlop! As I told your receptionist, Ontario's Heroes learned about the break-in last night. Given the vital, confidential and high-profile nature of Helical BioSpectra's work in the biotech sector, I'm here to offer whatever assistance you might find helpful...?" She paused briefly, before solicitously adding "...I'm Heartforce? I'm pretty new, just hoping to do my part with my talents..."

The lawyer smirked behind tented fingers, violet eyes betraying clear amusement. "Oh, I know who you are. I saw your interview with *Xtra*, too! How's it been to be 'Toronto's first trans superhero' since then? Or really, 'Toronto's first government-backed, officially-out trans Hero, who's still a Hero, for the moment,' I suppose?"

The sheep-bear froze, unused to civilians who weren't slightly awed by their presence. Although, actually... between the receptionist, Mx. Gorgoni, Ms. Dunlop, and several passers-by in the corridor, they'd been getting an awful lot of unimpressed looks since they'd arrived. And attitudes verging on *hostile*, even. The Hero was starting to feel like something was just a bit off. "Um..."

"Anyway! It's Maddy, right? Please, call me Grace." The deer paused briefly. "And just to be clear — in case these antlers and volunteering my pronouns weren't enough of a tip-off — I'm trans, too. So why do *you* think I'm asking why you're here?"

"I, uh... I'm not sure what that has to do—"

She rolled her eyes in mild exasperation. "I'm asking why you're here, because the incident happened twelve hours ago, and we didn't report it to police; they only showed up because our landlord called about a trespasser in the common areas," the full-figured doe snapped. "When we declined their help, the cops were happy to — if you'll pardon the expression — fuck *right* the fuck off. We're privately held and self-insured, so we didn't need to make an official report for insurance purposes. As you said yourself, our work is *highly* confidential, and our leadership values privacy. This wouldn't appear, *prima facie*, to be an incident so unusual or potentially hazardous that it requires the attention of capes like yourself, and we've also already completed our own investigation. Given all that, what makes you think HBS is in need of your services?"

They were unnerved by the deer's gaze; she seemed to see right through them. They were, admittedly, also somewhat relieved to have confirmation of the suspicion they were talking to another trans woman, even one who dismissed her as just another cape. The two factors didn't *quite* cancel one another out, and the Hero was left still feeling slightly anxious. "Well, I…" Maddy cringed, looking to a small deskside ficus to avoid eye contact. "… You completed your investigation already? You're sure there's nothing I could do to help?"

HBS's chief counsel cocked an eyebrow. "Quite sure, thank you. You're not here to help us; you're here because — *among other things* — your handlers thought it might result in earned media and push the shitshow over that interview out of the news cycle. Am I wrong?"

"I'm not sure what you—"

"We have a very good reputation with the community, between our philanthropy with LGBTQ2+ causes and our dedication to patent-breaking the meds struggling queer and trans folks desperately need. We also have a nonbinary CEO who people *don't* say 'eat the rich' about, because they publicly take a very modest salary, and at every possible opportunity they shame their industry peers for not doing the same." The deer spun her chair a half-rotation towards the window and looked down to the traffic on University Avenue. "You, personally, could use our help; being associated with us would give you more credibility as a trans Hero. We don't need your help, and frankly, being associated with you is neutral PR *at best* for us. Probably a negative, all things considered. Have you considered why *that* is?"

The two sat in silence. Maddy hoped that the deer would answer her own question; they didn't like it hanging in the air. Eventually, she did.

"You're a cop, Heartforce. I'm sure you don't like thinking of yourself that way; the *Xtra* piece made *that* clear. But whether you like it or not, you're in law enforcement, and work hand-in-hand with the TPS, OPP, RCMP, CBSA, CSIS... you're still upholding the systems that oppress your own community. Foucault had it right, don't you think? Government-backed Heroes are all about 'hierarchical observation,' and 'normalizing judgment,' just as much as any of those other law enforcement agencies. And the thing about being a queer cop is that your own people have *very good reason* to presumptively distrust you, no matter how good your intentions."

"I'm... I'm making a difference. From the inside," Maddy said, unsure why she felt the need to justify herself to the calmly dismissive older woman.

"I'm sure that was the sales pitch. Do you think they'll really let you be more than a token, though?"

"Ms. Dunlop—"

"*Grace*, please."

"Grace. *Please.* I understand why you're hesitant," the sheep-bear pleaded. "But I have a gift, and — I think — a responsibility to use it for good. That's how I was brought up. I'm sure it's not what you'd do if you had my powers, but isn't it positive for the public to see trans superheroes, and not just villains and criminals?"

Grace pursed her lips, bleat-sighing disappointedly. "Maddy... watch this, would you?" She turned to her laptop and tapped something out on the keyboard, humming to herself. After a moment, she turned it around to show her guest. The screen was frozen on a scene of what the Hero recognized as one of the HBS corridors. Except, Maddy quickly realized, it wasn't paused; a shadowy figure slipped by alongside one edge of the video. The timestamp read 11:21 PM.

The lawyer raised an eyebrow. "Notice anything?"

"...No? You clearly had an intruder, and I don't understand why you don't want anything done about it?"

"Just keep watching," the deer said archly. She slid back in her chair, tenting her hoof-nailed fingers, expression unreadable.

The figure crept back into the frame, clearer this time. The intruder was clad in dark grey and matte black tactical gear, but was still unidentifiable, head entirely concealed by a hood. Then, they pulled it back and craned their neck over their shoulder, peering up at the camera with a satisfied sneer. It was a brown rat. It was a very *familiar* rat, one she'd met with just hours before. It was Neal Salton. Fucking *Slider*.

Maddy narrowed her eyes and clenched her fists against her muscular thighs, rage rising up from deep within her. "What. *What*," she seethed through gritted teeth.

Grace scrubbed the video back to pause it on the rat's clearly-captured face. "I told you," she said mildly. "We completed our investigation. We know exactly who broke in — the Ontario's Heroes operative Neal 'Slider' Salton — and we know that he didn't meaningfully *do* anything. He *thought* he disabled our security system, and then rifled through some desks and knocked over a recycling bin; just enough to leave evidence of a break-in, such that the police would get called, OH would hear about it officially through your information-sharing protocols, and someone like you would have an excuse to come knocking at our door this morning." She met Maddy's gaze with a sympathetic expression. "Given your reaction just now — and, I'm sorry, but it's true: a general lack of investigative subtlety — I'm satisfied you had no idea until just this moment."

"But that's—"

"Yes, it is." She again let the moment linger; the sheep-bear's skin crawled with discomfort. "I'm not going to tell you it's impossible to deepfake something like this; of course it isn't. But this is real, and I bet you can think of some way to verify it on your own, too. Also, frankly, I don't need to justify anything to you? You showed up on our doorstep unannounced." After a pause, she continued, with a faint note of genuine concern in her voice. "I don't think they trust you, Maddy. If they did, don't you think you'd have been in on the whole plan here? Whatever it is?"

They fumed, teeth gritted and looked out the window. The round central courtyard of Grange Park was visible in the distance. "I don't... why aren't you more upset about this?"

The older woman shrugged noncommittally. "We have the situation well in hand. No actual harm was done, and the PHL, the police, and our industry competitors all being what they are, it's not in our strategic interest to take this public right now. So, how fortunate for me that you just happened to stop by, offering to ever-so-*helpfully* snoop around, hmm?" She cleared her throat, and then reached over to close the laptop. "I think we're done here. By all means, *please* pass on that we're not terribly impressed."

"Um. Thank you," Maddy mumbled. The ground felt like it had shifted (figuratively) under her feet, much as she'd (literally) applied her powers to Slider earlier.

"Any time," the deer said unctuously, grinning as she stood up to usher the sheep-bear out of her office. "Lovely to meet you, Heartforce. Have fun with your bosses, eh?"

Maddy sped her motorcycle back towards the OH facility in Mississauga, continuing to seethe at... *whatever* was going on.

Ontario's Heroes maintained multiple facilities in the Greater Toronto Area, but this, commonly referred to as OH Lakeview, was one of the most extensive. It was located beneath the waterfront site of what had once been the WWII-era Long Branch Arsenal, with parts reaching as far as the long-demolished Lakeview Generating Station. The site was technically confidential for security reasons — with OH customarily refusing to confirm or deny the existence of any facilities beyond their official suite in the Ministry of the Solicitor General's downtown office tower — but the Hero had quickly come to learn that it was a widely-known "secret" in the industrial neighbourhood.

Turning off Dixie Road, Maddy slowed and clicked a tab on her headset. As a loading bay door opened for her, she pulled into the nondescript warehouse that served as the secured entrance and parking garage for the facility.

They hit the Yamaha's kickstand, stowed their helmet, and proceeded to the elevator. Several sub-basements lower and a brisk walk later, they made their way to the director's office. Nodding at the guard as he swiped his keycard to allow the young Hero access to the executive wing, they proceeded to alert his secretary (an elderly, perpetually unamused mourning dove named Lola) of the need to meet immediately. She squinted and clicked her tongue sourly, but waved Maddy in.

Hagen turned away from his computer monitor as the sheep-bear entered, removed his headset, and crossed his arms impatiently. "Well? Out with it already! Report, Heartforce, I'm a busy man!"

"Is there anything else I should know about the HBS break-in, sir?"

Hagen's eyes narrowed. "That's not a report, Oakes. What are you saying?"

"I'm saying that I, ah, was able to review the evidence, and it appears that the intruder may have been, um… one of ours…?"

The Director took a deep breath and stared them in the eyes. "How in the *fuck* did you come to that conclusion?"

"Well, there was video, and—"

Hagen's eyes narrowed and his nostrils flared in rage. "Goddammit, Slider," he fumed.

Maddy boggled. "You… knew it was Slider, sir?"

Hagen growled, a deep, threatening rumble. "HBS is a Korps front, Oakes. This was a need-to-know op, and you didn't need to know yet."

"No! Are you sure? They were a little rude to me, but I don't think anyone I saw there looked like a *supervillain*…"

"That's the point of a 'front,'" the wolverine snapped. "The plan was to give you an excuse to make direct contact. You're one of *their* types, and I just gave you a hard time. A *well-deserved* one, I will fucking remind you. They'd be sympathetic about the bad press you're getting and the leash I put you on, and assuming you didn't shit the bed again, they would eventually try to recruit you, and you'd accept… but as a double agent," he leered.

Maddy, for her part, was quietly horrified. She tried to mentally brush off her boss's grumbling about whatever "*their* types" meant; the generalized phobic sniping seemed less urgent, for the moment.

"It would have worked better as a slow burn with a more substantial public profile, and if you didn't know it was a setup — more organic that way, and you'd have had an easier time getting through their telepathic screens — but Salton had to make a fucking soup sandwich out of covering his tracks," Director Hagen grunted, pondering. "We can still do something with this, though. Scratch the Team B plan, you're going to go to the Infirmary right away. Doc Gallant has an experimental, new and improved psi-blocker formulation he's been working on, to protect you from the mindfuckery. I'll have Lola clear my schedule for a strategic briefing next Monday—"

"But that's not what I signed up for! I don't want to be a spy, I want to *help* people..."

Hagen stared her in the eyes and spoke at first with terrifyingly calm intensity. *"Madison Skylar Oakes.* Listen very carefully to me, you ungrateful little *pissant.* You would not even *be* part of this organization if not for your father's good name, *and* your usefulness as a... a *mascot* for the God-forsaken wokeness that's taken over this country. It got the Premier's office off our back about profiling for a whole six *months,* just to pass along we were keeping you in our back pocket as a *prospect.*"

The Hero gasped. She... she knew that there was *some* cynical PR element involved in her rapid rise, sure, she was supposed to play ball and be "Heartwood II" in all but name...

"I knew Roger," the Director barked. "He wasn't the best or the brightest, but Jesus, that was a Hero you could point at a soft target and just watch him charge in and win. That was his strategy; he'd *win.* He'd never get bogged down in this bleeding-heart nonsense; he knew that there are white hats and black hats, and if you're not ready to shoot it out with the black hats, you're a liability. *Like Sunrise,"* he sneered.

As the wolverine worked himself into his trademark rage, he became louder and louder, until it was a bellow that shook the coffee in the PHL-branded mug on his desk and made Maddy cringe with every word. *"Get your head right,* Heartforce. You want to contribute to the public good? You want to 'help people'? Then you're going to do whatever I bloody well *tell you* to do. If I tell you to infiltrate the Korps, the next words out of your mouth should be 'How many tasteful snapshots of the stomach-churning reefer-den hypno-slave orgies can I surreptitiously take for you, *sir!'"*

Maddy nodded their head, furiously, and again fought back tears.

CHAPTER 3

October 20, 2022

Maddy had been camped out at a window seat of the cafe for nearly an hour, across the street from the office tower where HBS occupied the 21st floor; this was the third day in a row she'd tried staking out her potential contact. She wore civilian clothes — jeans, a loose grey hoodie, and a cap bearing the team insignia of the recently-renamed TMU Bold, the latter courtesy of her varsity hockey-playing sister — and hid her eyes behind wide sunglasses. The sheep-bear sipped at her increasingly lukewarm latte, keeping an eye out for Ms. Dunlop. She had to use the building's front door *sometime*, didn't she?

Soon enough, a figure strode out the revolving doors on the other side of Adelaide Street: a chubby deer with petite, swept-back antlers, wearing a blowsy, rich purple maxi dress. It was her. They chugged the rest of the coffee and hustled outside, making sure to keep eyes on their target constantly.

Maddy's burly frame wasn't built for stealth, but OH basic training had taught the sheep-bear rudimentary investigative techniques. Walking at a brisk but conspicuously casual pace, it wasn't difficult to get closer to the deer, then closer still. The Hero weaved through the foot traffic of similar white-collar workers on their way to lunch, eyeing the environment carefully, alert to the motions of every surrounding figure; she *had* to get the steps right. Suddenly, she realized the deer had slipped from her sight. She whipped her neck back and forth, panicked. That was when the sheep-bear felt a tap on her shoulder, and spun around, already reflexively raising her hands to defend herself, until she looked down and faced—

"Ms. Dunlop…!"

The deer's arms were crossed, and she calmly raised an eyebrow. "Hello, Maddy. I told you, you can call me Grace; 'Ms. Dunlop' — heavy sarcasm on the 'Ms.', and usually prefaced with 'my learned friend' — is what I get called by asshole opposing counsel. How long have you been waiting to spontaneously run into me while I went out to grab lunch?"

They lowered their hands and cringed. "I, uh, don't know what—"

Grace narrowed her eyes, patience clearly ebbing. "*Maddy.*"

The Hero was silent, chagrined.

"Anyway, I *am* getting lunch, so you may as well come with, if you want to talk; there's a great noodle place over near Bay and Temperance," the deer shrugged, looking eastward. "I take it you're not thrilled with what you found out from the boss, eh?"

Maddy walked alongside, nodding nervously. After half a block, the sheep-bear finally worked up the wherewithal to say something. "...You were right," they mumbled. "Hagen — the Director — doesn't trust me. Neither do my teammates. I really am supposed to just smile for the cameras and be the diversity poster child. And I wouldn't even be *on* the team if not for my dad."

"I am, genuinely, sorry for that," the doe said sadly. "You deserve better."

The sheep-bear hesitated briefly but decided to just say the really worrying part out loud, to get it over with. "Oh, and my boss, he thinks your company is a Korps front. Wild, right...?"

"We know. And *he* knows we know, and *we* know that he knows that we know. But he *doesn't* know a way to get to us without compromising his *own* position in several matters."

"...Wait." Finally the Hero gasped, inhaling sharply, feeling like her jaw must have comically dropped to the sidewalk. "Oh my God, you *are*—"

The deer rolled her eyes and flicked her wrist at Maddy dismissively. "Oh, please, we're barely even hiding! There are *two* big magenta flags in our name alone! I'd expect *any* PHL operative to get at least the one, but a trans Hero ought to catch both, frankly."

"Huh?"

"*Helical.* As in, shaped like a helix." She gestured, drawing the twin lines of the Korps's insignia in the air with hoof-nailed fingertips. "And, okay, the other one is kind of a deep cut. 'HBS' is also a joke on 'Harry Benjamin Syndrome,' which—"

Maddy couldn't help herself. "Which is some antiquated transmed garbage, right up there with 'autogynephilia' and 'true transsexualism.'" The shock of confirming she was making a social call on a supervillain — well, at least, a *lawyer* to supervillains — was pushed to the back of her mind when she realized that the older woman seemed impressed. The Hero felt pleased, somehow. "You weren't expecting me to know that at all because I'm so young, huh?"

"I wasn't, no," Grace mused as they arrived at the restaurant, cocking one eyebrow. "You just might surprise me yet, Heartforce." She opened the door to a room decorated in kitschy florals and bright translucent orange plastic highlights and gestured for Maddy to go inside. The pair joined the lineup to the counter. "So, Madison Skyler Oakes, duly-licensed Hero of the Province of Ontario: What can I do for you?"

The sheep-bear's eyes darted from side to side, trying to add up all the other customers. "You... you just told me, uh... and you want to talk about this *here*?" Maddy choked out the words in a low voice, incredulous.

"Why not? We're just two professional women in high-pressure jobs, bitching about work," Grace smirked. They came to the cash register, where she ordered the seafood laksa with Hokkien noodles and a Diet Pepsi. "Want anything? On me, of course!"

"No, thank you," the Hero insisted. "You're being *way* too chill about this. Is this some kind of trick? Are you—" They dropped their voice to a bare whisper. "Fuck, are you hypnotizing me right now? Is this what happened to Sunrise...?"

"Suit yourself," the doe shrugged, picking up her tray and navigating to a booth. "Anyway, no, right *now* I'm about to have some delicious soup while I wait to hear what you want from me. Sit down, and tell Auntie Grace all about it; no mind control, I promise. I don't know what you may have heard, but we tend to do that to folks who are *into it*," she said with a wink.

They squeezed into the opposite banquette, trying to avoid thinking too deeply about what the deer's last words had meant, and rubbed agitatedly at the back of their neck. "I'm not naive, you know! I know what's wrong with the system," Maddy continued morosely. "It's just that I don't... I don't know what to do, or who else I could talk to, even! If I quit, then I feel like I'm letting so many people down! There'd be nobody on the inside of OH trying to make them improve anything. And the kids, oh my God, the kids — I met this adorable little girl a few weeks ago who was able to come out to her parents because she could tell them she's like me, I'm some kind of *role model*, and—"

Grace nodded along as she finished slurping a long noodle and swallowed. "I think the question you need to ask yourself is: Do you want to be a role model in the sanitized little box OH intends to build around you? Will you be able to live with yourself like that? Being their token trans team member, attending press conferences and flag-raising ceremonies and doing little workshops on pronoun best practices, having to explain to the cable pundits every other month how *of course* you know in your heart that your teammates aren't bigots, when one gets caught mouthing off about immigrants or sex workers or affirmative action? Can you really 'Do Good' or 'Make a Difference' from the inside, or will you be compromised by even trying?"

Maddy sighed. "What do your parents do for a living, Grace?"

The doe took a long sip of her drink. "They were teachers, before they retired."

"Did anyone ever push you to be a teacher?"

"Not specifically? But my parents did impress on me that I had to do *something* impressive with a higher education. I picked law, and I, uh… I haven't always felt great about that, admittedly, especially before I signed on with the 'bad guys.' But I did have a choice, and I assume you're about to say—"

"Yeah. I definitely have to live up to Dad's legacy. I have to 'make him proud.' People have been telling me that my whole life, and even if I actually *don't*, they'd rather just pretend I am, for the sake of his honour or something, I guess. My grandparents, my teachers, the League… I even met the prime minister once, when I was eight; he gave some big speech about valuing the sacrifices of our brave Heroes, fighting against the forces of anarchy."

"And what do *you* want?"

There was a long silence between them. The sheep-bear looked away, out the window to the narrowest part of Temperance Street, where a delivery truck was being unloaded. "I wish… I wish I didn't have to do the legacy thing, or be a Hero, let alone a *trans* Hero. As great as it feels to be, like, a role model for that girl… it's like I can't really be *me*, if I'm 'representation.' For whatever good I can do, I still have to be this big public symbol of progress, above everything else."

"That must be tough, being under the spotlight," Grace said kindly.

Maddy continued, growing more agitated as the doe opposite them calmly continued eating. "Nobody asked me, you know? I hoped so hard when I was a kid that I wouldn't get any powers, just like I hoped that my voice wouldn't get any deeper and that I wouldn't grow big ram horns," they groaned. "At least I could get puberty blockers, for the other stuff. But, no, Dad was a big *fucking* deal, 'The Pride of Grande Prairie,' so when the telekinetic flashes started happening, shit, turns out I've got powers too... I didn't get much of a choice, no."

"Maddy, I'm sorry for everything that happened when you were younger. I truly am. There's no such thing as 'parental rights'; no parent or family should be forcing their children to be anyone other than who they are, and that you weren't given the choice from the get-go is *vile*. But you're an adult now! Independent, and fully capable of making your own decisions. Right here and now, is anyone *making* you be Heartforce?"

Maddy clenched her jaw. "I mean, *you people*, if anyone! If he hadn't died in a fight with a villain, maybe I wouldn't have had to do all of this..."

Grace held up a finger, indicating she had something to say, while she finished swallowing the last of her noodles; her companion waited with some irritation. The deer kept holding it up as she downed the last of her drink as well. Finally, only after she took a deep breath, did she begin to speak. "That's not how your father died."

They narrowed their eyes. "What. *What*."

"Roger Keith 'Heartwood' Oakes. Born January 26th, 1972 in Clairmont, Alberta; died August 3rd, 2005, in Edmonton. Your father. He didn't die in a fight, let alone a fight with a Korps operative."

Maddy huffed, anger rising in her gorge. "Okay, I'm done," she said in a hoarse whisper, standing up. "You showed me the video of Slider, and thanks for that, I guess, for showing me how apparently my teammates think I'm a joke, just some useless diversity hire. Great. Good job. This is how you get me, right? This is... you're trying to confuse me, aren't you? Trying to make me quit. Convince me you're *so* harmless and innocent and well-meaning and didn't have anything to do with my dad's death.

Fucking… Hagen was right, you're trying to *recruit* me! You're trying to get me all sympathetic and demoralized so I'd come crawling. Well, *fuck you.*"

The deer looked disappointed, somehow. "That's not—"

"And you know what, you didn't even get the *fucking* day right! Or the place! I've seen the death certificate! He died on August 4th, in *Calgary!* God." She pulled down her cap, tears welling up in her eyes, and was about to storm off — until she felt the older woman tug at her sleeve.

The doe's overall vibe was *soft,* but in that moment, there was steel in her eyes. She made a small, pained smile. "It's the truth, and I can prove it. Please, Maddy. Just let me show you something."

Chapter 4

Maddy was reluctant, but sufficiently intrigued by the older woman's promise of an explanation that they bitterly agreed. Maybe it was a trap, they considered; maybe they'd be kidnapped and taken to a secret facility at the top of the CN Tower, held down and brainwashed out of every deeply held belief she'd ever had. Sunrise would be there, she was sure; the lioness would probably even try to seduce her to the dark side, grinding those gigantic tits in her face. Maybe they'd just interrogate her until she spilled her (admittedly limited) knowledge of OH tactical operations, then kill her.

Or maybe it was only a psych-out, an exercise in humiliation, and she'd be brought before dozens of Korps agents just so they could point and laugh at the silly, useless babytrans who somehow had the delusion that she was actually a decent person who helped her community, let alone a competent *Hero*. It hardly mattered, the sheep-bear huffed to herself; all Hagen thought she was good for was PR (and holy shit, had she ever whiffed on that front) or being a double agent (unlikely, as a laughably bad liar). But at least she could maybe find out something — anything — new about Dad, and maybe that would help her figure out what she wanted her *own* legacy to be. In any event, the two walked back to the corner of University and Adelaide together.

On their second trip to the 21st floor, Maddy realized something was different, but couldn't place what, exactly. They'd passed the boardroom and stopped just long enough in the doorway for the deer to vaguely gesture to Maddy, breezily noting to her fellow executives that everything was under control. It was only after following the doe a different direction through the cubicle maze that the sheep-bear twigged to it: they weren't getting the stink-eye from anyone. Not the tiny, intimidating receptionist; not Grace; and not even Mx. Gorgoni, or the other senior staff.

(Well, maybe still a *little*, from the anole.)

Finally, the sheep-bear and their escort arrived at what seemed to be a back corner of the office, at a very ordinary-looking door signed with the placard FACILITY CONTROL B // AUTHORIZED PERSONNEL ONLY. Grace waved near a sensor, not even an ID badge or key fob in hand, and the door unlocked with a series of heavy clicks, hydraulic shifts, and mechanical creaking noises. She pulled it open and waved Maddy in.

It was… just a room. Something like a security or IT office, with a series of small flatscreen displays clustered around one enormous one, at a long console desk with three workstations. Proprietary-looking hardware and peripherals were mounted to every surface, including a small rack of servers. The Hero looked around and saw no signs of restraints or ray guns. But for a decor motif built around shades of magenta — and what she recognized as the Korps's helix insignia — it could have been any kind of control room or small lab, or even a compact recording studio.

The doe noticed Maddy's confused expression and smiled gently. "It's for real, Heartforce. No tricks." She pulled two of the rolling task chairs out, took a seat, and gestured with one hoof-nailed hand to do the same. With a series of keypresses, the system booted up; a stylized rose icon flickered by quickly.

Grimacing, the Hero sat down and folded their arms defensively. They wouldn't be *fooled*, at the very least; they'd hear the older woman out, and judge for themselves. *Independently*, they thought, with a tinge of bitterness.

Working through an OS interface Maddy didn't recognize, Grace quickly brought up a video clip with the touchpad. Rather than click on play, she turned to the Hero, folding her hands. "Now, I have to warn you. This is a cable news feed of your father, shortly before his death. It's not a fight, and it's not even exactly *violent*, so much as a tremendously sad medical episode. But it's your father, and if you want to know how he really died, the clip is right here."

The sheep-bear pursed her lips and looked downward. "Yes. I've… I've come this far."

Grace smiled sympathetically and reached back over to hit the play button. It was indeed from a cable network — CBC Newsworld, per the caption — and the on-screen graphics similarly indicated the date: Wednesday, August 3, 2005.

Maddy recognized the scene. It was a press conference on the steps of Prairie League (Alberta Division) HQ in Edmonton, PHL pennants strung proudly across the building's central pillars. They'd watched a hundred press conferences just like it in Dad's clippings but had never seen one from this date. There hadn't been *any* League media availabilities recorded for the week before his death, as far as they knew...

...And she *did* know, because Granddad had made certain of that. She — "the boy," as he'd usually called her to her mother — would need to *understand* the legacy of the man she'd have to live up to, the martyred Heartwood. He'd drilled her on her father's exploits every day, those summer weeks she and Brianna spent at the Oakes family cabin as children. In between swimming in the lake and playing in the woods, she'd been sat down on the dock and quizzed on Roger Oakes' Hero career statistics. She *knew* her father's life from front to back, Alpha to Omega; a closed circle, his whole life fitting inside. It was, therefore, freaking her out the *tiniest* little bit to peer up at the giant screen and see Dad lumber in from out of frame, to join a group milling around a podium, in a way that didn't quite match any of the press conferences in her memory.

The anchorwoman spoke, offscreen. "Coming up in just thirty seconds, we're waiting on the Prairie League spokesperson and two of their top Heroes, Heartwood and Reclaimer, discussing successful enforcement operations today against illegal logging protests in Kananaskis. Okay, I see now — thank you, Tony, yes, I have confirmation, we're live with PL media officer Alexis Westerhaven now." The audio clipped out abruptly as the feed zoomed in to the conference, where a blonde wolf in a pantsuit approached the lectern.

Grace looked solicitously to Maddy. "Still doing okay there?"

"Fine, thank you," they lied.

After Alexis spoke briefly to the details of the day's activities against the so-called "eco-terrorists," including arrests handed over to the local RCMP detachment — Alexis who had come to Thanksgiving Dinner for years, Alexis who'd *babysat* for Maddy and her sister while the family grieved in Calgary, afterwards — it was Dad's turn. The massive brown bear grew animated quickly, denouncing the activists as if they were plotting sedition, rather than merely trying to halt provincial approval for old-growth logging permits. This wasn't quite like anything she'd ever seen before; he was beginning to rage like *Hagen*, for fuck's sake, all jowly and spittle-flecked and white-hot incandescent with fury. A vein in his forehead throbbed rapidly in close-up 1080p.

"…AND I SWEAR TO YOU, NO COWARDLY GODDAMNED TREE-HUGGERS WILL BE PERMITTED TO IMPEDE THIS WORK, SO VITAL TO THE ALBERTA ECONOMY; IT JUST ISN'T, WON'T—"

At that point Roger Oakes began to pant rapidly, roaring and gasping. After a moment of apparent distress, his eyes rolled back; finally, he toppled face-first into the spray of microphone mounts, limp. Audible gasps arose from the crowd, with a faint yell to call 911 audible in the background as the audio signal blipped back to the unseen anchor.

"Ladies and gentlemen — *Tony, cut away, cut away now* — we're going to come back to this in a moment, it appears one of the speakers may need medical attention." The video changed again to show the anchor in-studio, a severe-looking hawk in a sober blue blazer. "Returning to our top national stories, reliable sources in the Prime Minister's Office indicate that he will announce the appointment of a new Governor-General tomorrow…"

Grace paused the video a few seconds before the end. "It was a ruptured brain aneurysm. He worked himself up so much that he burst a blood vessel in his head and died not long after being transported to Emergency at the U of A Hospital. The Prairie League pressured the networks to withdraw the footage and go along with a cover story that your father died of injuries from a fight. Too embarrassing, you see; normally the PHL could throw their weight around to just bury it and move on, whenever your dad went off half-cocked on a hot mic, but *raging* himself to death live and on-camera? Well, *that* required extra effort to fix for public consumption."

The sheep-bear said nothing, stunned.

"The next Prairie League press conference," Grace continued, "And I'm betting you *have* seen that one, was the next day. Ms. Westerhaven announced that Heartwood had succumbed to wounds sustained in the *previous* day's battle. And that battle was no longer just a beatdown of passively resisting protestors, but mysteriously now also included a local villain and his henchmen."

Maddy stared straight ahead, gazing into the beady eyes of the avian anchorwoman on screen. "I don't… no,,,? How can it have been like that? I've never seen him that *angry* when he wasn't even in an actual fight…"

The doe shrugged sadly. "The PHL gets a *lot* of embarrassing shit buried. Easier to manufacture consent to law enforcement-by-*Übermensch* that way. Our Archive and Records Division saves as much as we can of what they try to memory-hole, and it usually comes in handy at some point." She tentatively, gently patted the sheep-bear next to her on the shoulder. "Maddy? Are you going to be okay…?"

They took a deep breath. "There's more like this? More of him being fucking terrifying? More that nobody ever showed me?"

Grace nodded.

"I want to see *everything*."

Many hours later, the troubled Hero was in the kitchen of their mother's Malton home, having called ahead to ask if they could come over for dinner. It was a quieter house than they'd remembered, between them being assigned their own apartment as part of their OH stipend, and their sister Brianna moving into the TMU residences for her sophomore year. Mom was always glad to have Maddy visit, and they worried that she was a bit lonely.

"Mom? Can I ask you something about Dad?"

Deborah Gillespie turned her woolly neck to smile at her daughter, who was sitting worriedly at the kitchen table, before returning her attention to the dishes in the sink. "Of course, honey!"

Maddy looked at the linoleum floor. "Um. How… how did he *really* die?"

They saw their mother tense up as they asked the question, her arms stiffening as she grasped the front lip of the sink. When the sheep spoke, her voice was faint, her tone stilted. "What… what do you mean, honey? He was in a fight with a supervillain — then at the hospital — I couldn't make it in time…"

"Mom."

"I, I tried to get there — the League, they called me, but I was too late, I—"

"*Mom.*"

She turned around, tightly clasping her hands, still dripping with dishwater. "I… I have to go lie down," the sheep murmured nervously, wiping her hands on her jeans and scurrying out of the kitchen on delicate hooves.

Maddy followed her towards the master bedroom and called at her mother's retreating back. "*Mom.*"

Deborah cringed, and stumbled to her neatly made bed, where she sat unsteadily on the hand-sewn quilt. She held a hand over her mouth and looked at her daughter — standing in the doorway, their arms folded and jaw set — through watery eyes. She choked down a sob. "I'm… I'm sorry, honey. They thought it'd be better this way…"

"*Who?* Who's *they*, Mom?"

Maddy sat down beside their mother and hugged her tightly. They stayed like that, silent for a few moments, until finally Deborah spoke with a cracking voice.

"The League. And — and your dad's family. Grandma Patty, God rest her soul, and Granddad Garth, and Aunt Marilyn and Uncle Gary and Aunt Joan. They didn't want…" she cleared her throat, sniffling. "How did you find out? Did someone tell you? Is that what happened?"

Maddy considered lying. She chose not to. "Yes. Someone thought I should know the truth and showed me the cable news clip of the… the press conference. A friend, I think." *I hope*, she silently added to herself.

"I didn't want to keep it from you. I didn't. But you were so young, and we'd just lost him, and then… he was your hero, honey. *Everyone's* hero, back in Grande Prairie, I guess, even before he was a real official *Hero*. But especially yours, and I didn't want to take that away from you. You were just a little b—" The sheep caught herself. "You were so young, Maddy." Deborah hugged her daughter tightly and wept.

"Was he… was he like that a lot?"

The sheep looked up, wincing. She took a deep breath and held her chin high. "Madison. You *should* know. Your friend, please, thank them for me. I'm sorry I wasn't strong enough to tell you myself." She paused, peering away. "Your father was a giant piece of shit, honey."

The sheep-bear hugged her mother, chagrined. "That wasn't the only video I saw today. I'm figuring out that part."

"He hit me," Deborah said flatly.

"Mom…!"

"It's true. Every time one of the bad guys got away. He'd drink, and he'd hit me. It was bad enough when he was just working around Peace River Country, dealing with burglars and biker gangs. When he got called up by the PHL… well. There was this one time, about a year before he died. Your dad and I went to Ottawa by ourselves one summer for this big oil industry party. You were staying with your grandparents for a couple of weeks, remember?"

Maddy nodded, recalling. "I was five. They said he was going to see some big men in Ottawa, and I got it mixed up and thought that meant, like, giants…"

Deborah chuckled sadly. "He ended up chasing one of those… *Korps…* people. It was the only time he ever went up against one alone. He never cared for them much, but back when we first met, it wasn't personal, you know? He got *obsessed*, though, after he was with the League. He'd talk and talk about how much he hated them, how disgusting they were, what he wanted to do to them, but it wasn't really about *them*, exactly; really, what he meant was—"

"—People like me," Maddy said with a sudden, stomach-churning clarity. "He wanted to be able to hurt *people like me* and still be the 'good guy.' That's what being a Hero really meant to him, in the end." They shuddered.

"Oh, *honey*," Deborah said, holding them tightly. "Yes. I think… I think it was. And when that man got away, the lizard, it made him look bad. I remember him coming back to the party afterwards, and he was just so *furious*; he would hardly say two words to the bigwigs before we left. He dragged me by my arm and grabbed a bottle of rye from the bar. And then, when we got back to the hotel, he…"

Tears filled Maddy's eyes. "Mom, you really don't have to—"

The sheep looked down into the deep-pile bedroom carpet. Her voice dropped to a near-whisper. "The hotel called the police. And when they got there… he gave them *autographs*, Maddy. They were *fans*. I was sitting in an ambulance with the paramedics, and he was just standing around with them ten feet away, joking about how… how… h—"

"*Mom, please—*"

Her mother nearly shouted out her next words. "*How rough I like it,*" she said, her ovine eyes blazing with fury. She clenched her fists, and took several deep breaths before continuing, more calmly. "Like I said. Roger Oakes was a real piece of shit. I would have left, but with you and Brianna, I mean… the League would never let me get custody. Who do you think an Alberta divorce judge is going to believe?" She clasped Maddy's hand tightly and began to sob. After a moment, Maddy joined her, her composure crumbling.

"Mom?"

"Yes, dear?"

"This stuff… this is part of why we moved from Calgary too, isn't it. Not just that Granddad didn't like that you let me start transitioning."

She nodded.

"I think I'm going to go get a legal name change after all."

"Why? I thought you liked Maddy?"

"I do. I just… I think I'd rather be Maddy Gillespie than Maddy Oakes."

Maddy stayed the night in her old bedroom; she and her mother ordered a pizza, broke out the ice cream and wine, and had the girls' night they needed.

When the Hero returned to their own apartment, there was an HBS business card slipped underneath the front door. It was Grace's, and had a handwritten note on the back:

WHEN YOU GET TIRED OF BEING THEIR CHAMPION
I KNOW SOMEONE YOU SHOULD TALK TO

Chapter 5

Maddy Oakes concentrated, gritting her teeth as she strained to flex her telekinetic powers, staring at the transport truck grill inches from her face. She breathed out deeply.

The truck began to move, slowly, from where it had jackknifed and overturned into the barriers on the highway overpass. Traffic continued to speed by on the 401 below as the sheep-bear telekinetically pushed and pulled at various parts of the vehicle's transmission and chassis, carefully rotating the shapes in their mind to accomplish the same movements upon the physical objects. They eventually managed to right it, but great heaving creaks and groans from the metal made clear that there would be much to repair.

However, the future roadworthiness of the vehicle wasn't Maddy's problem; she was concerned only with removing the road hazard, as she'd been dispatched to do earlier that morning, being the nearest available Ontario's Heroes operative with suitable capabilities for road accident cleanup. This was the kind of Hero work she could enjoy on some level: acting in the public good, achieving results quicker and more effectively than those without her gifts. Had her telekinesis not been conveniently at the disposal of the Ontario Provincial Police's highway patrol unit, it could have taken several more hours for tow trucks and cranes to clear the accident.

They sighed sadly at the part of that equation that involved working alongside police. The cops who'd radioed in a request for OH assistance leaned lazily against the side of their black-and-white Ford Explorer, sipping their coffees and kibitzing as they watched the sheep-bear work. Maddy's eyes narrowed in irritation.

She also wasn't thrilled to be helping out this particular truck driver, a sour-faced newt who was inexplicably wearing a Confederate flag-emblazoned baseball cap, despite the owner-operator information on his cab doors indicating he was based in Lévis, Quebec. When she'd pulled up on her motorcycle and introduced herself moments before, the man had mumbled something in French that Maddy hadn't quite caught; from his bitter tone and refusal to look her in the eye, however, she was *reasonably* certain it had been transphobic. The newt stood apart from the OPP officers, thumbing at a smartphone and periodically wincing as his truck was moved haltingly off the roadway.

Finally, it was done; although substantially the worse for wear, the tractor-trailer was at least no longer blocking the overpass and could be easily towed away. Anxious to depart, Maddy exchanged perfunctory acknowledgments with the police and gave a sarcastically cheery salute to the trucker; the newt scowled and looked at the ground. Straddling their Yamaha V-Max, the sheep-bear donned their sleek maroon motorcycle helmet and sped off to their destination on the Mississauga waterfront.

Maddy waved at the guards as she swiped her access badge to the reader and proceeded through the security gate of OH Lakeview. She was just about to proceed down the wide corridor when one of them popped out of the security post's door and called after her. "Miss Oakes?"

They turned, hesitantly. "Yes…?"

The guard was a lean bloodhound, and he held a notebook in one hand, reading it off to the sheep-bear before him apologetically. "You have a priority order from Director Hagen. You're to, quote, 'Get your fucking head in the game,' unquote, and meet with him immediately." He rubbed at the back of his neck with the other hand, a hangdog look on his face. "Sorry. Just the messenger here."

Maddy winced. "Thank you, officer. Understood; please let the Director know I'll be with him shortly," they forced out in a clipped, professional tone. The bloodhound gave a polite nod and dipped back into the doorway to his side.

She'd been dreading returning to duty; the revelations of the previous week had thrown the young sheep-bear for a loop. After all, it wasn't every day that Maddy found out that her nascent career as a legacy Hero was based on a lie: her father, Heartwood of the Prairie League, had been anything but *heroic*. Roger Oakes had been a hateful, festering sore of a man, openly bloodthirsty about the prospect of inflicting pain on the petty criminals, leftists, foreigners and queers he despised — to say nothing of *equally* violent and abusive to Mom, in private.

It was all, Maddy considered, A Lot to Deal With.

They'd begged off sick for the weekend — they *were* sick, in a way, sick of being lied to and manipulated by cruel old men who saw them as nothing more than a tool for their frustrated ambitions — but could no longer avoid what would happen next.

She was going to have to talk to her boss, Director Hagen. The talk was going to be about his plans for Maddy to infiltrate the Korps.

Maddy took the elevator down through several sub-basement levels, arriving at the executive wing, where another guard had to manually release the electronic door lock for them to enter. Hagen's office was just down the hall, and they opened the door to be on the receiving end of an utter death glare from his personal secretary.

"Good morning, Lola," Maddy sighed politely.

The elderly mourning dove woman continued to scowl. "He's *waiting*," she enunciated bitterly with a cluck of her tongue.

Maddy took a deep breath and opened the door. Gathered around the conference table at one end of the long, windowless office were the high-strung wolverine himself; Maddy's team leader, Jules "Lightbox" Lafusée, a lanky flying squirrel; and her god-damned fucking nemesis, the slippery, skeevy little bastard of an 'infiltration specialist' who liked to antagonize and misgender her subtly enough she'd never had enough evidence to make an issue of it, the short brown rat known as Neal "Slider" Salton. Finally, joining by videoconference, was Lawrence Rockwell, the head of the Provincial Heroes' League; he was distractedly reviewing a briefing binder, his microphone muted. The Toronto skyline was visible through the window behind his desk.

Slider grinned menacingly. "Heeeeey, buddy! Guess who's going to be your handler for this job," he sniffed.

"Zip it, Salton," Hagen growled. His sleeves were rolled up, and his tie was somehow already loose and rumpled at ten in the morning. "Oakes, take a seat. Care to tell me why you're a whole fucking *hour* late? And with Mr. Rockwell here, as well?"

Her heart raced. At least this time, unlike their meetings the previous week, she wouldn't be alone with the rage-prone director. "Answering an emergency call, sir!" she spouted, body tensed as she sat down. "It came in from Dispatch, and I was in the right place at the right time to clear a road hazard."

The wolverine's eyes bulged, and he took a deep breath. "*Oakes.* Did you happen to *mention* to Dispatch, in the course of accepting the assignment, that you were supposed to report at 0900 for this intel strategy meeting?"

Maddy gritted their teeth, internally screaming. They had *deeply* hoped that arriving this late would have resulted in postponing the meeting. "Didn't think of it, sir…? I thought protocol was to prioritize all emergency calls involving civilians in potential danger, unless specifically instructed otherwise by a superior, or the Ministry chain of command," they said tersely. "Sir."

Hagen grumbled, eyes narrowing as a sneer curled his lip. "Of course," he snapped. He slid a standard-issue tablet down the conference table to the sheep-bear. "First of all: everything about this mission is classified on a need-to-know basis. The only personnel who need to know are the five of us in this meeting and Doc Gallant. Do I make myself clear?"

Maddy nodded dutifully. "Yes, sir."

"Speaking of Doc Gallant," he mused, scanning his own tablet, "how are you adjusting to the psi-blockers?"

The sheep-bear had in fact met with OH's medical director the previous Tuesday, before beginning their stakeout of HBS. Gallant was another last-generation Hero retired from the field, an unpowered super-science type with a brusque, patronizing manner to the less technically-inclined; he reminded Maddy of the first doctor they'd seen at the gender clinic in Calgary, years before. The bespectacled bull had handed them an unlabeled bottle of red and white capsules, his own novel formula, supposedly better than the standard bulwarxine, instructing them to take two daily — brushing off questions about side effects as 'not relevant to the necessary requirements of efficacy and reliability.'

The doctor had merely insisted that the medication — he refused to even describe its contents, beyond "experimental" and "in testing with Health Canada" — would prevent having any thoughts or memories accessed by outside forces, whether organic wielders of psionic forces like Maddy, or the Korps's dreaded Rose-Coloured Glasses (to say nothing of consumer-grade technological knock-offs, such as the personal assistant headsets made by the Thorn Corporation). These were *far* better than the standard-issue psi-blocker meds used by most government-sponsored Hero teams, allegedly.

However, she wasn't... actually... on the medication, *per se*. The first time she'd tried them, the pills gave her a dull headache and blunted control of her powers; trying to do something relatively simple, like hovering a can of seltzer from her fridge to the living room couch, had felt like playing a video game while wearing oven mitts. The bottle had consequently sat on her bathroom counter untouched for several days.

Anyway, I have the blockers if I really need them, right?

"No complaints, Director," said Maddy, looking down at the table. The issued tablet blinked, full dossiers on Helical BioSpectra, Inc., and other known Korps operations in the Greater Toronto Area ready for access.

At that, Rockwell peered up and unmuted his mic. "Caleb, I've got another meeting to make. Two-thirds of the Prairie League is... *concerned* about the leadership of the other third, and it seems like you've got this well in hand. And, Oakes? Good luck." The display abruptly blinked out to an idle screen.

"Good," the wolverine grunted, rolling his eyes. "Let's get down to business. Here's the top-down view for the short term: You're going to stake out the HBS office and find a pretext to casually bump into their chief counsel, *Ms.* Dunlop, since you've already met them once. That's your 'in.' Start crying about how *cruel* and *abusive* things are around here for your kind, some soft-hearted bloody nonsense like that. Make up something about having a bad childhood, if you need to. They won't be able to resist trying to 'save' you," he sneered, chuffed. "You'll have an invitation to meet one of their recruiters before you know it."

Maddy once again bit their tongue at the director's terminology of 'your kind,' as the events of the previous week flashed through their mind. After a moment of what they hoped looked like deep thought, rather than simmering frustration that threatened to boil over into rage, the sheep-bear spoke. "Of… of course, sir. That makes sense…"

Hagen continued in a vaguely irritated tone. "That's your first progress metric. You'll check in daily with Salton for updates, got it?"

"I look forward to it," Slider said unctuously. "I've always thought we'd make a good duo, *pal.*"

The director rolled his eyes silently at the black-clad rat and turned to the flying squirrel at his other side. "Salton, in turn, will be reporting back to Lightbox and myself as needed, but otherwise staying out of your way in the field. When we reach the point of setting up a meet, Jules will handle logistics and arrange for further backup or law enforcement involvement as needed; Salton will have your backup on-site."

Maddy nodded slowly, jaw set. "Sir? Am I expected to be on the regular duty roster at the same time?"

"No, Maddy," Lightbox said kindly. "The official version will be that you're still on sick leave. But at the same time, Director Hagen will arrange for a strategic leak that you're in the penalty box for all the blowback to that interview you did and aren't taking it very well. It'll look better for your cover story if there are rumours you're unstable, and vulnerable to 'help' from the bad guys."

"Exactly," Hagen grunted. "Now, if you'll turn to the slideshow queued up on your tablets, I'd like to review timeline projections, ongoing expectations, and refresh your memory about intel and counter intel operating procedures…"

The meeting had continued for another hour and a half before finally, mercifully, it was interrupted by the wolverine needing to take a new conference call — not from Rockwell, but from his *actual* boss in the Deputy Solicitor General of Ontario's office. Hagen had dismissed the three remaining attendees gruffly and instructed Maddy to do anything *but* publicly return to the field, for the moment.

She wasn't looking forward to having to spend time with Slider, but to be fair, she wasn't looking forward to any part of the mission. Somehow, she couldn't restrain herself from feeling unreasonably grateful to the Korps at large, for what Grace had done; the idea sent a shudder down her spine. The sheep-bear had already begun to doubt whether she really knew anything at all about the field of her chosen — no, not chosen, not really, *arranged* — career. She'd been lied to her whole life about what it meant to be a Hero. Wasn't the corollary of that, necessarily, that she'd also been lied to her whole life about what it meant to be a villain?

Maddy stewed on it as they slowly ambled towards the cafeteria. Lunch would help their mood, at least. They ordered a huge salad, slathered in sweet honey mustard dressing, and topped with dried cranberries and several chicken breasts' worth of lean white meat. As the sheep-bear carried their tray from the serving line into the seating area, they looked for their usual ideal seat — adjacent to others so as not to stand out too much, but alone at a table wherever possible. They found a good spot along the east wall, back to the panel of massive flatscreens running satellite channels from throughout Canada and around the world. A group of technicians and administrative staff were at the next table over, chattering dully.

Maddy momentarily considered scanning through the tablet's dossiers in further detail — despite the length of the meeting she'd just escaped, Hagen had left that reading to her own time — but drew back her hand right before touching the fingerprint scanner. That was top, *top* secret information, and reading it in a common area, around staff lacking her particular security clearances, would be apt to make the director go ballistic. Instead, she pulled out her phone to flip through Instagram as she ate. Soon, though, despite the distraction, she couldn't help hearing the conversation nearby. She looked over; the speaker was Ruth, a business analyst with whom she'd sometimes made small talk when they passed in the corridors.

"So that transgender, the one who works at my salon — the first time I saw him he was a male and then the second time a few months later he was a female; good for him? It's so nice they can live their truth nowadays," the peahen opined. There was a collective mumble of vague concurrence around the cafeteria table.

"Um," the sheep-bear hesitated, tentatively raising a hand, "That's, uh… not the best terminology, Ruth? You were talking about a trans woman. So, she was always female; you shouldn't be saying 'he' and 'him' even in retrospect..."

The older woman looked taken aback. "No, no... I said 'she,' I'm sure of it? I must have. Anyway, you know, I've just had a lot on my mind what with Gary in the hospital, I'm sorry if I slipped up," Ruth sniffed as she looked away.

"Oh, gosh, how's Gary doing?" the technician to Ruth's right asked solicitously. "You know we're all supporting you two, right? It's just awful, I hope your cousins are able to travel in." Her other dining companions chattered with similar soothing words; the peahen smiled sadly, nodding, almost basking in the attention.

Maddy shrank into her seat, her face burning. Great; now *she* was the asshole for bringing it up. She quickly choked down the remainder of her lunch and fled the cafeteria.

This really was no place for them, the sheep-bear realized, pained, on their way back to the secured garage area where their beloved V-Max was parked. It never could be. They'd been deep in denial about the indignities of the situation, but this wasn't okay. It hadn't been okay for a long time, if ever. They had to do something about it while they had a chance. They had to do something *soon*.

She came to her parking space in the above-ground warehouse that served as the Lakeview facility's concealed, secure parking garage. It was a narrow stall with a wall-mounted bracket for her helmet, and she reached for it. As she did, she heard a scuffling noise behind her. The sheep-bear tensed up as she instantly spun around, reflexively lashing a tentative telekinetic wave of force out in all directions around her. It wobbled her motorcycle on its kickstand, but more importantly, it had caught Slider off-guard; the rat staggered back from where he'd once again tried to sneak up behind her.

"So just what was that about being a good duo, Neal?" Maddy spat acidly as they held the helmet to their leather-jacketed chest. "Not sure how that adds up with skulking around, making like you're going to stab me in the back. Or trip me up. *Again.*"

Salton seemed mildly chagrined, but resentful. "Uh. Hi. Look, dude — um, Madison — I didn't mean anything by the skulking. I'm… *sorry,*" the rat forced out. "For today. And the thing — the thing last week."

The sheep-bear growled. "Are you? Are you *really?* Or did you get chewed out for doing the class clown routine in front of Hagen?" She put on her helmet, flipped up the visor, and folded her arms in front of her chest, scowling. "Stay away from me when we're not on an op, Neal. We're not friends. You're not some charmingly roguish comedian; you're just an asshole. I have to *work* with you, and I can do that *politely* and *professionally,* but don't insult me like that."

Slider's expression hardened. "Fine," he whined. "You heard the bossman. I want a status update once a day, and if you do *anything* to make me look bad, you…" The rat rolled his eyes and bared his buck teeth. "…You *reliable, valued teammate,* he's going to hear about it. I'm not getting on his shit list because the diversity hire can't get the job done."

"You think I don't know what I'm doing? Just watch me, 'buddy.'" Maddy flipped their visor down, mounted the bike, and nudged Salton back with their powers again — he stumbled slightly as he realized a tendril of force was pushing him out of their path, and yelped with irritation — before they rode home in a chilly rain.

After she'd doffed her boots and jacket in the apartment's narrow entryway, she proceeded to the bedroom. She flopped her ursine bulk onto the fluffy purple comforter, groaning, and looked over to her small bedside table.

The HBS business card was still there, right where Maddy had left it.

CHAPTER 6

October 25, 2022

Maddy blinked open her eyes, groaning. The sheep-bear had fallen asleep in her clothes on top of the covers, surrounded by her pillows and plushies, Grace Dunlop's business card in hand. The previous day, her boss had ordered her to make another contact with the deer — chief counsel of Helical BioSpectra, Inc., the Korps front company she'd been sent to investigate the previous week — and determine how she might be extended an invitation to be recruited by the supervillainous organization.

They were presently trying to square those instructions with the fact that they'd... already done all of that, without the short-tempered wolverine's knowledge.

Maddy flipped the card over to re-read Ms. Dunlop's handwritten note. She winced; under the circumstances, the sheep-bear had in fact grown *intensely* tired of being Ontario's Heroes' "Champion."

She knew what she had to do. She had to call Ms. Dunlop — *Grace*, the older woman had insisted — and admit that she couldn't handle any of this. She needed help. She wanted *out*. She didn't want to be a Hero any more — least of all an Ontario's Heroes operative.

Maddy gulped, uncertain. Whether or not that meant joining the Korps was... something they were trying to avoid thinking about, for the moment. They weren't a *criminal* — or at least, they weren't inclined by disposition to be.

But the clock was ticking on her current assignment, regardless. Hagen would want results, or an explanation for her *lack* of results, soon enough.

They picked up their phone and tapped in the number.

Later that morning, Maddy was again in the Financial District of downtown Toronto, again dressed low-key in their civvies. They'd parked their motorcycle underground, and after taking the skyscraper's elevator up to the 21st floor, were ushered warmly to the HBS legal department for their appointment with Grace. The difference in *vibe* from the previous week continued to astonish… except with regards to Mx. Gorgoni, the firm's CEO. When they passed Maddy in the hallway, the anole had nodded cordially, but still coolly at the Hero.

The deer looked up as Maddy knocked tentatively at her open door. "Ah! Come in, please. Grab yourself a drink if you like?"

The sheep-bear nodded, carefully closing the glass-fronted door of the chief counsel's office, and once again took a Perrier from the minifridge alongside the near wall before sitting down in one of the guest chairs. "Thank you," Maddy said hesitantly. "And — thank you for seeing me again. I feel like I've taken up so much of your time already," she mumbled.

The doe shrugged. She was today wearing a pink pantsuit with a light mauve blouse and took off her cateye-framed glasses to set them on the desk, rubbing at the sides of her muzzle before smiling warmly at the troubled Hero. "Maddy. Please, don't worry about it. I'm happy to; I know you must be going through a lot right now."

Maddy sighed sadly. "Yeah… I am," she said. "I've been thinking some more about, uh, the things we talked about last week. The 'being compromised' part."

"Understandably," Grace nodded.

"And, well, now — I mean, I told you part of this already — since I know you're all part of the Korps here, my boss wants me to get inside and infiltrate you."

Grace giggled, cocking one cervine eyebrow. She fluttered her lush eyelashes theatrically and pursed her dark lips into a pouty moue. "Get inside *me*, in particular? I'm flattered, dear, but I think you might be a *little* bit young for me. What are you, 20?"

The sheep-bear flushed, flustered, suddenly realizing her phrasing; the unbidden but inviting image of a soft, chubby transfem deer in lacy lingerie, lounging in a gently-lit boudoir with a glass of wine and just *waiting* for her, briefly invaded her mind. Gasping, she shoved the thought back down into her subconscious. "No! I'm — I'm 23," Maddy sputtered defensively.

"24 in a couple months. And, no! I'm — no, sorry. I *mean*, he wants me to infiltrate the Korps. To get recruited to be a double agent for him." She gripped the bottle of water in her hands so tightly she was afraid it might shatter. "Sorry," she said again. "*Sorry*. I'm sorry."

The deer leaned over her desk, gently chuckling. "Maddy. I'm *teasing*. Yes, I made the logical inference about what you meant, and we had assumed that was one of Hagen's potential angles in sending you here in the first place." She reached out and patted the sheep-bear's hand, still death-gripping the Perrier bottle to her desktop. "I'm gathering that you're not as comfortable about that idea as you might have been in the past? Are you having a bit of conscience weighing on you?"

Maddy relaxed, slightly, as the older woman comforted her. "I'm... not thrilled. And honestly, I'm not sure what I really know about you people, at this point." She looked down, breaking eye contact with the deer. "But, I do know that you were telling me the truth when you showed me those videos of my dad. I asked my mom, and she told me... she told me a lot of things about him. Scary things." The sheep-bear paused for a long moment. "He beat her. Every time he didn't catch a bad guy, he'd take it out on her. *Every time*." Her eyes began glistening with tears.

Grace frowned sadly. "I'm so sorry, Maddy." She reached down to a desk drawer and took out what was soon revealed as a box of tissues, setting it gently on her desk near the sheep-bear's hands. "Please, by all means."

Maddy sniffed. "Thank you," they mumbled, pulling out a tissue and dabbing it around their eyes. "But why, though? Why are you helping me so much? Aren't we, um, enemies? What makes you think you can trust me?"

"I — we — *could* help you. And you needed it."

That set Maddy off, and she began blubbering piteously. Grace looked on with concern and patted her hand again.

"Where we go from here is up to you. What can I do?"

After several more moments of weeping — at one point, the sheep-bear began grasping the older woman's hand, and squeezing tightly — they eventually collected themself. Pulling back their hand and folding their arms in front of their chest, they tried to resume a professional, cautious mien; the effect was somewhat undermined by the pile of crumpled tissues on the desk before them.

Maddy inhaled deeply. "Okay. H-here's what I was thinking: you clearly want to recruit me, and Hagen wants me to try to be recruited. I have complete cover to be here, and I want to hear you out before I decide what happens next," she pleaded. "I'm… I'm *done* with being a Hero, one way or another. I know that. And I'm going to have to make a decision about what that means. But you've been kind to me, and I feel like I owe you something for that…?"

"We're not actually going to let you spy on us for the PHL," Grace said matter-of-factly. "You do understand that, right?"

Maddy nodded. "Of course. I assumed you haven't shown or told me anything that Ontario's Heroes doesn't already know about. And I'm sure you *wouldn't*, unless you think I can be trusted."

"Very astute, dear. I bet Caleb Hagen's never even noticed you're so sharp."

The sheep-bear shrugged. He *hadn't*, but that wasn't the point. "So… I'm listening. How is it you usually pitch Heroes on abandoning their ideals and coming over to the dark side?"

Grace chuckled, snorting. "Dramatic, aren't we? You might just fit in around here better than you think." The deer reclined into her high-backed executive chair and gave herself a half-spin to look out the window. As she spoke, she gazed at the towering weather beacon of the sprawling old Beaux-Arts Canada Life Building a few blocks up the street. "Look, Maddy. I'm not a recruiter. That's not my field of expertise. I really am a lawyer, and this job isn't a cover; this is genuinely what I do for the cause, as a member of the Korps Legal Affairs Wing, 'K-LAW.' Most of my work involves fucking with our enemies *within* the bounds of legality." She paused, before turning her head back to the sheep-bear and smirking. "Of course, it helps that all our litigation and regulatory tribunal shenanigans are funded by the assets that other divisions liberate from hostile billionaires, corporations, governments, megachurches, and what have you…"

Maddy made a faint noise of disappointment. She'd grown… not fully *comfortable*, exactly, but certainly somewhat less anxious, about the idea of discussing these things with the matronly, gently sardonic doe. Meeting with someone else would be different. "What does that mean for me?"

"It means exactly what I said in my note: I know someone you can talk to. She's a field agent, and a super, like you. When she's not on, uh, *other* missions, she's one of the Korps's best recruiters. She's trans, too, and closer to your age, and she can give you that pitch for what 'the dark side' would mean in your particular circumstances. She can surely share some thoughts about 'ideals,' too. Much better than I could from my quiet little office job, frankly."

The sheep-bear nodded, rubbing their arm nervously; that made sense, they supposed. "Field agent," they said with some trepidation. "So, I'd be expected to, like... use my powers to fight Heroes and help with those heists that fund K-LAW? Is that the deal?"

The deer tented her fingers and leaned forward again. "Not at all. If you wanted to help, though, there's plenty of jobs that need doing and *aren't* also indictable offences. I saw on Twitter yesterday that someone spotted you on the job from the highway, clearing an accident on the 403 off-ramp with your powers; the Facilities and Disaster Relief teams can always use telekinetics of your calibre for things like that. And that's not to say you'd have to *do* anything at all, really! Ever heard the joke about 'fully automated luxury gay space communism?' The punchline is that the Korps actually does it. We take care of each other, since the world at large can't, or won't." Grace's expression changed slightly at that, a hard glint in her eye. "Not yet, anyway."

"Huh," Maddy mouthed, more uncertain than ever. "So, um, this recruiter. When could I talk to her?"

Grace turned to her laptop, tapping something gently into the keyboard and scrolling about with the touchpad. The deer hummed brightly. "She's planning on being in Toronto on the weekend, actually," she said in a surreally brisk tone, as if they were scheduling an ordinary business meeting rather than discussing the reluctant superhero's potential defection to villainy. (Or possibly non-villainous following of one's personal bliss, merely *funded* and *logistically supported* by villainy; Maddy was uncertain if that was a distinction without a difference.) "Is your schedule open?"

"I'm... off the team duty roster right now," Maddy mumbled. "No public Hero duties. This is my only assignment."

"Keen," the deer said brightly. "Then I'll leave it to her to make contact. We know where to find you."

The sheep-bear nodded, trying to put on a brave face. "Thank you. I really mean that." Maddy inhaled deeply, and started gathering themself to leave, thinking about the rest of their day. They'd have to check in with Slider, at some point. They weren't looking forward to it.

As she stood up, though, something else occurred to her. "Can I ask something? You've been so kind to me, and I'm guessing I'm, like... under your protection, or something, so I haven't been getting the cold shoulder around here anymore. *Mostly*. But, um. What's with Mx. Gorgoni?"

The doe leaned back, and sucked air in sharply through her teeth, wincing. "That's complicated, and it's not really my story to tell. It was a good *year* after I met them until they were willing to share it," she said thoughtfully. "But... I think it's fair for me to say that your father hurt a lot of people, in his career as Heartwood. A *lot* of people," she emphasized, significantly tilting her antlers towards the executive suite, like an aircraft marshaller directing a jet to its runway. "Killed some, when he really got worked up. Others lived, but..."

Maddy's heart sank. "O-oh," they said in a small voice. Of *course*, their father would have been a painful memory to his other victims, too. Mom wasn't the only person he'd abused, and they and their sister weren't the only loved ones of the survivors of that abuse. And here they were, just walking around as a living, breathing reminder of that violence, weren't they? Especially — in this particular front company's office, at least — as long as they were officially following in his Heroic footsteps. "I see," they mumbled.

Grace tilted her head upwards, pondering. "What's that line from the Jimmy Stewart movie? 'Each man's life touches so many others, so if he isn't around, he leaves an awful hole in the world?' Some people are... the opposite of that. Some people would have left the world an awful lot more *whole* if they hadn't touched anyone else's life at all." She stood up, and walked around her desk to open the door, patting Maddy gently on the shoulder as she did. "Anyway, please don't dwell on it. You're not responsible for what he did, and Rin doesn't really think that either. They don't hate you, I promise."

"I'll take your word for it," she sighed.

"It was lovely to see you again, Maddy," the deer said with genuine warmth. "Give me a call if you ever need someone to talk to, eh?"

The sheep-bear weakly smiled, melancholy. "Grace? Can I ask just one more thing?"

"Yes, dear?"

She pulled a slip of thermal printer paper from the pocket of her hoodie. "I've, uh, got my motorcycle in the parkade downstairs. Could you validate my parking…?"

Maddy ended up wandering over to the Eaton Centre after departing the HBS office with a friendly wave. They passed the great neoclassical heap of Osgoode Hall, the sweeping space-age towers of City Hall, and the stolid Romanesque-revival bulk of Old City Hall in turn as they walked down Queen Street to the downtown mall. Eventually, they browsed the stores for a few hours before giving up, proceeding to the basement food court to chow down on a trio of burritos, each as big as their head.

Much as she gazed with curiosity at the selection of dresses that might actually flatter her bulky frame in the Torrid, or the vast panoply of makeup filling every brightly-lit square centimeter in the Sephora, she felt frustrated by her lack of savvy in the ordinary business of… well, being a young woman. Mom and Brianna had tried to help, and so had her (brief!) high school girlfriend Emily, but she'd never felt she had the time to learn how to be… pretty? Not that she was unhappy with her appearance generally — she could rock the butch look *very* well, all things considered — but it would just be nice to have those skills handy, if she ever needed them.

There'd always been too much pressure to train, to prepare to be a Hero and carry on the Heartwood legacy. First Granddad's unbearable drilling on her father's career trivia, then the doctors who assessed and tested her powers once they manifested, and then the after-school and weekend obligations to the Prairie League Cadets. It didn't leave much bandwidth for thinking about anything else, especially once the sheep-bear had graduated high school, and had to channel full-time attention into the OH Junior Development Program.

Maddy was idly people-watching, zoned out as they sipped their fountain Coke, when their phone vibrated on the food court table. Glancing at the screen, there was no caller ID listed. The sheep-bear answered cautiously, holding the phone up to one fluffy ear. "...Hello?"

A sullen, nasal voice emanated from the tiny speaker; it was Slider. Of *course* it was Slider. "Why aren't you picking up on your secure communicator, Oakes? Why am I having to call you on your fucking *civilian cell phone* to get your attention...?"

She groaned, rolling her eyes, and set down her half-eaten third burrito. "Neal, how do you think it would look if I was trying to play nice with our friends on the 21st floor — I'm supposed to be making them think I want to be on *their* side, if you recall — with my... usual... gear on me? Should I just walk in wearing my full costume? They're not stupid! They'd scan me for standard-issue bugs and trackers."

The rat growled peevishly. "Fine," he grumbled. "Whatever. You infiltrate the gay anarchist weirdos your way. What do you have to report?"

Maddy was reflexively about to share the events of their morning, when they suddenly remembered: as far as the sheep-bear could tell, neither Slider, nor the Director, nor anyone else in the OH chain of command seemed to be aware of their activities in the previous week. That could be an advantage, later. "I, uh... I staked out the building from across the street. For like six hours. I left when the cafe staff started getting suspicious. No luck making contact today, so I'm getting a late lunch."

Slider huffed, dismissive. "What's your plan for tomorrow?"

"More of the same, until I can talk to Ms. Dunlop again. I mean, you just said I can do this my way, right?"

"One week. I'm entertaining this for *one week* until I tell Hagen you can't fucking get the job done. Better make the most of it, pal," he sniffed dismissively, before ending the call.

Maddy shoved the phone into her pocket and picked up her burrito briefly before setting it back down, staring off into the crowded food court. Suddenly, she wasn't that hungry.

CHAPTER 7

October 29, 2022

The sheep-bear took a sip of their Baja Blast and looked out the window at the headlights flickering by on Eglinton. It was just after five on Saturday afternoon, but dark and overcast, and Maddy caught a glimpse of their reflection after the cars passed: a Pepper's Ghost of worried-looking ursine bulk buried in a puffy black ski jacket, white toque pulled down past their modest horns.

The Taco Bell was empty. A handful of drive-through customers had driven through, but no one else had entered in the forty-five minutes she'd been sitting in a corner booth. The employees, as far as she could tell, were hiding in the back of the kitchen prep area, quietly bantering amongst themselves. That was all the better while she waited for her meeting with the Korps recruiter.

They'd been spending the wait agitated, scrolling through social media. Maddy had never bothered unlocking their profiles since the previous week's shitshow with their ill-chosen interview, but regardless, couldn't stop name-searching themself. People were sharing a brief Vice article on them, alleging that a "well-placed source" with Ontario's Heroes had shared stories of Heartforce's erratic, negligent behaviour in the past two weeks. The sheep-bear scowled. Martha from the Comms department had clearly done what Hagen had asked of her, to give cover for the undercover Korps-recruitment mission, but it really didn't have to lean so far into "look at the crazy tranny" territory.

On top of *that*, Maddy was growing increasingly anxious about dealing with the scheming fuckboy/technically-a-Hero Slider. She'd been stringing him along with increasingly elaborate stories of striking out in her attempts at infiltration but could tell he was impatient and growing angry. The rat already thought she was a useless, hopeless "diversity hire," though, so at least he was unlikely to realize she'd already gone *much*, much further in her interactions with the Korps than she'd seen fit to officially report.

They just needed to do this on their own, the shaken Hero reassured themself. They didn't want Slider or Hagen to know what was going on *quite* yet... if ever. Their new friend (they hoped?) Grace had made the arrangements; just as the deer had promised, an anonymous note had turned up slipped under their apartment door with nothing but a time, date, and the words TACO BELL and TOMKEN.

Despite Maddy's apprehension about meeting with a straight-up *villain* — probably a wanted fugitive, maybe even a killer! — who was surely a high-profile target of the PHL (if not also the federal Aurora Squadron, and probably their American counterparts with the NHA, too), the older woman had assured Maddy this was preferable to anything she herself could tell the young Hero. Grace may have been with the Korps, but it wasn't as if she *personally* got her hands dirty working in their legal department. The recruiter was both a fellow super and transfem and could speak to the experiences of a potential defector in her circumstances much better than the office-bound doe, she'd claimed.

A defector, they thought with a wince. That was what they were or would be. That was what they were seriously, genuinely considering: turning their back on Ontario's Heroes, and on being a good, safe, PR-friendly little diversity mascot for their super-team in order to side with the clandestine motley crew of anarchic, gleefully queer criminals that made up the Korps. It repulsed Maddy on some level but intrigued and provoked her longing even more on another. Quitting being a Hero was one thing — they'd already made up their mind they couldn't be Hagen's pet publicity stunt for very much longer — but there'd be no going back from a decision like this. And yet...

After all, it had been Grace who'd taken pity on the sheep-bear, and shared the Korps's records of their superhero father's embarrassingly memory-holed death, leading them to the epiphany that his legacy was nothing to uphold or take pride in. Ontario's Heroes had concealed the truth from them, the Prairie League had concealed the truth from them, the *whole damn PHL* had concealed the truth from them. They resented it. They resented the hell out of it.

She felt obligated to... do *something* in return. At least hear out the recruitment pitch, consider it in good faith; she owed Grace that much, didn't she?

Their reverie was broken by the realization that a figure had approached the table (even though they could have sworn they hadn't heard the restaurant's doors being opened) and was calling their name. The voice was rich and dark and sinuous, and they bit their lip as they spun towards the new arrival.

"Maddy Oakes?" It was a grey tabby cat in a leather jacket, curvaceous and vaguely threatening in her manner. She radiated confidence and *demimondiale* disdain for the strictures of polite society, Maddy noted, feeling unaccountably impressed. She was also *extremely* fucking hot. "Carmen Rayne."

"Um. Hello. You must — I mean, of course, yes, who else would you be." Maddy looked away, flushing, and paused for a beat as the woman squeezed into the seat opposite them, a minor feat given the feline's bodacious curves. "Can I, uh, ask why we're meeting at Taco Bell?"

"Call it a tradition," the cat sneered playfully. "So. I'm here, you're here. You're curious. You've seen that the Korps aren't the soulless monsters the capes make us out to be, but you're not sold on the villain life. Is that our starting position here?"

The sheep-bear winced, still avoiding eye contact with Carmen. "Pretty much...?"

"Let's be clear about something up front," the tabby said. "The Korps is my *family*. If someone were to take advantage of my *goodwill*, to *hurt* my family, they would never get another opportunity. Do I make myself understood?" Carmen bared her fangs through a sweetly menacing grin.

Maddy growled under her breath, hackles beginning to raise, and looked at the cat. "I have a family too. A very, very *normal* mom and sister. They've got no powers, they're not political, they're not rich or famous or powerful, they're just... ordinary. They *might* understand if I quit being a Hero, but I don't know I could make them understand *this*. What happens to them?"

"That depends on just how cool they are," Carmen said blithely, gazing with indifference at the back of her extended claws. "And how much *they* would want to be in your life, if you changed teams. As for their safety...

we're capable of sending some very *harshly worded* messages to the PHL about leaving them alone, if necessary."

Maddy pondered the cat's words for a moment. "I've got powers, and OH invested a lot into training me," the sheep-bear murmured tentatively. "What kind of protection would *I* have, even if OH left my family alone?"

Carmen raised an eyebrow. "If you're with us, you're *with* us, Maddy. There are hundreds of Korps members who've been in the same place you are now, disgusted with the hypocrisy of being a government-backed Hero. You know what we call them? Comrades. Friends. *Family.* We all have each other's backs; that's what mutual aid means." Her expression softened the tiniest bit, but she continued. "If you want to help people, there's all kinds of ways you can pitch in. If you just need a clean break from the PHL, to heal and reflect on what the hell you actually *want* from life, that's an option too."

The sheep-bear took a deep breath. Was the tabby *sure* she understood the stakes here? "Director Hagen—"

"*Asshole,*" Carmen coughed out theatrically into a clenched fist. "*Psychopath,*" she coughed again. The cat tilted her head and locked eyes with Maddy, smiling brightly. "Oh, I'm sorry, forgive me; please go on?"

Maddy shifted uncomfortably on the hard bench. "—Wants me to be a double agent spying on you. He was setting me up without my knowing it, and then gave the order this week."

Carmen looked thoughtful and sipped on her own drink. (*Wait,* thought Maddy; did she *have* a drink, a minute ago?) "So I heard," the tabby said pensively. "I also understand from your K-LAW contact that you've been keeping him out of the loop about when you've already met with her, and honestly, I didn't expect you'd want to keep that up for long anyway. Playing both sides of the field is high stakes, especially if they both think you're really on *their* side. And you know, with respect? You don't strike me as a very good liar. But, yeah, we could do that, if you want. As long as we can trust you to double-agent for *us,* not the PHL. Can we trust you, Maddy?"

The sheep-bear wrung the pads of her blunt hoof-nailed hands. The recruiter wasn't *wrong;* she couldn't help but think Hagen was growing suspicious by this point, and she was afraid she'd crumble and let something slip, if pressured. Carmen's tone rankled her, though, and she pursed her dark lips. *They* were the criminals! *They* were supposed to be selling *her* on giving up everything she'd worked for — much as she'd hated it all, in the end — for a life outside the law. "I... don't really want to do that, no. Anyway, how do I know I can trust *you*, though? How do I know this isn't some trap to brainwash me?" Maddy's heart rate began to climb. "People... people disappear, and then they turn up with the Korps, and they're completely different. Their personalities, their bodies, I've seen the videos—"

"And where did you learn *that?*"

The sheep-bear's mouth hung open briefly, as her train of thought was derailed. "Um. From OH, I guess. The broader PHL. And the news?"

Carmen sighed, bitterly smirking. "Let's *talk* about the PHL, hon. They hid the truth from you and made you believe lies. They moulded you into a tool to be used at their convenience, leveraging your power — not just your *powers*, but all of you, the incredible strength and resilience it takes to just *be* different like we are, in this world — to turn you into something *lesser*. They built a cage around you, a persona that wasn't really yours, but an extension of your father's," the cat scoffed. "*And* they had the full cooperation of every major media outlet in Canada to do it. If he'd lived, you'd have been his sidekick, right? Tell me I'm wrong. And after you've been through all that, you still think that *we're* the propagandists and brainwashers?"

"But—"

"Madison. I've read your dossier. You started transitioning at 14, which, *fuck* yeah. How did your family, your friends, react? Was there anyone who didn't accept it? Is there anyone who *still* doesn't accept it?"

"Well..." The sheep-bear winced again and looked away, clenching their jaw as they thought back.

May 10, 2013

The adolescent sheep-bear hid under the blankets and tried to cover their ears. It didn't help; they could still hear Mom and Granddad shouting at each other down the hall in the living room of the suburban Calgary home.

"Deborah, I can't believe you're letting the boy *do* this to himself. He's just confused, don't you see? His head's all messed up, from that boondoggle with the Cadets trip last winter. Do you think the PHL is going to want him to be the new Heartwood if he makes himself some kind of *freak?*"

"I've been talking to Alexis," Mom said in a shaking voice. "The Prairie League doesn't like it, sure. But Ontario's Heroes—"

The elderly bear growled. "You'd move out east? Just so he can keep playing dress-up like this?"

Mom took a deep breath. "The — the director knew Roger. Mr. Hagen. Do you remember, he was Canadian Shield? Alexis put me in touch and I spoke to him, and he's open to it. He said the government told them they had to be more 'diverse,' so it wouldn't be a barrier to a licensed Hero career there. It might even be a benefit, you know, like affirmative action? I mean, the new premier is a lesbian, they're very modern about these things in Toronto—"

"*Toronto?* Bloody hell, Deb, you're not talking any sense. You'd take the boy away from his family so he can go join the junior transvestite brigade in *Toronto?*"

"*I'm* Madison's family, Garth. Me and Brianna. And he — *she*, I mean, *she* — has to do this. I didn't get it at first, but this is who she is. Brianna knows it too, she's been so happy to have a big sister. I saw how Maddy couldn't concentrate at school, I'd hear her crying at night, and she's got *no* real friends, just those squad mates in the Cadets…"

Maddy began sobbing a little, at that. It was *true*, but the way Mom said it broke her heart. It hadn't always been like this. She used to have actual friends, when she was younger, before she had to transfer to a new school and her powers started flaring up. She'd stopped seeing them at hockey practice, or the after-school club at the community centre; there was no time, not when she had to *train*.

They had to make their father proud. They *had* to. They had to be strong and try to hang on; this was all there was for them. It was, in fact, what had convinced Mom, and the stern bison doctor at the Children's Hospital gender clinic, that they were mature enough to start transitioning.

Next to that, what were friends…?

"Maybe the boy *would* have friends if he wasn't a God-damned *weirdo*," Granddad muttered. "I heard about this. He's been brainwashed by the TV and the MySpace, he thinks it'll make him 'cool' to start calling himself a girl. Who could actually *want* this? I remember all the times he was splashing around in the mud, going fishing with me, getting into fights... it must be that something's gotten to him. You've got to take away the internet, keep a closer eye on who he talks to! It's like his personality is completely different."

"Please, stop calling her 'the boy.' She's afraid to say anything to you, but I know it hurts her. Until her — her *powers*, you'd only been seeing the kids in the summer and for Christmas! I see them all the time! Madison is the same sweet, shy, thoughtful person she's always been. You just don't want to believe this is really her."

"It isn't. I'm sure of it."

Mom sniffed, and made a low, angry bleating noise. Maddy could tell from the tone that she was holding back tears against her father-in-law's hectoring. They wished — they wished she didn't have to. Sometimes they wished so hard that they could have been *normal*, no powers, no...

"We're moving to Ontario, Garth. She's proved she's responsible enough, and I want to let Maddy be herself. That's final. I'm not sure if she'll even *want* to follow in Roger's footsteps in the end, but if she does, Ontario's Heroes will look out for her."

"If Grande Prairie—"

"Garth."

"—if it was good enough for Roger, then the boy—"

"GET OUT OF MY HOUSE, GARTH."

Granddad growled with irritation, but Maddy soon heard the front door open, and then slam closed. Mom's hoofed footfalls went past their bedroom door, alongside the sound of tepid sniffling. The master bedroom door closed. Several minutes later, it opened again, and then, the young sheep-bear's own door slowly creaked open.

Deborah Gillespie's tone was soft, and pained, and beaten-down. "... Honey?"

Maddy faced away from the door, pulling the blanket down from over her head. "Yeah, Mom?"

"I'm sorry. I'm sorry that you had to hear all of that. I'm sorry for… well, I'm sorry your Granddad can't see you for who you are, right now. I'm sure he'll come around. He just needs some time to get used to it," the sheep said plaintively.

"It's okay," Maddy mumbled.

It was not okay.

"Let's — let's all sit down tomorrow, after I bring Brianna home from her swim class, and we can start planning what to pack, okay?

"I love you, Mom," the sheep-bear murmured, before pulling the covers back up.

October 29, 2022

"…I think I understand what you mean," Maddy gulped. "But you're saying that every single time that's happened, it's been voluntary? No… no mind control hypno-goggles, no torture, no threats?"

The brash feline raised an eyebrow. "I *know* you know that they're called Rose-Coloured Glasses. And yeah, sometimes people need some help, to realize what it is that they really want, and it's not always just a leg up on transitioning. We can offer that help."

Maddy screwed up her snout, quizzically. "What *does* 'help' mean, then?"

Carmen shrugged; her expression seemed more genuine now, a gently supportive smile. "It means *help*. It means giving people what they need, even if they don't know they need it yet. And sometimes that does mean a little nudge towards conclusions that wouldn't have occurred to them otherwise, and *yes*, sometimes a chat with ROSE inside your frontal lobe can be that nudge. We'd rather have accomplices than nemeses, after all."

"You want minions to rule the world, is what I was told." Even as soon as the words were out of their mouth, the sheep-bear realized they weren't sure if they really still believed that.

The cat took a deep breath, flicking a drop of condensation off the side of her waxed drink cup. It landed on the table between them. "Let's try thinking about this from a different angle," she said warmly. "What is it you want, Maddy? What is it that you've been denied all your life? What's been just *eating away* at you with its absence?"

The sheep-bear snorted. "What, are you trying to bribe me?"

"Everyone has a price," Carmen asserted.

"Not me."

"Don't you?" The cat began counting down on her elegant, clawed fingers. "You don't want anything to do with the Heartwood legacy, especially since you learned your father was an abusive rage monster when he wasn't waving for the cameras — much like a *lot* of your present co-workers, *just saying* — or being a capital-H Hero at all, really. You don't want to be a weapon, or a tool, getting manipulated by people who see you as a pawn. You especially don't want to be the token queer, leading your team's float in the Pride parade. Except, hah, I heard capes got banned from the parade here; fuckin' A? Anyway, *most* importantly, you want your mother and sister to be safe. Them not being disappointed in you for giving up on a Hero career would be nice, too. How am I doing so far?"

"...You're still not wrong," the sheep-bear winced. "But so what?"

"So? That's your price," Carmen smirked, tenting her fingers over the hard plastic tabletop. "The Korps can give you all of that, and more. *Just let us show you.*"

Maddy was more twisted up than ever. She didn't know, couldn't know — how was she supposed to feel, right now? How could she be *sure* that the cat wasn't tricking her, wasn't setting her up to be exploited and manipulated in a whole new way, wasn't playing on her feelings of guilt and inadequacy and longing for validation, just like *everyone else in her life* — and she sniffed, snout trembling, eyes beginning to water. After a moment she steeled her jaw again, took a deep breath, and met Carmen's gaze with as much bravery as she could muster. "Show me *what?*"

The cat turned her head, nodding eastward out the window of the Taco Bell. "What 'home' could look like for you. What *a life after OH* could look like for you. That is, if you wanted it." She paused. "You know Yorkdale, yeah?"

"Of course," Maddy said, uncertain. It was a huge old mid-century shopping mall in North York, at Allen Road and the 401, near the defunct

Downsview Airport. The Korps couldn't possibly have a secret base *inside*, could they?

"I've got something else to take care of first, but I think I need to give you a *tour*, girl. Meet me there, by the Sunglass Hut, in an hour?" Carmen smirked, smugly. "I'll show you all *kinds* of things. And lucky you — tonight's the Halloween party."

Chapter 8

October 29, 2022

Maddy Oakes was at Yorkdale on a Saturday night. It had been an elegant suburban shopping destination, and briefly the largest enclosed mall in the world, when it opened in 1964. Decades later, it retained a faint aura of its former grandeur, even though the most upscale retailers had fled back downtown to the so-called "Mink Mile" of Bloor Street, and the sprawling complex had come to feature a tackily giant multiplex and a Rainforest Cafe. The sheep-bear had parked her beloved Yamaha V-Max underground and meandered through the mall on her way to her destination. At one point, the sudden echo of her footsteps made her look upwards; she hadn't realized when the architecture had shifted but noted the dramatically steep arches of the vaulted ceiling as she traversed the oldest section of the building.

They were here to meet back up with Carmen Rayne, the Korps recruiter who'd gently, but smugly, raked them over the coals earlier that evening... at *Taco Bell,* of all places. Maddy was trying to reconcile their curiosity about the freedom and support the supervillainous organization could offer in breaking away from her unbearable role as a token trans member of Ontario's Heroes, with the fact that the Korps were still, you know, *criminals.* And overwhelmingly queer criminals, at that — the kind of people her late father, the rage-prone superhero Heartwood (as well her current boss) tended to call "perverted terrorist subversives."

The sheep-bear was still torn, despite the heart-to-heart she'd had with Carmen to address some of her most pressing concerns. The cat had, in response, insisted on giving her a *tour;* of what, Carmen hadn't said. Maddy assumed it was a secret Korps facility of some kind, since the cat had mentioned tonight was their Halloween party. She imagined an underground lair hidden in disused stockroom areas, or a sealed-off portion of the parkade, something along those lines. In her mind it was small, dark, and cramped, but possibly... welcoming? She had to hope, at least.

Arriving at a crossroads in the wide walkways, they looked around and spotted the sign for their destination: the Sunglass Hut. Sure enough, there was Carmen — a curvaceous gray tabby in a leather jacket, languorously leaning against a nearby wall. She grinned like the proverbial Cheshire Cat on spotting the sheep-bear across the room. *Fuck*, Maddy silently huffed, biting her lip. The cat made villainy look so enticingly, effortlessly *cool*.

Carmen clapped Maddy on the shoulder as she approached. "Hey! Glad you decided to come."

The sheep-bear smiled weakly, confused. "I mean, you said to meet you here in an hour because you had something else to do first...?"

"Yeah, I did — and I didn't. Maddy, you get that that was a no-strings-attached opportunity to back out, right?" The cat purred smugly. "But you didn't take it! So, I'm glad."

"Oh," Maddy said in a small voice. She had not, in fact, realized that. "I guess — I guess I am, too."

Carmen nodded kindly, and started walking, gesturing for Maddy to follow. They proceeded along to a service corridor between two storefronts, following it to an unmarked door. "Okay," the tabby said candidly, pulling a small pile of magenta fabric — unfurled, it turned out to be a scarf — from her pocket. "Here's the part where you have to trust me. Maddy, can I blindfold you? It won't be for long, and it's the easiest way to do this." Suddenly very serious, she added: "I *promise* that no harm of any kind will come to you."

The sheep-bear looked around uneasily. The door was visible; what was there to hide at this point?

Still...

"I've come this far," she conceded. "Do it." She turned around, letting the cat carefully wrap the scarf around her eyes, knotting it in the back. It only caught once on the point of her left horn, and the villain mumbled a faint apology.

Suddenly, Maddy felt momentarily disoriented, and they lurched forward, their balance off-kilter. Carmen grasped their arm — was she already grasping their arm before that point? — to steady the sheep-bear.

"Sorry about that," the cat sighed, and immediately began undoing the scarf's knot, pulling the impromptu blindfold away. "Madison Oakes, welcome to your first Korps site. Well, second, I guess, if we're counting that one front downtown, but that's more of a satellite operation…"

Maddy boggled as she looked around. The two were no longer in the mall's cramped service corridors, nor some dingy sub-basement; far from it. Instead, she stood in a massive, brightly lit, high-ceilinged atrium. It might have been the largest indoor space the sheep-bear had ever seen, possibly bigger than the whole of Yorkdale itself. There was greenery everywhere, in massive planters and delicate hanging fixtures, and the walls were hung with warmly-toned wooden and metallic panels, magenta accents and helical iconography everywhere. She couldn't read the signage — it was written in a language she didn't recognize — but it was clearly directional in nature, pointing to various destinations down vast airport concourse-wide hallways. People of all shapes, sizes, species and gender presentations bustled around, many wearing the Korps's signature Rose-Coloured Glasses.

"What? *How…?*" Maddy's mouth hung agape, and they walked in circles around the recruiter, trying to take everything in. "God — God-fucking-*dammit*, Carmen," they sputtered, "where the *fuck* are we?"

"Told you," the cat smirked. "Could be home, if you like. Come on, let's go over to the LRT stop, and we can take a loop around the different sectors. We'll finish up at a tailor in the Quartermaster's; if I'm taking you to the Halloween party, you're going to need a *costume*, girl."

"There's *trains* in here…?"

Nearly three hours later, surrounded by throngs of costumed, lustily energetic partygoers — there must have been *thousands* of people in this "Dominion Club" Carmen had led her to — Maddy was still utterly stunned by the sheer scale of everything she'd seen. This was an entire underground *city*. It had residential areas, offices, research labs, and recreational facilities, as well as the kinds of vital infrastructure that might ordinarily be provided by some level of government, from medical clinics of all types (including one solely for transition-related care, the size of a city block!) to power, transit and telecommunications.

They felt vaguely ridiculous and unworthy, appreciating now just how overwhelmingly massive and *complex* the Korps's operation was. And this was just one site of many, Carmen had said! It made the drab gray tunnels and industrially-carpeted offices of OH Lakeview seem laughably tiny and under-resourced, by comparison; whenever Maddy went to the facility, they had to park their bike in a dingy former tire warehouse, for fuck's sake.

The sheep-bear insisted to her tour guide that it wasn't necessary to outfit her with a costume for the party, but Carmen had *insisted*. The cat had taken her to a small tailoring boutique alongside a row of similar facilities and introduced her to the proprietor — a short, wizened wallaby in a dapper vest, named Montgomery — who told her that money was no object, nor would it be particularly difficult to quickly fabricate anything she could think of. What, Carmen had asked, was Maddy's dream costume, that she'd never been able to pull off on her own? Who would she have dressed up as for Halloween when she was younger, given unlimited resources?

Disbelieving, Maddy gave the wallaby instructions for cosplaying one of her childhood heroes that she was *sure* he wouldn't be able to fulfill, let alone in the twenty minutes it took him to do so. And *that* was how she had wound up at the party dressed in snugly-fitted black suede and matte-painted lightweight Mockingjay armour, right out of the movie poster, complete with what she suspected was a fully combat-ready bow and over-shoulder quiver of arrows.

Carmen (costumed as her vintage edutainment software namesake, in a flowing crimson trench coat and broad-brimmed Cordovan hat) had briefly left them alone near one of the many bars in the club, having gone off to find someone she wanted to introduce. That had been several minutes ago, and they were getting antsy. The sheep-bear squeezed past the shaggy bulk of an older wolverine who wore a Ren Faire-esque blonde pageboy wig, tight white tunic and pink doublet. A tall, lithe ferret in the costume of a scarecrow, and cheerfully scarred brown bear dressed like a stereotypical hayseed farmer — the latter would have fit right in among Maddy's rural Alberta cousins, the Hero imagined — likewise had to part to let them pass.

Coming up to the bar proper, she passed a short, twunkish mouse in drably similar costume, green dyed fur and some kind of antennae, talking to a lean falcon femme festooned with gem-laden jewelry and wearing the loose wrappings of an ancient mummy — although Maddy, flushing, was certain that actual ancient Egyptians had likely left more to the imagination when dressing the bodies of their honoured dead. The two walked away, drinks in hand.

The sight made their dry mouth water. They were growing more anxious in the crush of sweaty bodies, too, and it crossed their mind that they wouldn't mind a bit of a buzz to take the edge off. When they were able to flag down the bartender, Maddy ordered a Cosmo, and immediately began nervously sipping at it.

Fixated on her drink, the sheep-bear stumbled; her bow, slung over her shoulder, had become caught in the frills of a huge, flouncy vintage-looking dress worn by a slim reptilian figure.

Maddy backed away, disengaging their bowstring from the tangle, then looked up and realized exactly who they'd bumped into. "Mx. Gorgoni," they gulped, eyes wide with panic.

The anole nodded cordially. "Hello, Maddy! I've been hearing a lot about you lately. I'm glad you decided to give us a chance." They preened, striking a pose with their slinky arms and delicate, long-fingered hands, before launching into an enthused infodump. "Do you like my Madame de Pompadour costume? It's a traditionally tailored Rococo *Robe à la Française*. You see, here I have the *paniers* to support the wide hips of the *jube*, and then the *manteau* portion goes over that, with the stomacher visible over the bodice; now, the *engageants* of the arm portion aren't actually sewn in, as such, but—"

Maddy opened her mouth and closed it several times, struggling for a response, and feeling ever more like the walls were closing in on her. She looked up and down Mx. Gorgoni's elegant teal-blue dress; it struck a fine contrast with their supple cerulean scales, admittedly, as they rattled off ever more details about 18th-century *Ancien Régime* fashion trends. But what could she even say to someone Heartwood had nearly killed in one of his brutal rages? Finally, she blurted it out anxiously: "*Oh God Mx. Gorgoni, I'm so sorry about my asshole dad—*"

The anole raised a hand, waving her anxiety aside. "It's *okay*, Maddy. And you can call me Rin. Grace told you about our history, eh?"

The sheep-bear cringed, rubbing the back of their neck. "Um. Thank you, Rin. Not... a lot. She said it wasn't her story to tell, but the upshot was that Heartwood, uh. He hurt, um — I mean, I assume you two fought, and — and he almost killed you...?"

"Oh, back when I was doing field ops out of Ottawa, yes. I got lucky, and got away from him before he could finish the job. That Canada Day party was the last time I ever went out on a covert mission; he basically ended my career in the field. But it's *not your fault*," the anole continued, "and we don't really believe in the 'sins of the father' thing around here, believe me; there's plenty of folks with abusive parents who've made their way to the Korps, myself included. *I'm* sorry for letting that resentment spill over to how I treated you last week; you didn't know. Although, to be fair, we had good reason to think you were hostile at the time."

"To be fair, I *was*," Maddy admitted regretfully. "Even if I was being set up, even if I knew I was personally compromised somehow by being a PHL Hero... I still let myself *want* respectability on some level. It was easy to believe that the Korps was just, you know... all dangerous, cackling maniacs, before I met Grace."

"Oh, we've got our fair share of dangerous cacklers," Rin cackled. "But it's an *aesthetic*. Mostly. Sometimes. Anyway, 'Be Gay, Do Crimes' doesn't necessarily mean destruction for its own sake," the anole said warmly. "One of my dearest friends in the world is a doctor with the Medical division, attached to one of our other sites. I recruited her back in the 90s, when she was working for the government. And you know what? *She's* never been particularly gung-ho about the villain thing, honestly. She was just happy to have a place to work on her biotech research, where her values wouldn't be compromised."

The sheep-bear gazed off into the crowd of revelers, dancing and laughing and gyrating joyfully. Several partygoers walked in front of Rin and Maddy, and she looked back to Rin. "Has... has it always been like this, for the Korps?"

"Not *exactly*," the anole said, slightly cagily. "But as long as there's been supers, there's been queer supers who figured out it was a better deal to find our own path and build our own world, rather than try to assimilate."

Rin sipped their drink (apparently champagne in a flute glass) and looked wistfully off into the distance at a well-endowed serval woman in a tuxedo and top hat. "I know he was before your time, and — Overlord love him — never had that much of a public profile, but have you ever heard of Degrade? Supervillain, biiiig buff stallion, active in the 80s and 90s, his power was that he could disintegrate inorganic materials at short range. He mostly used it to knock out alarm systems and do B&Es."

Maddy shrugged. "No, sorry. I don't really know that much about Heroes or villains from before I had to start studying in the junior PHL training curriculum with the Prairie League Cadets, and that was 2012. Mostly just the big names that everyone's heard of, like any civilian."

Rin raised a gold-ringed eyebrow, smiling sadly. "Well, we dated for a while, he and I. It was when I first got into this life. He got me into this life, actually, but we broke up. I wanted to join the Korps, and he didn't."

"Oh? What happened?"

"Rod liked working for himself, and not having to listen to anyone. For him, the supervillain thing was just a means to an end, a way he could carve out a little shelter from a hostile society and take care of himself."

Maddy nodded. "And you…?"

The anole shrugged. "A friend showed me the good that could be done outside the law, with a little bit of organization and mutual aid. Rod didn't disagree, but he just wasn't a joiner like that," Rin mused. "He's a sweet guy, but he had to go his own way. He retired to open a nerdy gay bar in Miami Beach — they do wargaming nights — and I stop by whenever I'm in the area. He's never quite wrapped his head around the nonbinary thing, but he tries."

Maddy smirked, rolling her eyes. "Tell me about it. Mom… well, as far as my mom is concerned, I'm just a girl. Maybe a slightly spicy girl, but…"

"I know it's not much in the grand scheme of things, but I can tell you that here, of all places, you are vanishingly unlikely to ever have anyone second-guess your gender or sexuality."

"It's true," said a familiar voice from behind the two. Maddy turned to see Grace Dunlop; the zaftig doe lawyer was a familiar-looking warrior princess, wearing a bright white short-sleeved tunic-dress with golden highlights, and a bejeweled tiara framing her swept-back antlers. She smiled widely on seeing the sheep-bear. "Hi, Maddy! I take it your chat with Ms. Rayne was a convincing one?"

Maddy beamed, glad to see a friendly face. "Grace! I love your costume," she said.

The deer giggled, throwing her head back. "Aww, thank you! *But*," Grace tutted, suddenly with a serious mien, "that statement was not responsive to my question, Ms. Oakes…!" Resuming her genuine good cheer, she added: "Really, though, how's it been?"

"I've learned some things. And Carmen did, uh, address some of my worries. I believe her even more about the Korps's ability to follow through now, though, having seen…" The sheep-bear gazed around the Dominion Club, still in awe. "…Seen all of *this*. It's amazing! How is it not, like, common knowledge that you have this whole Supervillain Bio-Dome thing underneath Toronto?"

Grace and Rin looked at each other, and then to Maddy, before speaking at the same time.

"So, you see, the thing about that is—"

"Okay, so *historically*, what you need to understand—"

At that point Maddy spotted the crimson-clad figure of Carmen Rayne off in the distance, beyond several milling groups of costumed partygoers, just past a bulky civet in a techwear-looking bodysuit and some kind of metallic orange gauntlets. When the tabby locked eyes with them from under her wide-brimmed hat, she waved, and gestured for the sheep-bear to come meet her.

"Oh! I'm sorry," Maddy said, interrupting the pair's explanation, "I think my tour guide is calling me. Thank you for being so welcoming. And Grace, thank you, for encouraging me to talk to Carmen. It's… it's helped," she said, with a curious sense of satisfaction.

The K-LAW agents smiled.

"Go, go! Enjoy yourself," Rin insisted.

Grace chuckled lightly. "I'm glad. Now, go, enjoy partying with people your own age rather than us old fogeys," the deer said warmly. She playfully patted Maddy on the back, gently pushing her forward.

The sheep-bear nodded, waving farewell to them over their shoulder as they began navigating through the crowd towards Carmen. The cat was saying something as they approached, but they couldn't make it out through the music and the buzz of the crowds, and Maddy gestured to their head to indicate they hadn't heard.

As she got closer, Carmen pulled on her sleeve, and leaned over to speak directly into Maddy's ear. The curvaceous cat gestured to her side. "Have you met my girlfriend?"

The sheep-bear turned, to find themself at eye-level with a filigreed, polychromed armour breastplate covering an ample bust. Their eyes were then drawn downward to a set of *very* impressively toned, rusty orange-and-white-furred abs, and a slit blue peasant skirt pinned to impossibly wide hips with a circular brooch. It was only when Maddy looked up — and then back down, and up again, to take in the entire figure — that their jaw dropped in shock.

She stumbled backwards a few paces, dropping her drink with a crash of tinkling glassware as her heart rate suddenly skyrocketed. Panicking, her hands shaking, the sheep-bear reflexively dropped into a defensive stance, and reached out with her telekinesis to ready for an attack.

The gigantic red wolf gave Maddy a quizzical look through angular RCGs as she calmly sipped her Rusty Nail. "Don't tell me this is the most bare fur you've seen on a lady at a party?"

Maddy didn't dare consciously move a muscle, for fear they might lose their focus. Their hands continued to tremble, regardless. They fixed their eyes on Carmen and hissed at the tabby through gritted teeth.

"YOU'RE DATING *REDLINE?!*"

Chapter 9

October 29, 2022

"You can call me Volta," said the wolf mildly, before turning to her partner with a sardonic grin. "God, Carm, you weren't kidding about how tightly wound this one is."

Every impulse drilled into Maddy Oakes by her training — the Prairie League Cadets, to the OH Junior Development Program, to the constant intel briefings she'd endured as a fully-fledged Hero — told her to keep her back up and be prepared for life-or-death combat at any second. Suddenly, she was second-guessing everything Carmen had told her at the Taco Bell; was it all enticing lies, an attempt to seduce her into becoming like the monstrous figure before her, a brutal, unrepentant murderer? Had *Grace* been lying to her too? Was the doe's kindness merely an act to get Maddy to let her guard down, and listen to… to the kind of cold-blooded puppetmaster who could *love* someone like Redline? Was she being used yet again, manipulated by the Korps just like her grandfather and Hagen?

Lost in spiraling doubt, heart pounding in their chest, the sheep-bear suddenly realized that someone was repeatedly calling their name.

It was Carmen, who had stepped directly in front of them, and was waving gently. "Maddy. *Maddy.* Come back to us, honey," the cat said soothingly.

The sheep-bear cleared her throat, and peered around Carmen, sputtering frantically. "B-But — I mean — she…!"

"*Maddy.* I can *make* you calm down, but I don't think you'd like it," the tabby said matter-of-factly. "Anyway, just think about it. You're surrounded by supervillains who have a wide variety of abilities, including a whole fucking lot who could take you down *without* powers, *and* without breaking a sweat. If the Korps wanted to hurt you, you wouldn't have been invited to the party, believe me."

Some of the tension in the sheep-bear's body dissipated, and their stance relaxed slightly. The recruiter was right, of course — they wouldn't stand a chance if they actually got into a real fight, here, in the heart of this secret underground base, festively decorated for Halloween though it might be. Swallowing, Maddy lowered their hands and cringed into their mostly-ursine bulk.

Carmen grasped Maddy's shoulder. "I promised that you'd be in no danger here, and I keep my promises. If you gave it a *moment's* thought, you'd realize that your physical, mental and emotional well-being are safer right now, in this room, than any time you've been within six feet of Caleb Hagen. Now come on, let's try that again," she said firmly, maneuvering the sheep-bear in front of her to face the wolf. "Maddy, meet my girlfriend, Volta."

"Never mind Hagen, I'm standing next to fucking *Redline*," Maddy mumbled, teeth still gritted.

The giant red wolf shrugged, eyes narrowed, and downed the rest of her drink. "Yeah, and I'm in a Halloween costume. I have a *drink* in my hand. What's your point? I'm not here to fight."

"*One more time*," Carmen whispered in the sheep-bear's ear, more than a hint of menace in her low, honeyed tone. "You say 'Hi! I'm Maddy,' and then *she* says 'Hi! I'm Volta.' *Can we please do that*," the tabby said, squeezing her shoulder hard. Maddy swallowed again and looked up.

"H-hi, I'm Maddy," the sheep-bear forced out bitterly, offering an anxious wave.

"Hi. Volta. Seems like my reputation precedes me, though."

"You! You — you killed — on *live television*, you electrocuted him, *to death*—"

Volta huffed, clearly irritated, crossing her broad arms in front of her massive torso. "Look. I know what the media and Bradley and the PHL says about me. Somehow, I'm both a mindless, unhinged beast rampaging around, and a calculating, cold-blooded mastermind, right? Well, I'll tell you this: *He had it coming.* I gave that asshole every opportunity to realize he was beaten and should quit, *every* opportunity to stand down, and he just *wouldn't.* So, I made an example of him, and *I'd fucking do it again.*"

Maddy thought back to everything she knew about Redline, all the briefings and news reporting she'd taken in during the course of her brief Hero career, even the (clearly, bombastically exaggerated, and vilely transphobic) alt-right news clippings that Hagen had insisted the intel officers include, alongside more sober items from staid old institutions like the CBC. She'd known the red wolf was with the Korps — she was hard to miss, considering her size and the destruction left in her wake — but it had been so easy to put specific wanted criminals out of mind when Grace and then Carmen had been so earnestly pitching her on switching teams. She'd *wanted* to believe there was a better option than her OH career and *hadn't* wanted to consider who in particular she might end up rubbing shoulders with, if she did.

And yet...

The sheep-bear frowned and gazed up at Volta's peeved lupine face with what they hoped was an appropriately forceful, judgmental expression. "*Why*, though?"

Carmen raised a sleek feline eyebrow. "Volts? I really think you two should talk," she said, gently pushing the red wolf and sheep-bear towards a nearby couch with an intense, sharp-looking grin. The two sat down, awkwardly. "Tell Heartforce about how you got here, and *why*. I'm going to go get another round... after I make sure the maintenance drones clean up that broken glass." She gave the two a meaningful nod before disappearing back into the Dominion Club crowds.

"*Heartforce?* That's... huh," Volta said, sneering with bemusement as she lounged into her seat. "You pick that out yourself?"

Maddy laughed bitterly, rubbing the sides of her muzzle with irritation, avoiding eye contact. "Fuck no. My dad was a PHL Hero, Heart*wood*. The Ontario's Heroes marketing department came up with the name, to make sure everyone could see I was 'upholding his legacy,' after I refused to be Heartwood II. I never really wanted to be a Hero at all, but... family, eh?"

"Yeah, I fuckin' know how that goes," Volta sighed. "Let me tell you about *family* and *legacy*. I actually wanted to be a Hero, you know? Helping people, protecting people, all that. Shit, I *idolized* True North. Got made fun of a lot for that; Canadians don't get much love in Texas. My parents put up with it as long as being a fanboy kept me quiet, and they could keep me and my powers under control at the academy. But y'know what they *really* wanted me to do, more than anything? The only real purpose I had for them? *Breed*. Make them a whole bunch of pure-blooded red wolf

93

pup heirs, to take over the family business someday. So yeah, 'Heartforce,' I *know* something about getting manipulated by shitty family into upholding their 'legacy.'"

Maddy's jaw dropped. "That's — that's *awful*," they choked out. They'd never seen *that* particularly eugenicist tidbit in any of Redline's profile information, even the classified sections they were cleared for. "I didn't realize..."

Volta nodded bitterly. "When they finally figured out I wasn't getting with the program, that was I was some kind of goddamned *queer*, they were about to send me to conversion therapy. Hell, they'd threatened to already, the first time I tried to come out to them. So right when I was going to be tortured back into being their perfect, obedient son, and giving them their *legacy*, that's when Carmen saved me. *The Korps* saved me."

Maddy's fear and loathing of the giant wolf woman ebbed away, gradually displaced by deep fury and empathy at what she'd gone through. The sheep-bear swallowed, realizing how lucky she'd been to at least have Mom and Brianna in her corner when she was figuring herself out, even if she'd been dragooned into her OH career at the same time. She began to feel guilty that she'd listened to *any* of those briefings, even after discounting the more hatefully click bait press clippings —"Redline and the Violent TRA Vanguard," for instance — for the propaganda they were (to say nothing of that one "ripped-from-the-headlines" docudrama Hagen had screened at their last team retreat in North Bay, *Turned Against His Family: The Austin Travers Story*).

They could hardly blame the wolf for being *angry*, under the circumstances. Did Redline — *Volta* — actually have good reasons for what she'd done? If pressed, could they have done the same?

What if *everything* she thought she knew about the Korps was just as skewed as the parts she'd already learned were untrue, first-hand?

Maddy cleared their throat and made an effort to look the wolf in the eyes. "But... the *execution*...?"

Volta paused for a long moment with an almost-imperceptible sigh; her gaze drifted away from Maddy's, until catching herself, and pointing her muzzle back at the sheep-bear's. When she spoke, it was as if from a very faraway place. "My parents are hateful assholes, but he was a bigoted shitheel *creep*. He hated people like us, but he treated us even worse. He had to *prove* that we're beneath him. I did *everyone* a favour."

The wolf grumbled, shifting in her seat with a shiver to fold her arms again, and seemed to become more present. "Look, Maddy. I understand, okay? I know how it feels to suddenly realize that, like, the whole Hero establishment was never actually on your side. I was tricked into thinking that *maybe* it could be a place for someone like me there, but really, I was all alone." She sighed again, but her expression became a happier one. "At least, until Carmen showed up."

The sheep-bear winced, looking away, afraid that a twinge of jealousy showed on their ursine face. What they wouldn't have given for a beautiful, intense, powerful woman to parachute into their own life, and decide out of the blue that they were *worth* saving, *and* worth loving. That, however, felt like it might not be the healthiest thought to dwell on, and Maddy pushed it aside, sighing.

"They... they really got into me, yeah. Be visible, be positive representation, be the face of the new, modern, *inclusive* Ontario's Heroes. A PR fix, after Sunrise. Is she here tonight, actually...?" With a shake of her horned head, Maddy pressed past the temptation to fangirl. "But that's *all* Hagen ever wanted me for. Well, that and infiltrating... um. You know, I'm still not sure exactly where I am, other than 'underground'...?"

Volta nodded sadly. "Some people are fine with being nothing more than tools. Fuck, I know a few who *like* it. But *they're* getting a choice."

Maddy huffed. "Anyway, it was plausible, at least? It's Canada, we have to at least *pretend* we're oh-so-progressive and benevolent and better than Americans; why wouldn't OH embrace a trans Hero? I tried to believe it could be real for so long; you have no *idea* how hard I tried. But you know who's had my back? Nobody. So, I've... I've been all alone, too." The sheep-bear snorted, a sound equal parts anguish and derision. "And I'm *so fucking sick* of trying to fit in where I'm not wanted."

It was at that moment that Carmen emerged from the crowds behind the couch to lean over the back and hand each of Maddy and Volta a new drink. "So? Have you figured out how much you two have in common yet?"

The sheep-bear shrank from the looming tabby, but gratefully accepted the cocktail glass and took a swig, wetting her dry mouth. She looked down at the floor. "Yeah. Yeah, I get it; thank you, and I'm sorry you had to talk me down from that freak-out. And I'm, uh, also realizing that I might have gotten some bad intel," she mumbled.

"No *shit*, hon," the tabby smirked. "Fuck, just think about how the media and the PHL covered up how *your* dear old dad bit it. They *lie*. They lie all the time, about shit that hardly even *matters* in the grand scheme of things. Roger Oakes would have still had a Hero's funeral either way, but they still lied, just to keep his myth alive. Just so you wouldn't doubt that you had to carry on a 'family tradition' for his sake."

Maddy fidgeted uncomfortably in their seat. They... needed to talk to Granddad, they realized. They needed to understand why *he'd* taken part in the deception as he had. The sheep-bear closed their eyes and downed the rest of their drink in a few brief gulps.

She then took a deep breath before she turned back to the supervillain on the couch next to her. "I'm sorry, R — *Volta*," the sheep-bear said, sheepishly. "Even for how much trying to be a Hero has fucked me up, I've never had to face the things you have. And it was stupid of me to still believe that *you* were uniquely dangerous, already knowing how much I've been lied to by... well, everyone." She tentatively extended a hand to the towering wolf. "So, uh. Sorry I, um, called you a murderer. Truce...?"

Volta reached out, nodding, and shook just a *little* more roughly than necessary. Her giant hand dwarfed the sheep-bear's. "Truce. *Heartforce*," she snickered.

"And with that," Carmen sniffed, taking Volta's hand as the wolf rose from the couch, "*We* ought to be turning in for the night. We're heading out to New Jersey in the morning, to fill in on a KDARC extraction op. Quick in-and-out, probably not even a fight if we play our cards right."

"Kay-dark...?"

Carmen smiled that fierce, cryptic Cheshire Cat grin once again. "You'll learn about them later. Assuming you *want* to, that is."

Maddy nodded nervously, biting her lip. She *did* want to; it wasn't just the second Cosmo talking. (Maybe.) She was onboard; she wanted to be part of all this. (Probably.) At that point she spotted Grace and Rin again, making their way through the crowd, and waved; the two waved back, and changed direction to approach the trio by the couch.

"You've already made some friends here," Carmen said with satisfaction, looking at the K-LAW agents as they approached. "*Good*. Stick with them."

She called out to the anole and deer. "Hey, Backchannel! Grace! I can leave the Hero with you, right? I've made my pitch, but I think they could use some 'local liaisons' right now."

"Of course, hon!"

"Oh, yes, by all means!"

"Cool, cool," Carmen murmured. "Be seeing you," she said with a wink of an amber eye and a tip of her broad-brimmed red hat, as she and Volta put their arms around each other's backs and began to walk off.

The red wolf looked back over her shoulder as they moved. "Hey, Heartforce?"

Maddy swallowed. "Y-yes?"

"Good luck with making the right decision," she said with an easy lupine grin. The pair walked off through the crowd, which parted with respect — and not a few affectionate nods and waves — to let them pass.

As the night wound on, Grace and Rin introduced the sheep-bear around to many more people, all of whom were just as enthusiastically friendly about the potential recruit. They had another Cosmo, and another, along with a quite good cinnamon appletini (before the anole insisted, in a kindly but avuncular tone just slightly discordant with their Madame de Pompadour costume, that that was probably enough for the evening), and began venting at length to their companions about their plans. Maddy would ride out to Alberta first thing Monday morning, they tipsily explained. They'd talk to Granddad, confronting the old bear where he lived, and *demand* an explanation... even if they were afraid of what the answer might be.

Laughing, smiling, aching with the joy of feeling more connected to a community and *alive* than she had in... well, ever, frankly... she didn't want the evening to end. Eventually, however, Maddy drunkenly drifted off to sleep while sitting in one of the Dominion Club's plush booths, leaning against Grace. The soft bulk of the deer's body felt *safe*, somehow.

Maddy woke up with a start and looked around in a daze. She was at home, in her own bed, wearing the camisole and shorts she'd had on underneath her costume. She smiled weakly despite a splitting headache; she'd had so much *fun* the previous night, notwithstanding that she'd gotten (at least) one or two drinks too deep.

Sunlight was streaming in through the bedroom window. Beneath it, stacked neatly, were the breastplate, greaves, bracers, and the rest of the lightweight armour pieces. The bow and quiver leaned against the wall, next to a manila envelope.

The sheep-bear shakily stood up, hungover, and leaned on their dresser to peer outside. Sure enough, parked in their space, six stories down, was their bike; they chuckled, quietly appreciating they wouldn't need to take an Uber back out to Yorkdale just to retrieve it. Their new friends were downright thoughtful, they mused through the pain in their temples, right behind their horns. Yawning, they scratched themself, blinking still-bleary eyes, and lumbered out to the living room for parts beyond; they were halfway to the kitchen when they heard a pointed cough behind them. Panicking, they spun around in a defensive posture, heart racing, now *wide* awake.

"Hey, *buddy*. You didn't check in yesterday." sneered the rat calmly sitting on the couch, legs crossed. He was picking underneath his claws with the point of a pearl-handled pocket knife, and contemptuously avoiding eye contact.

"*WHAT THE FUCK*," Maddy roared at Slider furiously, spittle flying from between her bared teeth. "*GET OUT OF MY FUCKING HOUSE, NEAL...!*"

She reflexively reached forward with one hand, instantly lashing out with her telekinetic power at the couch; it tipped over backwards with a loud thump, but the conniving rat had anticipated the move and hopped forward to neatly land on his feet. Maddy panted, enraged, and once again tried to telekinetically swat Slider to the ground. The rat tumbled forward from the space Maddy was focusing upon, dodging again, and strode towards her. He calmly folded up the knife and stowed it in one of the many pockets of his sleek camo-patterned gray tunic, sniffing derisively.

The sheep-bear didn't like using their telekinesis directly on people (rather than on their surroundings) if they could help it, or pushing around waves of force through the air — there was always a risk of causing more bodily harm than intended — but Slider's audacity pushed their buttons past their usual restraint. Maddy grasped the rat's ankles with their powers and held them together tightly. Off-balance, as if the victim of a tied-shoelace pranking, he tripped forward and landed on the carpet with a yelp and a groan.

"You *motherfucker*," she growled with anger, gesticulating wildly. "It is the *weekend*. How the *fuck* am I supposed to tail a target at her nine-to-five office job on the *fucking weekend…*?"

Slider looked up. He attempted to get to his feet, but the sheep-bear was still mentally gripping his ankles tightly together, and the rat could only kneel; he tried to make it look dignified, largely unsuccessfully. "C'mon, Oakes," he taunted from the floor, as Maddy panted and shook with rage. "Hagen never said you could have weekends off with this bullshit assignment, and it's not like you've even accomplished anything yet. *Right…*?"

Maddy took a deep breath, and spoke coldly and abruptly, when they did. "No. No, I haven't. Not a thing. Been a *little bit* preoccupied with some family stuff lately." They released Slider, scowling. "Go ahead and tell Hagen that on Monday if you want, Neal; I won't be there for it. I need some time off. Urgent. Got to go see my grandfather in Alberta. In the meantime, please get the *fuck* out of my home."

The rat scoffed as he rose from the ground and began walking towards the apartment's front door. "Don't think I won't," he said with a sniveling leer. "But how could you possibly blame me for being *concerned* about the safety of a teammate, when — entirely out of the kindness of my heart, and my profound sense of *duty* — I drop by to check on them, after they don't answer their secure comms *or* civilian phone. For all I knew, you could have been murdered in your bed! We've got intel that a top Korps assassin from the States is in town. Not that you bother to keep up to date on that kind of thing," Slider smirked cruelly, his chin held high.

The sheep-bear bared her teeth again. "You were sitting in my living room watching me sleep, you goddamned *creeper.*"

Slider sniffed again, shrugging, and nonchalantly scratched at his whiskers. "Just where were you last night, bud?"

"Not that it's any of your business, but I was at a Halloween party. You know, a party? Those things that people with *friends* go to?"

"Oh? Didn't realize that was a category that included *you*; imagine that! And your friends got you home safe to sleep it off when you overdid it, eh?"

Maddy's jaw set, and she stared down the rat. "Yeah. They did. They're good friends like that."

Slider nodded with evident suspicion, making a low chitter of disgust. "Fuck, go to Alberta instead of actually doing your stakeout mission. See if I goddamn care. Just more proof that diversity hires can't get the job done. But," he added, "Since I'm *such* a nice guy, and I believe *so* strongly in the importance of family, I'll cover for you with Hagen… just so long as you actually check in every day. *And* you give me a nice detailed update of what you've done to infiltrate the Korps that day, as well as everything you *haven't*."

Maddy grunted, pursing her dark lips. "*Fine.* Sure. Whatever. Just fucking *get out.* And don't you *dare* pull this shit, ever again, or I'll show you exactly how a 'diversity hire' *owns* your skeevy ass."

The rat opened the front door and seemed as though he was about to walk through it when he suddenly looked back at the sheep-bear and spoke again.

"Funny thing, *Madison.* I happened to be taking a leak while I was waiting for you to wake up and noticed something on your bathroom counter. Those special psi-blocker pills Doc Gallant hands out, the ones that are supposed to stop the Korps's hypno-goggles or high-powered telepaths from getting all up in your head? *Bottle's full.*"

A chill ran through Maddy's bones as the door slammed shut behind Slider.

CHAPTER 10

October 30, 2022

Maddy stood in their living room, listening to their bitter nemesis creep away down the condo hallway. They panted rapidly, trembling with fear and fury at what the rat had just said, before casually slinking out the door.

He must have *known* something. He had to. Never mind that he'd broken into their apartment (supposedly out of 'concern' for the sheep-bear's safety) and had been watching them sleep for who knew *how* long, after they'd gotten home from the Halloween party. If the rat turned them in to Hagen, the director was likely to excuse the fully improper invasion of their privacy.

Maddy padded back to the bedroom, fuming, and threw herself back into bed. She roared with rage for several minutes (into a pillow, to muffle the noise, which mostly resulted in a damply spittle-flecked pillow) before lying still, staring up at the ceiling. She growled and rubbed wearily at the sides of her muzzle.

What *exactly* did Slider know? What was he playing at? They tallied up the evidence. The rat had continued needling them about failing to make contact with their potential Korps contact, but they *had*; not just meeting with Grace repeatedly, but also Carmen, the actual, dedicated *recruiter*… as well as attending the Halloween party at their secret base.

Well, maybe not *dedicated*, the sheep-bear considered; Grace said the tabby was a working field agent, and she had mentioned some kind of hush-hush op in New Jersey. Despite her anxiety and waffling, though, and the anguish of revelation after revelation that she hadn't known as much as she'd *thought* about the world of professional heroics, Maddy was cognizant that she was circling ever closer to actually signing on with the Korps.

Maybe. Probably? They *wanted* to join; they'd never felt more connected to queer peers than they had the previous night, where they didn't have to be *any* kind of Hero, *or* hero, but couldn't. Not yet. First, they would have to quiet the naysaying voices in their head, the ones screeching about how disappointed their family would be.

It was ridiculous, Maddy knew, but she would have to make peace with those doubts before officially coming to a decision. Pressing Granddad for answers, about *his* role in the cover-up, would hopefully help illuminate matters.

Was Slider aware of any of that context, though? Was he merely suspicious? Or did he genuinely think that Maddy wasn't capable of such subterfuge? They groaned, paralyzed with worry.

Still, the sheep-bear thought, if the rat had planned to move against her, he probably wouldn't have told her to go ahead, fucking go out to Alberta to see her grandfather, what the fuck did *he* care, and so on. So, she must still have had time. Maddy swung her legs off the bed, intending to start packing; if she was going to start riding out the next morning, she'd need to be ready. She breathed a sigh of relief that the OH motor pool had just serviced her beloved Yamaha V-Max a few weeks prior.

As they got up, they looked again at their Halloween costume, neatly stacked by the bedroom window. Next to it was a fat manila envelope. They'd noticed it earlier when they'd woken up but struggled to recall what would be in it; the previous evening (that had admittedly lasted well into the small hours of the morning) was a bit of a blur, past a certain point. Maddy bent over and picked it up, quizzical.

Then she looked at the address label — to the Ontario Office of the Registrar General — and everything came flooding back.

Maddy was just starting on her fourth Cosmo of the night and feeling very loose. After Carmen and Redline — *Volta*, rather — had departed the party, she'd been left with Grace and Rin as her minders in the labyrinthine secret Korps base. (She realized, in retrospect, that she'd never stopped to ask if it had a particular name.) The K-LAW agents had gladly taken responsibility for the sheep-bear.

Several others had joined them around their table at the Dominion Club. To Grace's left was Dawn, a tiny dik-dik dressed as a classical mad scientist in a fluorescently UV-reactive pink Howie coat and oversized goggles; she smugly held leads of chain that wrapped around her giant eland husband Orion, costumed in erotically-distressed rags and prosthetic stitches apparently suggesting him to be the scientist's escaped, sexily-hulking monster.

To Orion's left and Rin's right was Vixie, a short demimorphic fox girl. She was a friend of Carmen and Volta, apparently, also new to the Korps (alongside her sister Ellen), and had tagged along for their brief trip to Toronto. She recounted in a slight stutter how Ellen was laid up in intensive care at another facility, where she was *currently a skeleton*, yet had still insisted that Vixie go and enjoy herself because villains *must* throw the best Halloween parties. Maddy was fairly certain that they'd tipsily misunderstood at least part of that story.

Next to her, Rin was recounting tales of field agent sluttiness past; they evidently had quite the reputation for finding a way to turn any covert op horny. While Maddy had caught parts of the first few — flushing intensely at the shameless details they offered (complete with illustrative gestures in some cases!) and gasping at the hot gossip of closeted queerphobes the anole had bedded for *kompromat* purposes — she'd tuned out while talking with Grace. However, Vixie had been listening intently. The demivixen's eyes were wide as saucers at the anole's anecdotes, to say nothing of Rin's candid answers to her extensive questions about their analingus technique and experiences.

For Maddy's own part, the sheep-bear had spent the last half-hour or so spilling their guts to the deer, first venting at further length about their exhausting teen PHL experiences, and then sharing more of the previous week's conversations with their mother.

"An' — an' so I said to Mom, y'know what, I thiiiink I wanna change my name after all. So of course *she* says, oh, I thought you liked *Maddy?* An' I *do*, though! M' lucky 'Madison' still works f'r me, *hah*, fuck yeah, weird gender-neutral 90s names. But *no*, what I meant was, I don't wanna have *his* last name anymore. Mom kept her maiden name, an' Brianna changed hers a coupla' years ago, but *I* had to stay an Oakes, f'r the *legacy* thing."

Grace smiled, nodding along with heavily-lidded eyes. The deer didn't drink or smoke, but *was*, Maddy had learned, partial to chocolate edibles; she'd been pleasantly, affectionately high and giggly for the past few hours. It took her a dizzy moment to focus. "So just… um… just your last name? That's all you want changed? To what?"

"My mom's name," the sheep-bear mumbled proudly. "She's, uh. She's not perfect, okay, an' she took a bit to um, *work through it* when I came out — she grew up, like, *super* small-town Alberta Baptist — but she packed us up an' moved alllll the way to Ontario just so I could transition without Dad's family gettin' in the way. So, *yeah*, I, I wanna be a *Gillespie*."

Grace chuckled lightly. "Is *that* all? Well, *heck*, I can do that for you right now, hee!" The doe shuffled out from the curved banquette seat, and gently tugged at Maddy's arm to join her. "C'mon, up, up, up! *We're going to K-LAW!*" she said, punching the air, a gleam in her eye. Standing proudly in her costume, the words might as well have been "For the Honour of Grayskull!"

Maddy shrugged and unsteadily rose to their feet, grasping the doe's offered hand for support. They turned away briefly, flushing, but managed to steady themselves well enough.

Vixie piped up, leaning past Rin's bodice as they sipped at their champagne. "Oh! M-Miss Grace! Can I c-come see K-LAW t-too? I always w-wanted to get p-pounded on a t-table like in the l-lawyer shows!"

"…Don't you mean pound on a table?"

The demivixen beamed at the deer innocently. "W-why would I m-mean that, M-Miss?"

Grace opened her mouth for a moment, holding up a finger quizzically, then closed it and took a deep breath. "Maybe, um, later," she giggled. "Gotta focus for a l'iiil tiny bit right now. Be right back!"

The two squeezed out through the crowds towards the club's main entrance. Luckily, Maddy learned, they didn't have to go far; the K-LAW offices were right next door in the "Base Operations & Support" sector, apparently. Grace led Maddy down a corridor signed with what the sheep-bear assumed must be the legal department's divisional crest —

the magenta Korps helix, but with the silhouette of an open book's pages substituted for the standard winged motif.

Finally, they came to the right suite; Grace tapped her wrist to a wall-mounted sensor, just as she had in the HBS back hallway, and the door slid open with a faint, possibly trademark-infringing *chff*. The deer ushered Maddy inside and invited her to sit in a very plush task chair (much nicer than the uncomfortable guest seat in her downtown high-rise office, Maddy considered) while she slid bonelessly into another, behind the desk.

"Mmmmkay," Grace mumbled. "I… oh, you know what, let's make this a little easier. ROSE, can you… eh… oh, right; can you sober me up for a bit?" Suddenly something in her expression changed, and the deer straightened up, no longer floppy or dazed-looking.

Maddy looked around in confusion. "…Rose? Wha? What happened…?"

"Oh! ROSE is… well, to abstract it rather a *lot*, think of her as the AI behind our operating systems. It's more complex than that, but," the deer tapped the temples of her cateye-framed Rose-Coloured Glasses. "She can be right in your head with RCGs, and help out with things like mental focus, or adjusting physiological processes or neurotransmitter levels on the fly through biofeedback. I'm still *very* high right now, technically! But ROSE is — and again, this is something of a simplification — temporarily helping me route around the parts of my brain that are full of cannabinoids, at the moment."

Maddy's own head swam through the explanation. The Korps's trademark RCGs didn't just… hypnotize their wearers? Although, she realized, what sense would that make? She'd seen Grace without them, in public, wearing identical frames without the pink lenses; the deer clearly wasn't having her mind constantly controlled, as such, if she voluntarily put them on and took them off. (Or, at least… it wasn't happening against her will? *That* was a peculiar thought that stuck in Maddy's mind, despite her inebriation.)

The sheep-bear propped their face up, elbows on the desk, as they leaned forward. "Issss, uh, that all they do?"

"Oh, no, that's not the half of it," the deer said, typing away furiously as she spoke. "There's also long-distance secure, encrypted communication, fully mental if you prefer — two people wearing RCGs can have a silent conversation as if they were telepaths — as well as complete integration into wider Korps systems. I'm sure you must have noticed me waving near doors to open them? I have a subcutaneous transponder implant in my wrist to manually trip the sensors, but I could also just mentally trigger the wireless locks through ROSE as well."

"Huh," Maddy mumbled. "So, what're *you* doing, though?"

"Just… one sec. Okay, done!" Grace said cheerily, tapping the Enter key with a flourish. A chunky inkjet printer to her side — squatting low on the desk like some hunched beast — spat out a sheaf of pages in the space of a few seconds. She picked them up, as well as a few pens and a strange-looking squared-off tool from a drawer, popping out a tab to turn it into a clamp-like press of some kind. The deer fanned the pages out in front of Maddy like she was dealing cards. "Here we go. Ontario change of name forms, falsified *mandamus* order to waive the fees and guarantor requirements and expedite processing, including transmitting the registration to the Alberta Vital Statistics Office; also an application for a new Alberta birth certificate, and another *mandamus* order to make that one free and high-priority too. Madison Skylar Oakes, do you solemnly declare that you want your name to be Madison Skylar Gillespie?"

"Um. Yes…?"

"Excellent. Sign here, here, here, and initial here," Grace smiled, affixing tiny arrow flag stickers throughout the pages and handing them off to the sheep-bear.

Maddy smiled wryly when she saw what the lawyer had typed in the field questioning the reason for the application: "I don't want anything of Roger Oakes', including his last name." She signed and initialed as she was told, handing the sheets back to Grace. The deer then demonstrated the purpose of the curious square device; it was a notary seal, and she embossed several pages with the words "GRACE ELIZABETH DUNLOP ✤ NOTARY PUBLIC ✤ PROVINCE OF ONTARIO" before also signing off.

Grace hummed brightly, stepping over to the adjoining room, and returned with a fat manila envelope — there was already something inside, it seemed? — to stuff the stack of papers into before handing it to Maddy. "I know you're a little drunk right now, dear, but take a look at these when you're sober? If everything is correct, just pop the envelope in the mail on Monday, and it'll all be taken care of. No fees, no publication in the Ontario Gazette — *that part is a little perk for trans folks, thankfully* — and you should have a new, corrected birth certificate in your hands within two weeks, with the surname 'Gillespie' backdated to your date of birth." Maddy's mouth hung open as Grace stood up and walked around the desk. "Does that sound okay?"

"Grace, I... *thank you,*" the wobbling Hero said in a near-sob. She hugged the deer, who patted her on the back.

"Of *course,* Maddy. You're very welcome. Now," the doe said, smiling, as she pulled away from the sheep-bear, "let's get back to the party, eh?"

It was all there. Applications, signed and stamped; what appeared to be orders from judges that she'd never heard of, with the Ontario Superior Court of Justice and the Alberta Court of King's Bench; there was even a metered postage sticker attached. And then, at the bottom of the envelope, making up the mysterious bulge...

"Oh," Maddy said out loud, taken aback. "*Oh.*"

She drew the object out with a shaky hand, and her heart skipped a beat. It was a lightweight, bubble-shaped pink visor, as wide as her face. It was a set of RCGs. *For her.*

They weren't ready for this. They wouldn't — they couldn't dare. Could they? No. *No!*

Not... yet, anyway.

The sheep-bear gulped, and carefully set the device down on her dresser while she began to gather up clothes and toiletries in a worn military-surplus duffel bag. Her V-Max wasn't really a touring bike, and lacking panniers or a top case, Maddy would have to fit everything she needed for a 7,000-kilometre round-trip highway ride inside. When it was packed near to bursting, she happened to glance again at her dresser.

Sitting on top were the set of RCGs, and their secure Ontario's Heroes comm headset. They looked to the open top of the duffel bag, and then again to the dresser. They couldn't just *leave* the RCGs there, Maddy thought. Not with Slider sniffing around. Then they gasped at the realization: Slider had been *here*. The rat had spent… hours? Just sitting on their couch, no more than a few metres away from the envelope, on the other side of the bedroom wall.

Huffing, Maddy hesitantly packed the RCGs, setting them in the pocket with her phone charger and wallet. She was about to close the bag when she thought better of it, and carefully wrapped the visor inside a folded hoodie before zipping up.

After scarfing a hastily-made, extra-extra-large chorizo-and-Oka cheese omelet — they wouldn't want to leave all the perishables in the fridge to go bad during the few weeks they'd be away, after all — Maddy closed and locked the front door behind them. Duffel bag over their shoulder, motorcycle helmet under one arm, they strode purposefully down to the parking lot. With one last glance back at their building, they straddled their bike and rode away towards Highway 400. Why wait for tomorrow? They could probably make it to Sudbury that night, at least. Maybe even Sault Ste. Marie.

It was several hours later, while she was refueling her bike at an Esso station outside Parry Sound, that something occurred to the sheep-bear.

"Wait a minute. Demimorphic fox girl, with a twin sister named *Ellen?* It couldn't be…"

Chapter 11

November 1, 2022

Maddy sighed disgustedly and held her phone up flat to her mouth, tapping the app icon to start recording a voice memo.

"Neal. 6:18 AM, room 3, Lakehead Traveler's Inn up here in Thunder Bay. Slept like shit. Non-smoking room, which is nice. From the outside, everything about this place looks like it ought to stink like mildew and fifty-year-old cigarettes. But honestly, it's clean, reasonably priced, bathroom's in tip-top shape. Terrible coffee in the lobby, though. Just *godawful* coffee. Anyway, here's your fucking *check-in*," the sheep-bear spat out acidly as she reclined in the room's sole chair.

"I have made no effort whatsoever to infiltrate the Korps, as per Director Hagen's instructions, in the past twenty-four hours. I'm on the road, traveling to see my grandfather outside of Calgary, for an urgent family matter."

Maddy made a noise somewhere between a grunt and an irritated snort and gazed off into the distance out the window of her motel room. Somewhere nearby, a truck was backing up with an insistent beeping tone. "I mean, 'urgent,' well. It's… it's complicated. It goes back a long time…"

September 23, 2011

Madison Oakes jogged briskly out the front door of the middle school as the bullies chased the young sheep-bear. "Come on, guys, leave me aloooone," they screeched plaintively, hunched down in their hoodie and gripping their backpack's straps tightly.

Jeremy was their leader, a scruffy beaver wearing a Calgary Flames jersey emblazoned with PHANEUF and the number 3 on the back. The biggest, meanest boy in Grade 7, he and his cronies — Kyle, Brandon and Zeke — had immediately taken to harassing Madison when they'd sensed the sheep-bear's weakness.

Their previous school had only gone to Grade 6; when they'd had to transfer to the larger middle school that fall, they were surrounded by cliques and battle lines that'd been drawn for years and were easily isolated from their peers. Madison bleat-growled weakly and tried to hurry away; if they could get across the street, the dental office where their mother worked as a receptionist was just down the block, and they'd be safe. Or even if they could get within view of the front door — the bullies had proven hesitant to pursue the sheep-bear with adults watching.

(Adults who weren't driving, at least. Madison had found, to their distress, that the occupants of the SUVs and minivans that sped down 52 Ave. NW were unfazed by the sight of a sad, chubby preteen curled up on the sidewalk, being kicked and spat on by a group of larger boys.)

They were in luck, that day; there was no sign of traffic in either direction, and they scampered across the suburban thoroughfare and up the concrete stairs of the strip mall plaza, Jeremy and his goons in hot pursuit. Madison ducked between station wagons and sedans at the corner of the parking lot, and was almost in sight of the dentist, when a huge pickup truck zoomed down the lane in front of them; they jumped back, spooked, and tripped over on a gash in the asphalt. The sheep-bear landed on their backpack between two SUVs and groaned.

A few seconds later, Jeremy was looming over them. "Hey, *Tardison*," he sneered through his buck teeth. "What's the *rush*, man?"

Madison tried to rise to their feet, but Brandon had circled around to the other side of the vehicles; the bemulleted, jean jacket-clad donkey planted a hoof squarely on their chest, forcing them back down. "Stay down, fag," he grunted monosyllabically.

"*Please leave me alone*," the sheep-bear whispered, tears welling up as their heart beat faster and faster. They attempted to push Brandon's hoof aside with their stubby, black-nailed fingers, without success, and sniffled piteously when they couldn't budge it. "I didn't do anything to *you*…"

"Sure you did. Bein' a *homo* all over the place," Zeke called out from behind Jeremy. The others all guffawed and hooted uproariously at this display of sparkling wit.

Madison knew by now, from experience, that it would make no difference to protest that they liked girls. The bullies knew, they just *knew* that there was something different — something *wrong*, even — about the young sheep-bear. They felt like an alien, sometimes. A *monster*. And Jeremy and his friends could see it, somehow. They braced for the inevitable kicks, trying to protect their face.

They just wished they didn't have to. They just wanted the bullies to *back off*, Madison thought with an anguished growl. The sheep-bear's entire body tensed up, and then... something happened; they cried out. Their head hurt, and they heard pained groans. When they opened their eyes, the bullies were no longer standing overhead.

Scrabbling to their feet, they saw Jeremy, Zeke, Brandon and Kyle on the ground. The SUVs, previously neatly parked within the painted lines, had skidded askew around the tweens. Madison felt dizzy but managed to leap over the prone elk and collie at their feet and stumbled away.

Jeremy propped himself up on one arm, touching his other hand to his nose; it came away daubed with blood. The beaver pointed at the sheep-bear. "You... you *freak*! You've got *powers*, don't you!" A wicked grin crept onto his face. "You're gonna be in so much *troublllllle*," he taunted in a sing-song voice as his erstwhile prey ran towards the dental office storefront.

November 1, 2022

"...And do you know what Jeremy does now? He's an insurance agent in Lethbridge. Ran for school board trustee last year on an *anti-bullying platform*, that absolute fuckface. Anyway, he wasn't *wrong*, I probably would have gotten in trouble for using my telekinesis on them, even if it was accidental, even though it was a textbook 'stress-induced adolescent breakthrough manifestation.' But my dad was *Heartwood*, 'The Pride of Grande Prairie,' so instead..."

September 27, 2011

Madison sat sullenly at the back of the conference room hunched over, hoodie pulled past their budding horns down to eye-level. They hated being Talked About, especially when they had to be in the room for it. The weekend had been a blur of grownups doing the same, at kitchen tables and in unnerving medical labs and on flights to and from Edmonton.

Mom, Granddad and Alexis Westerhaven — the Prairie League's head of media relations, and a family friend since their father's death — sat at the table with Principal Campbell and the school board psychologist. Granddad's ursine bulk towered over the others, especially the slight marten and chickadee representing the Calgary Board of Education.

"You are *not* going to punish the boy," the old bear growled. "He has a blessing like his father, and he's going to be a Hero. He's going to be the new Heartwood, some day."

Ms. Wilkins, the psychologist, shoved her small circular glasses back up her beak. "Mr. Oakes, we're not talking about *punishment* as such. We understand that Madison had… an *episode* when he was with the other boys on Friday, and while we appreciate that he has support from his whole family… *and* from the League," she said, nodding at the Ann Taylor-clad blonde wolf, "we can't have these kinds of outbursts around the other students, even off school grounds. The other parents are very upset about Madison. The children might have post-traumatic stress disorder," she chittered.

Alexis sniffed coolly and pushed two identical binders across the table to the school staff. "If you turn to page three, you'll see our proposed plan for Madison's next few years. First of all, he'll be joining our Prairie League Cadets program for youth with recently-manifested powers. He'll learn discipline and self-control; we take pride in teaching young people how to be responsible citizens with their special abilities. Best of all, he can stay enrolled here at Simon Fraser, to minimize any further disruptions to his life. His training and exercises with the Cadets will take the place of participating in school-organized extracurriculars, like the hockey team."

Flipping the principal's binder ahead several pages, Alexis continued her spiel. "If he's ready for it and shows the skill we think he can achieve — the testing we did at PLHQ on the weekend indicates *very* strong telekinetic potential, with a peripheral precognitive sensory aura that could aid in the development of exceptional agility and coordination as well — at 17 or 18 it'll just be a *formality* to get him approved for the PHL Junior Development Program." She flashed a toothy lupine grin. "And honestly, just think about the prestige the school could have for being associated with 'Heartwood II.'"

Principal Campbell leafed through the binder, nodding along blandly. "We can work with this. Madison will also have to apologize to the other boys, of course; we have a zero-tolerance policy for harassment and bullying, and from what their parents have told me, he's been giving all of them a hard time since the start of the school year," the marten tut-tutted sadly. "Given the extenuating circumstances — and, of course, the League vouching for him, I won't deny that's a factor, the Minister of Education was very clear I should take that into account in coming to an independent decision on the matter — I *think* we can forgo suspension, this time."

"No," Granddad thundered, baring his teeth. "The boy has nothing to apologize for. He says the others attacked *him*. Four of them, one of him. Does that sound like he was the instigator here? Are you calling my grandson a *liar?*"

"Mr. Oakes—"

"Mr. Campbell," the old bear snarled, "my son was a Hero. A *Hero*. He died in the line of duty, because cowardly little *shits* like those other boys ambushed him."

"—And we're very sorry for your loss and appreciative of your son's service, but—"

"But *nothing!*" Garth Oakes roared, standing to lean over the conference table on his huge, shaggy knuckles, causing Madison to flinch and shrink further into a huddled ball of tween sheep-bear. "You heard Miss Westerhaven. The boy's going to get professional training. He's not going to apologize for coming into his powers, or for fighting off a gang of low-class hoodlums. I'm not bloody playing around here. Just be glad I don't sue the school *and* all of them, for hurting his future Hero draft potential." The bear heaved his broad frame back down into the stacking chair, which creaked slightly under the weight. He then stared at Mr. Campbell and Ms. Wilkins until they looked away, abashed.

The principal gulped, and turned towards Mom, avoiding eye contact with Granddad. "Ms. Gillespie? You're Madison's primary caregiver. I'd like to get your perspective on this."

Mom blinked her ovine eyes, looking to Granddad and Alexis with a weak, nervous smile. "I, um, I think — I'm in full agreement with Garth and Alexis, of course. This is exactly what Madison needs," she said in a stiff, practiced tone. "And — and I don't think it would be fair to make him feel like he did anything wrong here. My husband told me about when he got his powers, and he just felt so out of control and *emotional* when it started happening… but when he was young, he didn't have the help that the PL is offering us now, of course."

The principal and psychologist looked to each other, sharing a moment of evident chagrin. When the marten spoke again, he closed the binder and gently pushed it back towards Alexis. "Understood. Madison can return to class tomorrow, as long as he's going to be under League supervision. And since we don't have a Super Ed program, he absolutely *cannot* use his powers on school grounds; that's not up to me *or* the Minister, that's right out of the *Education Act*," he said testily.

"Of course," Alexis said unctuously, offering her hand to shake. "You have my personal guarantee that the League will keep things under control here. We wouldn't want the public to lose confidence in our team, after all."

Madison, still quietly sitting in the back of the room, head in their hands, stared at the floor.

———
———

November 1, 2022

"So, I had powers, Granddad was my biggest cheerleader, and he wouldn't let anyone get in the way of my Hero career… least of all Mom, or *me*. How could he? His son was dead — by the way, Neal, I know how my father really died, it sure as fuck wasn't that he went down fighting in some supervillain ambush — and he had to live vicariously through *someone*. That wasn't the worst of it, though…"

January 5, 2012

"*Happy birthday, dear Maaadison, Happy birthdaaaay to youuuuu,*" the crowd around the dining room table crooned, off-key.

The sheep-bear blew out the candles and tried to look happy. It was difficult; the cake was decorated with the Heartwood crest, and the streamers and tablecloth were all in bright red and white, the colours of their father's costume. They couldn't help feeling like this was a party for *him*, as if Roger Oakes' parents and siblings had decided Madison could simply be slotted into the Heartwood-shaped hole in the world and were celebrating their son and brother returning to life.

The family had become a lot more *involved* in their day-to-day world, now that they had powers. They missed the days when it had been just them, Mom, and their sister Brianna, seeing the rest of the family only at holidays or over summer vacation. But it wasn't just Granddad and Grandma and Uncle Gary and Aunt Marilyn and Aunt Joan and the cousins; the *League* was around all the time now, too.

Alexis was a frequent visitor again, in a way she hadn't been since the year after losing Dad. So too were Danny "Sweet Crude" Johnson (an oil industry-sponsored Hero, and Alexis' boyfriend) and Ken "Reclaimer" Marcinko (formerly one of Dad's old teammates, retired from the field to become a Prairie League trainer, coach, and supervisor of the young sheep-bear's Cadets squad). Granddad and the three of them had formed an unofficial committee to oversee Madison's progress, brushing aside Mom's concerns that they were driving "Heartwood II" too hard. They were all present for the party, of course, laughing and joking and retelling old war stories — literal, in Granddad's case, from his stint in Korea.

"Okay, okay, everyone settle down," Granddad rumbled cheerfully. "We'll get to the cake, but first… this is for you, Madison," he said, pulling a long, flat gift box from the nearby pile and pushing it into the sheep-bear's hands. They looked up at his face; it was twisted up in an expression they'd rarely seen, a tear in the corner of his eye. Was that... *pride?*

"Open it, open it!" Coach Reclaimer urged, smirking through his leonine fangs and throwing back the contents of the tumbler in his hand. Alexis, next to him, had a camera at the ready. She grinned aggressively, and pointed at her teeth, evidently urging the young sheep-bear to smile for the photo op.

Madison took a deep breath and forced themself to comply before fumbling with the gift-wrapping, tearing it away in broad strips. Inside was a low cardboard box; they lifted the lid and winced upon realizing what Granddad had given them.

It was Dad's first costume, the one he'd improvised himself from hockey gear and a marching band uniform. They'd only ever seen it in old family photos. They held it up, hands shaking, as they heard the shutter of Alexis' camera snap over and over again.

"My boy, I am so bloody *happy* for you," Granddad gushed; he huddled in next to Madison, throwing a thick arm around his grandchild's shoulder, and gestured for the wolf to keep taking photos. "The League says you're on track for a real Hero career, just like your old man. You'll do his legacy proud, and I thought — we *all* thought, all the Oakes — that you deserved to be the one to hold on to this, now."

Uncle Gary started a round of applause and soon everyone else joined in, even Alexis, after she carefully set down the camera on the sideboard next to the punch bowl.

"Hear, hear," Reclaimer said, approaching to tousle the young sheep-bear's shaggy hair good-naturedly. "Madison, even though you're still just in the Cadets for now, from one Hero to another — you'll go further than anyone will ever expect, I'm sure of it. You'll make sure nobody *ever* forgets the name Heartwood."

"Um. Thank you, Coach. Thank you, Granddad, everyone," Madison forced out politely, feeling their heart rate rising. "*ExcusemepleaseIjustneedtousethewashroom,*" they mumbled, ducking out from under the old bear's grasp and hurtling down the back hallway. In the distance they could hear Granddad and Aunt Joan joking, something about the same jitters Roger had at senior prom. Reaching the bathroom, the sheep-bear slammed and locked the door behind them before sinking down to the floor, knees curled up against their chest. They couldn't hold back the panic any longer and began hyperventilating.

A few minutes later there was a soft knock at the door. "Just — just a minute, be done soon," they called out manically, before burying their face in their hands.

A high, soft voice murmured quietly from the other side of the door. "Are you okay?"

They pulled themself together and got to their feet, opening the door. It was their little sister, Brianna, an expression of concern on her tiny ovine features.

"There's cake...? Cake makes me feel better if I'm sad," she said gently.

"Are... are they looking for me?"

The younger sheep-bear shook her head. "Nuh-uh. Grandy said to give you time, 'cause it was a big respo... reshpon... a *big deal* to be Heartwood, and you were 'collecting yourself' now that you for-real have Dad's old stuff. But I thought you looked sad." She looked up at her sibling. "I think you look sad a lot."

Madison smirked, pained, and hugged their sister against their broad frame. "Yeah. Yeah, I guess I do."

"Why are you sad?" she asked plaintively, muffled by the older sheep-bear's best dress shirt.

"Bri..."

They considered telling her. They didn't want to be Heartwood. They weren't even sure they wanted to be a boy, for that matter... not that they could do anything about that. But how could they explain to their eight-year-old sister the pressure they were under, to be a *man* — the "man of the house," even — and a professional *Hero*, and carry on Dad's legacy?

What if they screwed up somehow? How would the family feel about that? How would *Granddad* feel? How could a little girl possibly understand what it was like to have their whole future laid out for them in an instant, all their hopes and dreams set aside by the grownups around them, just because they had to go and frigging — no, this warranted stronger language, they had to go and *fucking* — get *superpowers*, just like Dad?

Madison squeezed Brianna more tightly, beginning to weep, but managed to suppress the tears with a snort. No, they couldn't put all this on her. Or Mom; the sheep never discussed money around her children, but they could tell that all the League attention and resources were, somehow, making it easier for the exhausted receptionist to make ends meet for the three of them.

They had to be strong and try to hang on. For Dad. And for Mom and Brianna. They'd just have to make everyone proud, no matter how empty it made the teen sheep-bear feel on the inside.

Madison pulled away from their sister and crouched down to meet her at eye level. "I'm fine, Bri. I promise. Big brother promise, got it? I swear."

She appeared hopeful, if not entirely convinced. "Yeah?"

"Yeah," they grinned, patting her on the shoulder. "Let's go get some cake, Snotbrain."

Brianna bleat-giggled. "Race you for it, Buttface!"

November 1, 2022

"So that's why I need to talk to him. I don't... I don't want to be a Hero any more. I never did, but it took me a long time to be able to say that out loud." The sheep-bear winced and bit their lip. "And I'm going to have it out with my grandfather, once and for all, before I actually make that decision. I need to know why he did what he did. Because... if I quit, that wouldn't just be rejecting my shitheel queer-bashing, wife-beating rage monster dad; it'd be rejecting his whole family, *especially* Granddad. And he needs to know that he deserves it." They took a deep breath. "*I need to know that he deserves it.*"

Maddy sighed, and after a moment, hit the stop button. She set the phone down for a moment and took a long sip of (godawful) coffee, wincing, but grateful for the caffeine regardless. When she picked the phone back up, her thumb hesitated for only a few seconds over the screen before tapping to delete the memo and starting a new recording.

"Neal. 7:03 AM, room 3, Lakehead Traveler's Inn up here in Thunder Bay. Here's your fucking *check-in...*"

Chapter 12

November 3, 2022

Maddy sped along the Yellowhead Highway on her Yamaha V-Max. She didn't care for driving in the prairies; when she was young, she had always kept her nose buried in a book or her DS (until it ran out of power), or even just tried to nap, rather than look outside.

There was *too much sky*, was the problem.

It was worse in Saskatchewan — the sheep-bear had avoided taking the Trans-Canada Highway route just to circumvent the stretch of road between Regina and Calgary — but you couldn't really avoid it entirely, at least not until getting up in the mountains. The land was dead flat and stretched out for kilometres in every direction; in Maddy's view, it was just unsettling. Dwelling on the sheer scale and expanse of the prairie stretching out in all directions, apparently forever, was uncanny. *Creepy,* even. It was the closest they had ever come to truly understanding the cosmic horror concept of "alien geometries" driving the observer hopelessly mad.

But right now, she didn't have Mom to chauffeur her, nor any of her battered old Le Guin or Pratchett or Pullman paperbacks to take her mind off the emptiness of the distant fields. Those were all back in Mississauga. Right now, there was just herself and the highway; the bike thrumming beneath her and the occasional truck to pass; and that endless, maddening *sky*.

They'd checked in with Slider every day, sending a voice memo. The rat had immediately called them right after receiving it, a few times; not because he needed any particular clarification, but just to screw with the sheep-bear, condescendingly demanding point-by-point confirmation of all the things they *hadn't* done that day to fulfill their mission of infiltrating the Korps, through their contact with Grace. Did you try to watch her house? Does she maybe have a spouse? Did you hide behind a box? Have you seen her with a fox?

Well, actually, Maddy *had* noticed the deer consider Vixie's sweetly guileless come-on at the party...

...Wait, how old *was* she? Grace hadn't made a point of objecting that she would be too old for the petite demivixen, as she'd playfully teased Maddy about the previous week, and the sheep-bear couldn't have been *that* much younger.

This was a strange train of thought, and the sheep-bear tried to shrug it off as she rode down the bleakly flat plains in the direction of Edmonton. She most definitely was *not* attracted to Grace. Or Vixie. Or Carmen. Or Redline — or rather, *Volta.* Or that built honey badger girl who'd slyly smiled at her in the hallway on her tour, or the androgynous, pastel-gothy owl that gave Maddy an intrigued wink on the train. Or any of the dozens — hundreds! — of, okay, admittedly, *extremely fuckin' hot* women and enbies who'd been bumping and grinding to electronic remixes of vintage Halloween novelty songs in the Dominion Club. She grumbled, gritting her teeth underneath her helmet's visor.

Fuck, they had it bad, Maddy conceded to themself. That *shouldn't* factor into anything, should it? They probably shouldn't be deciding to join the secretive anarchist supervillain organization in part for the dating opportunities, and yet...

Maddy was still trying to shake off the thought when she finally pulled into the Sherwood Park Super 8, and exhaustedly trudged towards the lobby. There was only one more day of driving until she reached Granddad's house near Grande Prairie; for the moment, she had to get some rest.

...After, of course, a hearty dinner at the Smitty's attached to the hotel. The diner chain was one of the few things they had missed about Alberta, and alongside their daydreaming about pretty girls, Maddy had been thinking intensely about a giant Cobb salad with quadruple bacon, followed by a stack of fresh-from-the-fryer mini-donuts, for *hours.*

Maddy practically waddled back to her room from the hotel restaurant. She'd obtained the salad she'd been yearning for all day, and then some; the bemused server had brought half of the crumbled bacon on the side, apologizing that the kitchen had been unable to plate it in the neatly-arranged rows mandated by corporate. The aesthetics of her dinner didn't matter that much to the sheep-bear in the moment, and she happily sprinkled the surplus meat haphazardly over the rest of the ingredients before hungrily devouring the whole dish. She'd decided to have her dessert of fresh mini-donuts accompanied by a bowl of butterscotch ice cream, as well, and savoured every gulp of the combined fluffy, gooey, caramel-and-cinnamon goodness…

…All of which meant that, sated and dozy, it was time for the sheep-bear to have a nice lie-down.

Swiping the keycard at the door, they kicked off their boots, lumbered towards the bed, and hurled their wide, brown-furred bulk onto the soft mattress. After a quiet moment of relaxation, Maddy opened their eyes, and made efforts to get more comfortable. The sheep-bear undid their leather jacket and the flannel shirt beneath, letting their generous breasts hang out, before unzipping their tight jeans to release their stuffed, bloated gut from captivity. They sighed and grunted happily in contented relief, sprawling out and wriggling a loose nest into the bed covers.

Feeling pleasantly hazy, half-nude and halfway into a food coma, Maddy's thoughts wandered, returning to that afternoon's musing about all the attractive faces (and hot bodies of all shapes and sizes) she'd seen in the Dominion Club. Inspiration struck the sheep-bear: was there, perhaps — and she felt vaguely guilty yet remarkably excited at the idea — Korps-themed porn? It had never occurred to her before; she tended to get her kicks from spicy fanfics and soft-focus artsy indie lesbian content, but surely some studio (or enthusiastic amateurs) must have put out something along those lines.

They reached for their phone. Eyes reflexively darting from side to side despite being alone in the hotel room, the sheep-bear tapped on a VPN and flipped their browser to private mode – old habits died hard – and proceeded to carefully type "korps porn" into the search field.

Results: 419,000 hits.

Maddy boggled and began scrolling through. Sure enough, there was a *lot* of generically Hero-and-villain-themed porn from various professional studios; the scenario of a weary superhero, tied up in a classic deathtrap and not-so-unwillingly seduced by their archnemesis, was a popular one. But there were also a non-zero number of video clips with participants who were wearing RCGs, and they looked as real as the ones she'd seen at the Halloween party or buried at the bottom of her duffel bag. She bit her lip at a particularly tall, lanky transfem zebra, and a red panda with huge breasts and a truly astonishing cock but kept scrolling.

...Wait, *holy shit*; was that thumbnail *Volta*? The sheep-bear's mouth dropped open, and without even thinking, they immediately tapped the link. It was... a commercial of some kind? For milk? They watched, baffled, as a goat of ambiguous gender talked folksily about their farm's "top producers," and then, *wow, that sure was Volta, huh*. The gigantic wolf was sitting in some kind of industrial-looking chair, with a milking machine attached to her gigantic tits.

"Hey, I'm the infamous supervillain 'Redline.' You may have heard of me, and maybe you've already tasted me," the red wolf said from the tiny speaker of Maddy's phone.

"Tasted," the sheep-bear mused aloud, sleepily, as she became aware that she was growing hard. It had been a while, she admitted to herself. Not wanting to waste rare horniness — somewhat awkward though the source of it might be, *fuck* — she reached down below her broad belly to pop open the button of her plain black boxer briefs, allowing her chubby cock to peek out.

Maddy gave themself a sensuous stroke as they continued watching the video, which had cut to shots of a dairy production line. So, they could just... *drink* Volta's milk, if they wanted to? *Anyone* could? (At least, anyone with access to these "Korps Farms" products, she supposed.) The sheep-bear recalled sitting next to the huge she-wolf at the party, how their six-foot-zero frame put their blunt muzzle *exactly* at the larger woman's chest height, and pumped their shaft, hand bumping into the overhang of their muscle-gut to the thought of suckling at those voluptuous teats. It felt mildly wrong, somehow, and yet... with the effects of HRT on their libido, they couldn't *remember* the last time they'd been so ready-to-burst (in more ways than one) and riled up.

"Oh, *holy fuck,*" she exclaimed, eyes growing wide at the video's next scene. The demimorphic fox woman she'd also met at the party, Vixie, was sprawled on the floor at Volta's feet, licking and spit-shining the wolf's shiny black boots. Boots a lot like *her* motorcycle boots, discarded carelessly by the hotel room door, as she'd stumbled into this indulgent session of post-gluttony self-pleasure. Maddy's mouth hung open as she drooled at her phone's screen, and she began pounding furiously as her fantasizing shifted to the idea of the short, soft vixen at her *own* feet, eagerly and submissively servicing her.

Maddy couldn't help themself; they growled, they sobbed, they *roared* at the decadent sensations and the thought, the extremely visceral *realization,* that they could have this, if they wanted! They could be part of those orgies Hagen disgustedly raved about! The Korps was known for being horny as hell, that was genuinely one of the things that appealed to the sheep-bear, and that was fucking *great…!*

Two things happened at that precise moment. The scene in the video changed again — now *Vixie* was the one hooked up to the milking machine, and Volta's massive hand was *knuckle-deep inside her pussy,* Jesus! — and the sheep-bear reached a howling orgasm. Unable to stop herself, Maddy bucked her big beefy butch bear girl ass a dozen times and *exploded,* a spray of seed spurting from her chunky member across the treasure-trail shag of her bloated belly.

The sheep-bear panted as they closed their eyes, the phone slipping from their grip onto the bed. It had begun playing the next video, but Maddy hardly heard it. Having sated all their appetites, they pleasantly wallowed in their sweaty, sticky, and extremely soft nest of blankets, and began to drift off.

Tomorrow would be a big day, after all.

November 4, 2022

Grovedale was exactly the same as Maddy remembered it: same old Agricultural Society announcement board at the turn-off from the two-lane highway, same old general store ("COLD BEER — HOT FOOD — TACKLE"), same old stifling sense that if there was a bright centre to Canada, this was the hamlet it was farthest from. They slowed their bike, puttering carefully down the muddy, worn asphalt. At the end of the township road, past a swung-open gate, was Garth Oakes' tidy ranch house.

The sheep-bear carefully propped their bike's kickstand into the thin gravel driveway. Granddad's F-150 was parked by the porch, so she assumed he must be home. However, knocking at the front door resulted in no answer. Maddy stepped down from the porch and ambled around the side of the house to the long back acre. Sure enough, there he was, back along the scrubby brush forest, chopping firewood.

Garth Oakes was 89, but neither age nor the loss of his wife had slowed down the burly old bear; Maddy could see him swing the hatchet with as much force and precision as they'd recalled from him fifteen years earlier. When they were a few metres away, the sheep-bear called out. "… Hi, Granddad."

The man turned around, surprised. When he saw who had arrived, a range of emotions flashed over his face — first happiness, then a briefly uncertain scowl, until settling on a neutral expression, dark lips pursed. "Madison," he said quietly. For a moment the two stood staring at each other, arms folded, before he spoke again. "I'm getting a beer. Do you want one?"

Maddy nodded, uncertainly.

Granddad lumbered off to his shed and returned with an opened bottle of Labatt 50 in each meaty paw. He handed one to his granddaughter, and they perfunctorily toasted before sitting in two nearby plastic lawn chairs. She took a swig, wincing at the insipid taste.

"So," the old bear grumbled. "Haven't seen you in a few years. Haven't *talked* to you in a few years. Not since you went and… not since you moved *out East*," he said with more than a hint of derision.

"Yes," Maddy muttered. "I had to. You know that."

He shrugged, a motion like the slow turn of a battleship on the high seas. "Maybe so. I hear you're a full-fledged Hero in Ontario, now."

"Yeah. I am."

He took a long sip of his beer. "Madison, I was thinking, when I went to the fridge just now. I was thinking you probably wouldn't have come all the way out here, unannounced, if that was going well. Is it going well?"

"It's going like shit, Granddad."

The old bear snorted, a bitter grin spreading across his muzzle. "How's that? Toronto not everything you hoped for?"

Maddy swallowed another swig of the vile brew, and took a deep breath, looking away from her grandfather's gaze. "I know how Dad died. How he *really* died, I mean."

Granddad's grin faded. "I don't know what—"

The sheep-bear whipped their head back towards their grandfather, scowling. "He got so fucking mad at some logging protestors that he gave himself a brain aneurysm, *during a press conference, in front of Prairie League HQ.* It was on the goddamn *news.* Except, hey, it turns out the League pulled some strings and covered that up and told everyone he died from fighting a supervillain. And then *you* and the rest of the family made *my own mother* lie to me about that too, for nearly twenty years. I didn't learn any of this until a few weeks ago. Is this ringing any bells, *Garth?*"

He growled, and finished the bottle, then got up and headed back towards the shed. "I'm going to need another drink for this," Granddad growled.

When he returned, he had a new beer in each hand, confusing Maddy. When the old bear slumped into his chair, he downed the entire second bottle in one long gulp, before a briefer swig from the third.

"Madison—"

This time, the young sheep-bear growled at him. "It's Maddy. I *know* you know I prefer Maddy. And *by the way*, I know Dad was an abusive piece of shit who would beat Mom bloody on the reg, too."

The old bear was silent and stared at his feet.

Maddy grew louder, gesturing angrily with their free hand, and stood up to berate their grandfather. "I *never* fucking wanted to be Heartwood, or Heartforce. I wanted to play hockey with my friends! I wanted to write dumb little stories about Olivier Armstrong kissing Izumi Curtis! I wanted to have a *life*, and you and the fucking PHL took that all from me, when you forced me into being a replacement for your stupid raging asshole son, when I was all of *twelve!* I couldn't quit even when we moved to Ontario, because it was only since I was so 'responsible' and 'mature' that Mom let me start transitioning at fourteen! And now, here I am at twenty-three; I never got a chance to go to college, and I've never had a relationship that lasted longer than a couple months. I have no useful skills outside my telekinesis, and an encyclopedic knowledge of Heartwood's career and Ontario's Heroes policy, most of which is just *fake*. It's made up! Dad was a monster, and so are my bosses! The only friends I've made in *years* are… well, they're criminals! And they're *still* better people than you, or Dad, or anyone I've ever worked with from the PHL!"

She paused, taking a breath, now panting, spraying spittle as she spoke. Granddad looked unnerved. "And do you *know* what the *worst thing* is about this job? I'm basically just a *cop*! And I *hate* being a cop! Pretty much every other queer person in the country hates me being a cop *too*! So yeah, old man, the Hero career thing? *It's going like shit.*"

The sheep-bear roared furiously, and lashed out with one hand, flailing with their powers to topple a nearby tree to the ground; the old bear shuddered at that, but kept looking downwards. "I am *so glad* I changed my name to Gillespie. Who would *want* to be a member of this fucking family?" They huffed, eyes wide, and downed the rest of their beer before letting the bottle bonelessly slip through their fingers, landing on the scrubby grass.

Finally, Garth Oakes spoke, hesitantly, looking up at his granddaughter with damp eyes. "I did what I thought was best for everyone," he said, in an almost pleading tone. "You needed — you needed him to be a legend, to *inspire* you. You had powers, and you needed training to keep them under control. We were all so proud of you, of what you could *do*, and carrying on his legacy was, well… it just made sense! And Roger was — he was gone, he wasn't going to hurt Deborah any more…"

Maddy's reserve momentarily weakened at seeing her grandfather like this… almost expressing contrition, *regret*, for once in his long life. Was this necessary? Did she have to take this out on him? It was then that she remembered how Mom had broken down weeping in her bedroom, as she'd ashamedly forced out an admission of how her husband had hurt her. It had *broken* something in her. She huffed.

"You know what she told me, Granddad? He nearly *beat her to death*, one time in Ottawa. He couldn't catch some villain, a liz—" Maddy's breath caught in their throat as pieces came together in their mind, and the sheep-bear's jaw dropped. One hand flew up to their mouth, and they began to cry. "*Oh my fucking God*, both of them in the same night…"

Granddad peered at Maddy quizzically. "Both of who…?"

The sheep-bear turned her gaze back to the elderly bear, incensed, teeth bared and nostrils flaring. "Shut up. *Shut up*. Just shut the fuck up, old man. Just tell me this. How long did you *know* about him hurting Mom?"

He shifted uncomfortably in the plastic chair, jaw set defiantly. "Roger… had a temper. He told me he had it under control. That was just something men used to do, when I was a cub. When I came home from the war—"

"That was 1954. You got back from Korea in *1954*. When was the first time that you knew your youngest son, Roger Keith Oakes, who was fucking born in *1972*, liked to hit women? Liked to bash queers? Was a *bully?*"

The old bear growled, pained. He tipped up his beer, swallowing the rest, and then hurled the empty into the woods. There was a faint sound of shattering glass. "He had super-strength! How was I supposed to stop him? The last time I tried to correct him was when he was seventeen. He *broke my arm.*"

Maddy was incredulous. "He hurt *you* too? And you *still* went along with letting the world think he was a great man, once he was dead?"

"We did it for *you*, Mad — Maddy…" The bear's face showed his age, now that they were looking closely; his eyes were sunken, and he trembled in the fading dusk. Granddad seemed small, almost frail, *weak*, despite his massive ursine bulk. He couldn't meet his granddaughter's gaze.

The sheep-bear took a deep breath and gazed out at the scrubland. The sun was dipping below the horizon, and a chill wind blew.

"Goodbye, Granddad," Maddy said coldly as she walked away.

The sheep-bear sped away from Grovedale, up Highway 40, bitter tears stinging behind her helmet's visor. A few minutes down the road, she pulled into a Tim Hortons and spent a long time staring out the window as she sipped at her double-double.

Granddad had *always* known. Roger Oakes was a rotten thug from the get-go, but he and the rest of the Oakes had convinced themselves Maddy should not only uphold his legend but redeem the man behind it. The thought made them seethe.

She pulled out her phone. The sheep-bear was inside Grande Prairie city limits, and as long as she was there, she might as well see the Heartwood memorial. It was a statue, she understood; the city had commissioned it in memory of its favourite son. Despite the fact that he was born in nearby Clairmont and spent much of his early Hero career criss-crossing Peace River Country, all along the chain of towns sprawling through the surrounding valley, he'd been claimed by the citizens of Grande Prairie as their own. There were enough fans to support a local "Heartwood Memorial Foundation" responsible for raising funds for the thing, even. The sheep-bear wasn't exactly sure where it was, though, until the internet turned up the location: Muskoseepi Park, near the city reservoir.

Maddy (and Mom, and Brianna) had been invited to the unveiling, several years back, but had declined. The sheep-bear hadn't had much interest in attending — they hardly wanted to be called "Heartwood II" by gushing local media, right as they were insistently pitching OH to let them assume a different Hero name — but in the present, they *shuddered*, knowing how painful it would have been for Mom to see her abuser immortalized like that, and recalling how the sheep had refused even to look at the photos attached to the registered letter.

Maddy idly picked at the lip of her empty cup. She missed when "Roll Up the Rim to Win" had involved the tactile sensation of actually *rolling up the rim*, rather than just scanning a QR code into the Tims app, but it was a hard habit to break regardless. Crumpling up the tattered paper and trashing it on her way out the door, she returned to the parking lot, and straddling her bike, got back on the road.

It took only a few more minutes through commercial sprawl to reach the park, a gently sloping ravine that cut through the city on either side of a winding creek. The sheep-bear slowed down when they reached the turn-off to the paved waterfront path, and slowly puttered along; there was nobody around, thankfully, but they still didn't intend to draw undue attention. Following the creek, Maddy eventually reached the reservoir, and overlooking it, they found their objective.

The statue of Roger Oakes stood tall on a plinth, his arm raised in a cheery salute. She looked at his face; it wasn't a good likeness. It captured none of the hate and rage she'd seen from the fatal press conference, nor the callow arrogance he'd displayed in the other memory-holed news clips Grace had shown her, even when he *wasn't* seconds away from bursting a blood vessel in his brain. The whole thing was as grotesque as she'd imagined — Heartwood as the idol of some ancient god, patron of the city, *looming* over his eager worshippers — and her gorge rose.

They were going to join the Korps. That was a foregone conclusion; they knew they'd never see the inside of the OH Lakeview facility again. (Not with a security clearance, anyway.) Maddy was no longer a Hero, no longer an Oakes, and no longer willing to let their father's odious monument stand. They gulped, steeling themself as they prepared to commit their first real act of villainy.

Maddy Gillespie focused her telekinetic power, and silently extending a middle finger at the vile effigy before her, concentrated on the statue's head until it exploded in a hail of marble shards. She spent the next fifteen minutes meticulously breaking the rest apart with her powers, bit by bit, visualizing it as crushing the statue between massive fingers. By the time the job was complete, she was winded; it took a moment to recover before she was able to gather up every trace of the monument's remains, and with the power of her mind, hurled them across the surface of the reservoir. They skipped along the rippling water, and then sank.

The sheep-bear put on their helmet with a satisfied growl and gunned their bike along the path until swinging onto the highway in a wide arc. The gibbous moon shone on the former Hero's shoulders as they roared the Yamaha down the highway, leaving the stifling dust of Grande Prairie in their wake.

It was time to go back to Toronto and start a new life.

CHAPTER 13

November 4, 2022

Maddy's initial adrenaline-fueled euphoria of tearing ass out of Grande Prairie, after destroying the monument to her monstrous father in the city park, had ebbed. Several hours later she was getting sleepy; her thoughts drifted, which was definitely not ideal while riding a motorbike, after dark, down rural Alberta highways. The sheep-bear had pulled off the road to the unlit rest stop south of Little Smoky, and, flipping through her maps app while idling next to the small concrete toilet stalls, resolved to stop at the next town with a hotel. That turned out to be Whitecourt, another half-hour down the highway.

It ended up being past eleven by the time the sheep-bear staggered into their room at a recently-renovated ("UNDER NEW MANAGEMENT!!") independent motel. With a smirk, they observed it was conveniently right next to *another* Smitty's location; the diner was already closed by the time they'd reached town, but they'd be able to have an extremely hearty breakfast in the morning. Which was all for the good, since Maddy had consumed only a bottle of Granddad's awful old-man beer, a double-double, and a sack of A&W cheeseburgers since lunchtime.

It was then that Maddy realized a problem: despite her exhaustion, she couldn't manage to actually get to sleep. She laid tensely in bed, staring up at the ceiling, despite the adequate mattress and the television set to the comforting background drone of The Weather Network.

"Oh, fuck, what have I *done*," the sheep-bear murmured to themself, half-giggling, both pleased and slightly terrified. They were really, for-real, *committed*, huh? No more waffling. No more fence-sitting. They'd burned their bridges with Granddad and the rest of the Oakes clan; it was time to start thinking about how they'd do the same with Ontario's Heroes, once they got back to Toronto.

Wait. She *had* made a decision, hadn't she? And — buried at the bottom of her duffel bag, still carefully wrapped in (now-dirty) laundry — there was a set of the Korps's signature Rose-Coloured Glasses. The ones worn by members of the Korps. A set given specifically to *her*, for *her* to wear. Like a member would. Someone the secretive organization *trusted*.

That thought ate at them, somehow. In a matter of weeks, they'd made friends (slightly unsettling though they sometimes were) who'd been nothing but kind and supportive, despite their lives outside the law, and Maddy's hand-wringing indecision. People who'd encouraged them to take their time figuring things out, yet still trusted them with *this*, when and if the sheep-bear was ready.

Had Hagen ever trusted her like that? Had her teammates? Had Ontario's Heroes, or the Prairie League? Had any part of the PHL ever really expressed that kind of confidence in "Heartforce"?

Maddy threw the covers aside and rolled their fuzzy nude bulk off the bed, padding over to the floor where they'd dropped the bag, digging through until they found it. They looked at the bubble-shaped visor, turning it over and over in their stubby fingers, eventually finding a recessed toggle along one rim. With a deep breath, the sheep-bear clicked it, and slid the device across their muzzle.

Text flickered by in the HUD before Maddy's eyes, bold magenta superimposed on her view of her surroundings — at that moment, gazing at her visored face in the mirror behind the desk. It looked like the operating system Grace had been using to call up Dad's buried press conference, in the secret Korps communications post at Helical BioSpectra; she caught something about a biometrics scan and new user profile setup.

Maddy certainly didn't *feel* brainwashed yet.

Suddenly, they heard a voice, as clearly as if the speaker had been standing in front of them. Not quite *heard*, actually; it was like a memory of speech, rather than taking it in through her stubby ursine ears.

[*Hello, Maddy. My name is ROSE, and I'm so glad to meet you.*]

Maddy started. Grace had mentioned this too — the AI behind Korps electronics. "Um," the sheep-bear stammered. "H-hi, ROSE."

[*Your biometric readings are telling me that you're feeling fatigued and stressed right now. Is there anything I can help with?*]

She scratched the back of her neck, chuckling ruefully. "I need to get some sleep, and also figure out exactly how I, uh, logistically follow through on this 'defecting to the supervillains' thing once I get home…?"

[Of course! Which would you like to do first?]

"…Wait, really?" Maddy tramped back to the bed, and laid down, idly staring past the television's flicker. It was playing the segment on the week in weather history again; apparently a spectacular blizzard had struck the Great Lakes in 1913. "You can help me sleep?" Realization dawned on the sheep-bear. "Is that like when Grace — I mean, Ms. Dunlop — asked you to help her sober up?"

[She'd like you to call her Grace if you're comfortable with it, but yes, exactly like that! And similarly, with your consent, I can drop you into a deep sleep almost instantly. Think of it as having access to the 'software' controlling the various functions of your nervous system.]

"You have that backdoor, you mean, not me."

[Only with your consent, of course, as I said.]

Maddy pondered the offer, clasping hands across her furred sternum. "In… a bit, I think. First, uh, how do I…" Her face reddened, realizing she was about to ask how to "use" ROSE, and became uncertain — considering the evident personality built into the AI — how the… woman? Person? Construct? …would take it.

[Please don't be embarrassed to ask me anything, Maddy. I'm happy to tell you all about how to use me. By all means, please do use me! That's what I'm here for, I promise. May I begin the RCG Tutorial presentation?]

Despite having no visible face, the sheep-bear could swear the AI was winking at them, somehow.

November 5, 2022

The next day — after breakfast, of course, which had been the Ukrainian Skillet with extra smoked sausage strewn across the cheese-drenched perogies — Maddy was back on the road. There was one difference from the previous day, however. Rather than being buried at the bottom of her bag like a shameful secret, her RCGs (Her! RCGs!) were instead safely stashed in her jacket's inner chest pocket.

The sheep-bear thought happily about their conversation with ROSE. It had lasted another two hours before they finally took the AI up on her offer and accepted the help in drifting off. Their back-and-forth resumed in the morning, too, after the most relaxing night they'd had in *years*. ROSE had helpfully made certain to maximize Maddy's REM sleep, at that, gently awakening them with perfect timing to pack up for the latest possible check-out.

It also turned out that ROSE *did* in fact have a face, to Maddy's surprise. After very clearly obtaining the sheep-bear's consent, the AI had materialized in her RCGs' view as a warmly smiling vixen, superimposed on the surroundings of the motel room as an augmented reality construct. ROSE had virtually lounged cross-legged in the room's lone chair as the two spoke, listening to Maddy's giddy anxiety and offering comforting commentary. They planned out what the sheep-bear would do once back in Toronto: a heart-to-heart with Mom and Brianna, then... laying low for quite some time. Could she simply disappear off OH's radar for a while? If anyone could make that happen, it seemed like her new friends could.

More importantly, the AI had *also* informed Maddy of the nearest Korps facility (SCS, the "Saskatoon Command Site") and told them they'd be welcome to stop by, if highway motels were beginning to lose their charm for the sheep-bear. They were, and for that reason Maddy's route had changed, making a beeline back down the Yellowhead Highway towards "the Paris of the Prairies."

It was on passing the road sign welcoming drivers to the bi-provincial city of Lloydminster that Maddy's phone rang through Bluetooth earbuds, briefly confusing the sheep-bear; who would possibly be calling?

On the third ring, she realized, and her blood ran cold: Slider. She hadn't checked in, and he was, surely, going to be a dick about it. Sighing under her helmet, the sheep-bear pulled into one of the many parking lots of the bleak commercial strip stretching along the highway. Idling between a Princess Auto and a RONA warehouse, Maddy tapped to pick up the line.

"You owe me a report, *valued teammate*," the rat said testily, not even pausing for the pleasantry of a 'hello.'

"Made any effort to do your *one fucking job* lately?"

Maddy snorted, watching the traffic pass by in the distance. "Good afternoon to you, too," they mumbled.

"You think I don't goddamn *mean* it, bud? You want Hagen on your case? Don't get snide with me. Come on, quick-like, I want to hear *all* about it, since you couldn't be bothered to even half-ass a voicemail yesterday. What have you accomplished in infiltrating the Korps in the last thirty-six hours?"

"Well, I went to their Halloween party last week dressed up as my childhood hero, and got drunk after having a heart-to-heart with Redline. They gave me a set of RCGs, and I finally tried them on last night. Felt pretty good, very comfortable fit on the muzzle, no brainwashing to report; the virtual fox lady interface even helped me get to sleep, after I told her all about my defection plans," the sheep-bear snarked.

He made a whiny, irritated scoffing noise. "Go on! Funny. *Real* funny. My sides are *splitting*. Now try again."

Maddy took a deep breath, and repositioned their broad bottom on the saddle of their beloved V-Max. "You know what? Fuck off. After the Dr. Seuss shit, just *entirely* fuck off. I'm tired of playing these stupid little games. Do you like this, Neal? Do you like being the way you are?"

There was a long silence on the other end of the line. Finally, the rat spoke, with more than a hint of defensiveness in his voice. "I'm — I'm *good* at what I do."

Maddy turned, looking at a harried crane woman trying to keep her chicks from playing with shopping carts as she loaded a box of air filters into their minivan. "Are you? Are you, though? Because I feel like I've seen a lot of evidence to the contrary lately. What exactly are *you* reporting to the boss, if I'm such a fuckup? He's just letting you ineffectually give me shit periodically, good job, no notes?" She hesitated, before grinning, and deciding to twist the knife as hard as she could. "Hell, you're a joke to the Korps, you know. They weren't concerned *at all* about your little break-in at HBS. Threat level on par with a small-town cop, maybe? Just *beneath* contempt."

"At least I fucking *want* to be here," Slider snapped. "You don't. I pay attention, Oakes! It could not *be* more obvious that you've never wanted to be part of the team! I don't think you've ever even wanted to be a *Hero!*" He growled into the phone, exasperated. "But no, ungrateful little shits like you win the lottery with powers, and then you were oh-so-fucking-convenient to Hagen, a twofer of a diversity hire *and* someone for this whole *thing* with the Korps. Did you know he's been planning this mission since you were on the junior prospect roster? He's goddamn *obsessed*, he's only thinking about getting the best headlines of his career — who ever fucking *liked* him when he was Canadian Shield, hell — and he's willing to give you enough rope to hang yourself with. No skin off my nose."

"Neal. Hagen hates me, but he doesn't like you much either. Why are you so *loyal*, if you know he's gone off the deep end? And if you think I'm like... a disgrace to OH, or whatever... why wouldn't you just leave me alone to fail? To get fired — or quit, even — if I can't hack it? Why are you standing in my way, if you think I'm just a fucking useless 'diversity hire'?"

"Most people never get the things they want, Madison. Why should *you* be any different?"

The line went dead.

Slider was going to be a *problem* once she got back to Toronto, the sheep-bear realized.

A few hours later, Maddy was inside SCS, visor equipped. People waved and smiled, prompting the sheep-bear to wonder whether anyone at OH Lakeview had ever seemed happy to see them, and coming up blank.

It wasn't nearly as grand as the facility she'd seen the previous week, which ROSE had informed her was Korps Downsview Site, or KDS. (The virtual vixen seemed almost to be holding back giggles, upon correcting the sheep-bear's misapprehension that she'd been underneath Yorkdale, rather than the nearby decommissioned military base that had become Downsview Airport at ground level.) However, she'd still been welcomed, after blue-visored guards at a security checkpoint had reviewed her dossier, assigning her a guide to give her a tour of the base — and, Maddy assumed, keep an eye on her, despite ROSE's assurance that she had already been fully vetted by KDS's security team.

Although, "assigned" might have been overselling it.

ROSE had silently whispered to Maddy that the guards (a curvy zebra femme and a short, buff pintail drake) had merely pinged the local network asking for volunteers to "show a visiting new recruit around," which admittedly didn't quite *sound* like they were in need of a trusted minder.

In any event, that was how the sheep-bear had ended up sitting across a mess hall table from Lou, a stout, butch pine marten wearing black overalls and a dark flannel shirt, who had to be at least in her fifties. Maddy had been venting about Slider, while digging into a huge dish of mapo tofu liberally doused in pickled mustard greens.

"I don't get it," said the mustelid through a mouthful of hot and sour wontons. "This sketchy little prick is just giving you shit every day, and that's it? Seems to me the PHL would have more of a care about keeping watch on you, for this big double agent op they think you're doing."

Maddy slurped at the spicy, oily sauce around her lips as she carefully picked up another fat chunk of tofu with her chopsticks. "I took some leave to come out west and see my grandfather. Well, blow up at my grandfather. *Well*, actually, blow up at my grandfather and then also my dead father. But anyway, I think Neal is just… *freelancing* with this fuckery, honestly? Being a cowardly shitheel because he *can*. But I don't want to make waves by bitching about him to Hagen. More attention from OH is the last thing I need right now."

Lou nodded, the floof of her short undercut bouncing along as she did. "Oh, sure, sure, I gotcha. You about to do anything to knock him down a peg, though? Sounds like the twerp has it coming," she said before a belch, briefly pounding a closed fist against her chest to work down the indigestion. "*Ooof.* I'll tell you, girl, I can't half handle the spice any more. Best Sichuan food in town right here on-base, though! I always get some when I'm passing through."

Maddy raised an eyebrow. "Are you not, uh, *here*? Posted or assigned or billeted at SCS, or whatever? I mean, I assumed, since you showed me around—"

She laughed, a rich, smoky guffaw that spoke to a lifetime of *experience*. "Oh, I spend a lot of time here, but really, I mostly live on the road. Logistics and intel, see. I haul cargo between sites and keep an eye out for things the field ops and command folks like to know about. Nothing suspicious about an ol' trucker gal with a semi traipsing all over the continent, y'know," the marten said with a wink and a smirk of her bristly, greying whiskers. "And as a matter of fact, I'm on my way back east; got a shipment heading to BDB, with a quick stop at SHS. It's not all the way back to KDS, but you could take a break from riding, keep me company up front? Put your bike in the trailer behind the cargo pods, of course; couldn't expect'cha to leave it here, sweet thing."

That would be convenient, Maddy pondered. But also, was it her imagination, or was Lou hitting on her...?

[*Yes, she is.*]

The sheep-bear coughed and fumbled their chopsticks, eyes down; they'd gotten so quickly used to the RCGs, they'd forgotten ROSE was still active and listening.

[*I can go offline if you'd like! But yes, she's into you; the instance of me running on **her** hardware obtained her consent to share that. And from your current heart rate and brainwave activity, it seems as though you may be receptive? If it's a concern, I can tell you that Ms. Cartier's quarters here are very spacious and welcoming to overnight guests, as is her rig's sleeper cab.*]

"ROSE...!"

Although, this was what she'd been hoping for since seeing the crowds at KDS, wasn't it? Especially after her self-admissions and... *research*... the other night. It could be a chance to feel her oats, especially in the company of such a handsome older butch. Maybe she could even pick up a few pointers, to say nothing of gaining some confidence to flirt back, the next time Grace teased her about her age. The thought appealed, and she began to imagine what Lou might look like under the overalls.

[*I'll take that as a "Please give us some privacy, ROSE." Have fun!*]

Maddy flushed, and it wasn't just the numbing spice of the pepper that was heating up their face.

She looked up from her dinner into the older woman's weathered cherrywood-red eyes, and grinned in what she hoped was a cockily appealing way. "You know what, Lou? I'd be happy to hop in with you for a few days. I can always use more friends to show me the ropes of the villain life..."

Chapter 14

Maddy took a deep breath under her motorcycle helmet as she merged into the exit lane for Derry Road. She had parted ways with Lou in Sudbury earlier that day, with both promising to stay in touch; the sheep-bear had tremendously enjoyed her several days riding shotgun with (and nights riding) the trucker. Refreshed by the time off her bike, and the easy warmth of the older butch's company, the rest of her trip back home to Mississauga had been downright pleasant. This part, though… this was going to be difficult.

They pulled into the bungalow's driveway and dismounted their beloved V-Max. With no small amount of apprehension, Maddy knocked on the door. Deborah Gillespie appeared a moment later. The petite bighorn ewe smiled when she saw her daughter, before a look of concern overtook her face. "What's wrong, honey?" she said in a small voice. "You usually call…"

"Hi, Mom," Maddy said, exuberantly feigning cheerfulness. "Can we talk?"

She nodded, and the two proceeded wordlessly to the kitchen, the sheep-bear softly closing the front door behind her and dropping her duffel bag and helmet in the front hall. Deborah had already taken out two teacups and was filling the electric kettle by the time Maddy sat down at the table, lips pursed, unsure of how to even begin.

"You like that '*chay*' tea, don't you? I got some of that to try," the sheep murmured, as she busied herself rifling through the pantry. "I would have made some coffee cake if I'd known you were coming, but I think there's some biscuits in here…"

Maddy smirked at that. "It's *chai*, Mom. Yes, sure, thank you, but don't worry about a snack, I'm fine."

The sheep craned her neck around the pantry's folding door. "Are you sure, honey?"

"Yes. It's, um, it's okay, I promise."

Maddy went down the hall to the washroom while waiting for the water to boil. On her way back, she peered into her teenage bedroom; after the sheep-bear had stayed the night several weeks ago, Mom had re-covered it with the plastic drop-sheets that cut down on dusting. She sighed, sadly, and wondered when she'd next see this room (or Mom, or Brianna) in person again.

A moment later, cups of President's Choice Chocolatey Chai in hand, Deborah and Maddy sat at the kitchen table. Maddy took a careful sip and looked out the window. The gangly Norway maple in the back yard had lost nearly all of its leaves, with only a few die-hard stragglers still holding tight. "I can't be a Hero any more," they said bitterly. "It's just not — it's that — it's because of *Dad*. Sort of. But also because of me."

"Oh, honey, no! Please don't give up on your career just because—"

"I *never* wanted to do this. Never. You know that, don't you? Dad's side of the family pushed me into it. Pushed *you* into it, just like they pushed to cover up how he died, or how much he hurt you. It was all about the legacy, and I happened to be a convenient vessel for it."

Deborah sniffed, wincing. "I know. But you've been progressing so fast in your career, and until... until recently... you seemed to be more or less happy about it? I mean, you got to be the LGBT Champion! That's something," she said, patting her daughter's hand.

"LGBTQ2+, there's more letters now. Not that it matters; I was only ever window dressing, to make Ontario's Heroes look less backward. They're still like *Dad*. Most of the people I work with don't... really... *like* me, I don't think. My coworkers are transphobic all the time! And I found out that I wouldn't even be *on* the team if Mr. Hagen wasn't planning to use me to — uh, use me like that."

"Oh," the ewe said in a small voice. "I'm sorry, honey. I thought... I hoped it would be a good place for you."

Maddy took a deep breath and smiled weakly at their mother. "I know, Mom. I love you and I know you tried your best. *I* tried my best too, but I know now that I'm just not welcome there, not as *me*. What Ontario's Heroes wanted was a symbol; the 'Heartwood legacy,' but make it 'diverse.'

No accountability, no owning up to the way government Heroes have always been hurting queer people. They were willing to give me a seat at the table only as long as I could be co-opted to defend the status quo," the sheep-bear sighed. "But those new friends I was telling you about, they helped me figure it out eventually: I just *can't*. I respect myself too much for that, you know? I'm not a cop, and I'm not *him*, and I won't compromise on that ever again."

The sheep nodded with understanding as she sipped her tea, badly trying to hide that she clearly found the taste novel. "Oh! Actually, that reminds me," Deborah said brightly, turning around to pick up a stack of assorted mail from the shelf of the phone nook at her back. Shuffling through it, she found what she was looking for and handed two envelopes to her daughter. "These came this morning."

The addresses were from the governments of Ontario and Alberta, and Maddy looked at the envelopes only briefly before carefully opening each one. After a moment, the sheep-bear had in her hands a thick folded parchment, and a thin, translucent polymer document: her change of name and amended birth certificates, respectively. Mom peered at the papers curiously.

"I thought so! I wasn't sure why you had them sent here, but gosh, that was fast, if you only decided to change your name a couple of weeks ago," Deborah mused, a hint of pride in her voice.

Maddy smiled, chuckling delightedly. "I had a little help from those friends for this, too."

"Then you can thank them again for me. Welcome to being a Gillespie," the ewe giggled, before standing up with arms open. Maddy joined her, and the two hugged tightly.

"Mom? There's some other stuff I have to tell you," the sheep-bear murmured over their mother's shoulder. They pulled away, and sat down again, motioning for her to join them. "I went to see Granddad. I talked to him about... about Dad."

"Oh...?"

"If any of the Oakes ask, tell them I said they can all go to hell."

"Oh, honey, I'd be happy to! *Language*, though," Deborah smirked.

The sheep-bear took a deep breath, and laid a meaty paw on their mother's arm, squeezing tightly. "Do you trust me?"

"Of course," Deborah said, her expression suddenly worried.

"The PHL is going to tell you some awful things about me, soon. They're going to say I'm brainwashed. They might say that I'm a danger to you and Bri, or that they need to take me down, institutionalize me, for my own good. *Don't believe them.* They're lying, just like they lied about Dad."

The ewe grasped her daughter's hand in her smaller, more delicate, fully ovine ones. "Are you in some kind of trouble?"

"Maybe not yet, unless someone spotted me at Dad's monument in Grande Prairie. Soon, though."

"*Maddy!*"

"It's better I don't tell you too much, but… do you remember you were telling me about that time in Ottawa, at the party? Dad chased after the lizard?"

Deborah nodded. "Yes…?"

"Well… I met them. You have something in common, at least — he hurt you both very badly, that night." Maddy inhaled sharply, looking away. "They're pretty cool. Very kind, very thoughtful, very, uh, *forgiving*. I think you'd like them."

Realization dawned on the sheep. "So, your new friends are…"

"Yeah. Definitely *not* Heroes."

"And — and you trust them?"

"After learning everything I have in the last few weeks? Yes. With my life, I think."

"You know what? I think I trust them too, then," Deborah said, smiling.

Finally, Maddy arrived home to her apartment. Although, admittedly, it wouldn't be "home" any more, as soon as she abandoned it for KDS. (ROSE had assured her that she'd have assigned quarters waiting, whenever she decided to make the leap.) She looked around the space; after only days away, it somehow felt empty, almost *alien*.

The sheep-bear paced through the rooms rifling through shelves and closets for nearly an hour, before coming to a depressing conclusion: they didn't really have many possessions they valued. The apartment had come furnished, and the small amount of decor was mostly discount pieces from the HomeSense at Erin Mills. Most of their childhood mementos and adolescent nerd detritus were still in their old bedroom in Malton, underneath Mom's drop-sheets.

Nonetheless, she eventually stuffed her laptop and some personal bric-a-brac into the duffel bag, alongside a few favourite T-shirts. Maddy was about to do one last circuit of the apartment before heading out, forever, when she heard the creak of the front door opening. The sheep-bear urgently jammed on the RCGs from her jacket's front pocket before sidling up against the back of the bedroom door, peeking through the crack in the hinges into the living room. She saw the shape of a very familiar rat.

Slider.

An exhausted frown crossed the sheep-bear's features, and she silently messaged a query through her visor's mental link. "ROSE? *Can a new recruit call for backup?*"

[*Of course! I can definitely request assistance for emergency extraction, if you need it. Would you like me to do that now?*]

"Not... yet. If it's **just** him..."

[*Confirmed. Also, I've taken the initiative of tapping into your building's security system. The management really **should** go to the trouble of changing the default router password and updating their camera interface software. In any event, Slider appears to be alone, and I detect no incoming or outgoing signals from his communication devices.*]

Maddy's muzzle split into a sly smirk, upon learning that tidbit. "Thanks, ROSE. Stand by, but I think I can handle this one on my own."

The sheep-bear grasped the living room rug with her powers and pulled it sharply; Slider tried to steady himself but stumbled and fell on his chest with a grunt. She strode into the living room and mentally pinned him to the ground. "I *thought* I told you to keep your skeevy ass out of here," Maddy growled. "How'd you know I was back in town, anyway?"

The rat chuckled smugly into the floor. "What, you think I haven't been watching your mom's house?" As he craned his neck over his shoulder to face the sheep-bear, he looked Maddy up and down with an expression of disgust. "I *knew* it," he screeched upon registering that they were wearing a pink visor, before his expression turned to panic. "Wait, shit, already? You've already got a real set? Oh fuck, Hagen's gonna be right *pissed*..."

The sheep-bear folded her arms, looking down her muzzle at Slider. "Hey, *about* that. How much of the past couple weeks of jerking me around has been from our fearless leader, and how much was just *you* freelancing?"

The rat struggled, whining in a thin, scratchy voice when Maddy responded by holding him down even more tightly. "All of it was me, okay? *All of it!* I figured you were planning to defect for real if you could, once I saw the pills. I was going to let it happen, then ambush you once I knew you had a pair of RCGs and show Hagen the bottle. You'd at least be in deep shit for not following orders, enough to get kicked off the team; and maybe, if I got lucky and it triggered you into a big public meltdown or whatever, you'd catch a couple of conspiracy and terrorism charges on the way out, too. I didn't think you'd actually *done* it yet, though, knowing how fucking *useless* you've been until now," he whined bitterly.

"So, Hagen, right now, he thinks I'm doing *what* exactly?"

"Still tailing that fat bitch deer," he sneered, rolling his eyes. Neal then began hacking and coughing, as if he was trying to clear his throat without success. It took several more seconds before he seemed to realize that the cause of the obstruction was Maddy, slowly tightening her telekinetic grip around his neck with the gesture of a closing hand. "What're — you — *thhhhhk* — doing...?"

"Oh, this? I'm choking you out. You know, Reclaimer always wanted me to practice this, when I was in the Prairie League Cadets? 'Just in case,' he'd say. They even rigged up this whole dummy with a crushable windpipe for me. I refused, because I thought — I thought, in the infinite wisdom of a squeamish thirteen-year-old! — that I could never do that to a person. I'd *never* be in a situation where I'd have to seriously hurt anyone for real; there would always be an option to fight defensively and take opponents down without doing lasting damage." They scoffed and flexed their control slightly to allow Slider a deeper breath, tilting their broad ursine head to flash Slider a menacing grin. "Kids, eh? So innocent. So *optimistic*."

The rat glared daggers at the erstwhile Hero as he scrabbled at his neck with both hands, fruitlessly trying to gain purchase on the invisible force of Maddy's powers. "H — how are you even this *strhhhhk*..."

"*Oh my God.* Do you not get it yet? Neal, you colossal *asshole*, I have been *holding back.* I have been restraining myself for *years*, because I knew that podcasting maniacs, and fascist wine moms, and insecure little fuckboys like *you*, would bitch about how being aggressive — being *powerful* — means I'm 'really a man,'" Maddy roared, as she telekinetically lifted him off the ground and tightened her grip around his throat.

"I have repressed *so much* to keep other people comfortable. Do you know what that got me? All that caution and restraint and respectability, making myself *smaller*, being polite and earnest and not making waves, and just forever, endlessly volunteering to patiently educate you people that I'm a real person with a right to exist? *Nothing.* Nothing! It was *worthless*, you abusive piece of shit! It made Hagen see me as a pawn for his stupid cloak-and-dagger game, it made my family think they could railroad me into carrying on a wife-beating bigot's legacy, and it made *you* think you could gaslight and manipulate me for this... this petty little *ego trip*."

The sheep-bear panted, teeth bared, nostrils flaring in anger. "You know what, 'bud? I don't deserve to be barely tolerated as OH's pet diversity mascot. I deserve to *thrive*. I deserve to have a goddamn *life*, and *love*, and a motherfucking *purpose*. One that isn't betraying my fellow queers as, *basically*, a cop. The only people in the super business offering me any of those things are the Korps."

The rat sputtered weakly, kicking his legs in the air. With a glance, the sheep-bear's rage shaped itself into a cage of force around his lower body, locking down his movement there forcefully enough that they heard the sickening snap of a tibia. Tears streamed from Slider's bugged-out eyes, and for once — for once! — Maddy could see in his expression that he was truly *afraid* of something.

Maddy cackled with sinister glee, lowering her RCGs to give the rat a direct, baleful leer. "How's *that* for a 'diversity hire,' huh?" With a flourish of her hand, she contemptuously flung him to one side (leaving a Slider-shaped dent in the drywall) and then released him entirely, letting the rat crumple to the ground on his back, sobbing and gasping.

"You're... you're fucking *crazy*, you *bitch*," he roughly croaked through moans of pain, nose bleeding and face bruised. "You're — *aaaagh* — just as stunned as *Hagen* about this stupid Cold War shit!" At that, Slider began making deep, gurgling heaving noises, interspersed with his coughs.

Maddy, disgusted, half-kicked the rat with a sturdy motorcycle boot to flip him onto his front. She'd felt no compunctions about hurting him after all he'd done, but she wasn't going to let Neal Salton (vile little creep though he might be) die from aspirating his own vomit. Her timing in tipping him over turned out to be impeccable, as he began weakly puking on the hardwood floor. With a gesture, she telekinetically pulled his communicator earpiece to fly into her hand; dropping it, the sheep-bear proceeded to crush it under her heel.

"I am telling you this *once*, Neal. Pass it on to Lightbox, to the director, to the deputy minister, to fucking *CP24* if you want. I'm *done*. I'm out of the Hero game. I'm not being a double agent, and frankly, I don't feel up to committing any more crimes past this — what would a Crown call it, aggravated assault? — today. Leave me alone, *especially* leave my family alone, and you'll never hear from me again; I'll just chill at those Korps 'reefer-den hypno-slave orgies' that Hagen likes to get worked up about," Maddy growled. "If you or him or any part of the PHL ever give me a reason to want *more* catharsis than I'm experiencing at this exact moment, though... well, you're not going to like it, the next time you see this 'diversity hire.' Are we understood?"

Slider, still heaving and shaking, said nothing. Maddy used her powers to forcibly lift and turn his head in her direction. She bent low, and howled in his face; he shrank away, sobbing.

"I said, are we *fucking* understood?"

"*Hrrrrk* — yes, fuck, oka*uuuuurgh*..."

"Yes *who*? What's my goddamn *name*, Neal?"

"Y-yes, hngh, Madi–Mad*dy*..."

The sheep-bear released the pathetic rat to slump back down to the floor, where he continued to periodically gurgle into the puddle around his snout, moaning in pain.

Maddy made one last sweep of the apartment (ignoring the piteous noises Slider was making from the floor) before throwing the stuffed duffel bag over her shoulder and opening the front door. After a few seconds standing in place, she looked back over her shoulder and huffed. The sheep-bear couldn't help but feel the briefest pang of sympathy for the rat, awful as he was.

"Uh. ROSE? Can you make an anonymous call for an ambulance after I leave? I don't actually want this asshole *dead*."

[*Of course.*]

"Thanks, ROSE."

The sheep-bear walked down the stairs and out to the parking lot, where snow was beginning to lightly fall. They straddled their motorcycle and gunned the engine, pulling out to the street in the direction of KDS. It was time to start enjoying her new life.

Epilogue

January 26, 2023

Ray Delaney, *newspaperman* — well, "emerging trends and social media champion" for the *Grande Prairie Daily Herald-Tribune*, at least — was on his way back to the office from a Tim's run when his phone's notifications began exploding. The orca had just passed the Dairy Queen, his employer's building in sight at the next cross-street, when he began one-handedly thumbing through the comments; there certainly was a *lot* more activity on the annual Heartwood memorial posts, on every platform, than he'd seen in the past three years at this job. Suddenly, the phone rang, startling him into choking on his double-double. It was his boss, calling from the publisher's head office in Toronto.

The orca tapped to answer it, coughing to clear his throat. "Uh, Hi, Mark; what's up…?"

"RAY. THAT VIDEO. WHAT THE FUCK?"

"The video of—"

"Your dead local superhero guy! *Heartwood!*"

"The memorial post? It's just from the morgue files, like usual…?"

A truck passed by, honking at an inattentive pedestrian, and Mark paused for a moment. "…Ray? Are you out of the office right now?"

"Almost back from coffee, be at my desk in just a minute," the orca panted, beginning to lumber in a jog up 100 Street.

"Okay. *Okay*. Look at the video, pull all the Heartwood posts, and I'll call you back in ten. *Jesus*, man, where did that footage even *come* from?" The phone beeped dully to indicate Ray's boss had hung up.

He sprinted the rest of the way back to his cubicle. He faintly heard Jessica from Sales shouting something at his back about local advertisers threatening to boycott the paper, but the orca didn't stop until he was sitting at his desk, throwing his thick parka aside; taking a gulp of hot coffee, he pulled up Twitter first. He anxiously clicked on the video from the post he'd uploaded twenty minutes prior.

It was *supposed* to be a video from Canada Day, 2002 of the late local Hero, "The Pride of Grande Prairie," giving a patriotic speech in Muskoseepi Park about civic duty and vigilance. That was what he had posted every year on Heartwood's birthday. It was what his predecessor Dinesh had posted every year on Heartwood's birthday. As far as he knew, it was what *Dinesh's* predecessor had posted every year on Heartwood's birthday. After the mysterious disappearance of his monument in the park a few months prior, there'd been local debate over whether to install a replacement, and he'd linked to a yea-or-nay reader poll alongside the video.

The clip in the post, however, was… decidedly not that speech. It was instead a compilation of what appeared to be raw cable news footage from the early aughts, and Ray scrubbed through it, horrified. The burly bear in the red-and-white uniform was screaming himself hoarse in most of the clips, and none made him look particularly heroic, to say the least.

"—NO COWARDLY GOD-DAMNED TREE-HUGGERS—"

"—DIRTY FUCKING ILLEGALS—"

"—SHARIA LAW, IN OUR SCHOOLS—"

"—IF MY SON TURNED OUT TO BE A FAGGOT, I'D—"

"—THE GLOBALIST BANKERS' CABAL—"

Panicked, Ray deleted every one of the Heartwood posts, but it was too late; scanning through trending topics, he found dozens of reposts. Briefly clicking over to YouTube, it seemed as though several copies were already posted there too.

The orca removed his hand from the mouse and leaned back, staring at the wall. He took a deep breath, sipped his coffee, and waited for the phone to ring.

Bearing Down
Gracefully

November 29, 2022

Maddy Gillespie blinked their eyes open and yawned, well-rested, from beneath magenta sheets.

Two months earlier, the burly sheep-bear had been a licensed Hero with a government security clearance, vaguely dissatisfied by the burden of upholding her Hero father's legacy but giving her all regardless. One month earlier, she'd started off on the journey that ended in spectacularly quitting the Ontario's Heroes team, cathartically maiming her transphobic creep colleague/stalker on her way to defect to the Korps. In the present, in her cozy, den-like single quarters deep within the residential sector of KDS, she awoke once again relieved to be under no pressure whatsoever, and responsible for *nothing*. No duty rosters, no patrols, no status reports or security briefings or team meetings, and *especially* no dealing with fragile backstabbing fuckboys.

They'd hardly believed it at first, that the vast supervillainous collective would simply *help*. ROSE had been bemused, but insistent on encouraging the sheep-bear to explore and see it for themself. They had and inspected the shops and services and restaurants lining the avenues of the massive underground complex at length. In *particular*, they'd plowed their massive appetite through the various kiosks, stands, boîtes, bistros, cafes and clubs in the mess hall sector; the food was plentiful, delicious, and came at no charge.

Although, Maddy realized as she proceeded to get dressed, she'd need to resume regular training soon if she intended to keep up that pace. True, comfortable, flattering (and fucking *hot*) clothing — both decorative and functional — was similarly freely available in the quartermaster's sector. However, the favourite old pair of jeans she'd been wearing when she arrived were… starting to get just a *little* too tight. She leaned against the side of the unmade bed as she tried to wiggle into the nearly-black denim, eventually giving up and throwing herself back onto the mattress, groaning in defeat.

Exchanging the pants for a pair of lightweight synthetic leggings that hugged their bulky ursine ass and thighs, telekinetically pulled into their hand from the closet shelf across the room, the sheep-bear sighed with a half-snort. It was as good a day as any to get back in the swing of things, they supposed, grabbing their RCGs from the charging cradle on the sleek bedside shelf. The usual text messages scrolled by rapidly on bootup; it was surprising just how quickly the stylized rose icon had become a comfort, after those few seconds.

"Morning, ROSE," Maddy said brightly, as she pulled a sports bra down over her beefy shoulders. "Can you, uh, point me to the kind of gym facilities I'd need for a basic workout? And then, what kind of options do I have for training with my powers?"

[*Good morning, Maddy! I'd be happy to, and you're in luck — they're almost in the same place.*]

Two side-by-side beacons appeared in the map view of her visor's wayfinding app, and, as ever, the sheep-bear could *swear* that ROSE was invisibly smirking at them.

After some careful weight training and cardio (conscious not to lift too much or run the treadmill too hard, after a month of getting soft), Maddy proceeded at ROSE's direction to report to the personal trainers' bullpen. A masculine figure in behelixed, lightweight composite body armour waved as she approached. On closer inspection, it was a lean, weathered, older blue jay.

"Hi there, Maddy!" he chirped eagerly. "I'm Tommy, he/him, and I'll be sparring with you today." He shrugged, semi-abashedly, fluffing his blue-feathered neck. "Well, I say *sparring*, but mostly I'll be operating our standard telekinetic obstacle course and hazard scenario for you. There might be a surprise or two! But really, we just want to feel out your power and skill levels, get a current reading on classifying the strength of your telekinesis, so we can calibrate an experience more personalized to you for ongoing training. Sound good?"

The sheep-bear, still faintly panting from her regular gym routine, offered a hand to shake. "Yeah! Yeah. I pushed myself *hard* the last time I was using my powers for more than, like, convenience stuff," they admitted hesitantly, the sound of Slider's leg breaking still echoing in their head. "I'd like to at least keep up with regular practice, even if I'm not... well..."

The blue jay took her hand and shook it firmly, almost professionally. "Planning on getting yourself cleared to officially go out as a field agent any time soon? Hey, newbie, don't worry; I get it. Not everyone who signs on with the black hats wants to go on a roaring rampage of revenge," he nodded sagely. "At least, not *right* away."

"Something like that," Maddy said mildly.

The sheep-bear followed the blue jay to Training Bay F. It was a long hall-like space, floored in stainless steel grating. Tommy took his position behind a transparent blast shield at the room's control panel, twenty metres or more away from the centre of the room. He called out, his voice amplified into Maddy's ears by her own RCGs: "Ready?"

"Ready," she replied, taking a deep breath and flexing her hoof-nailed hands.

The program started, and the lights dimmed. True to his word, Tommy wasn't going for the gusto, at least to start with. The sheep-bear faced no more than a few volleys of glossy black rubber balls from cannons concealed in the walls — although some turned out to be augmented-reality overlays in their RCGs' view, which momentarily disoriented them when those projectiles proved immune to their powers. The difficulty slowly increased, and Maddy could see the blue jay nodding with approval as he activated one new hazard after another. They huffed, beginning to get winded, and had to be increasingly quick on their feet to deflect a gush of pink slime from a ceiling trapdoor and extinguish a series of mock-incendiary devices that rolled out from ankle-high chutes. Suddenly, the sheep-bear felt the ambient temperature drop slightly — was that the early warning of a cryokinetic device being activated…?

That was when her knees buckled from a series of dull thumps from behind, and she keeled over, tumbling to protect her face and bare arms. A buzzer sounded, and the program stopped, with full lights returning. A few meters away, a spray of water washed away the last of the slime trap's residue.

"Hey, Maddy!" the blue jay chirped perkily, looming over her prone form with what turned out to be a massive autocannon (its translucent ammo reservoir filled with the same glossy rubber target balls) in both hands. He seemed to be visibly *sparkling*, somehow, like an anime protagonist's object of affection. "That was really good! I did warn you there might be some surprises, though," he said with a warm smile, as he set down the weapon and squatted low to help up the sheep-bear. "You've got a lot of power and finesse! I can see that you've worked hard to streamline your motions to conserve energy and keep your defenses up, and I have to say I'm impressed! I reviewed your dossier; the PHL must have been *pissed* to lose you."

Brushing herself off with a Tommy-proffered towel as they exited, Maddy muttered darkly. "I'm sure Director Hagen was, but not because he thought my *powers* were worth anything. All he wanted was… anyway, uh, I'd rather not think about that right now."

"Ah, I'm sorry," he said with chagrin. "Me and my big mouth. I'd be happy to get you set up with another trainer, if you'd like?"

Maddy looked up and down at the older man's exceptionally earnest body language. "No, no, that's okay. This was… this was a good workout. How often can I use these facilities?"

"Any time you like! And if you want to book me, well, ROSE knows where I live," the blue jay said brightly as the two walked down the hall.

The sheep-bear bid Tommy goodbye partway back to the bullpen, diverting down a side corridor to a vending machine of sports drinks near the cardio equipment; parched, they impatiently punched the button for a glass bottle of the unnaturally-neon blue raspberry flavour, and guzzled it in a matter of seconds while leaning sweatily against the paneled walls. That was when they spotted a familiar-looking set of swept-back antlers bobbing up and down, a few rows of machines over.

Maddy pitched the bottle in a nearby recycling chute and ducked behind a bank of elliptical trainers, squinting at the back of the broad cervine figure pumping the pedals of a stationary bike. She gulped as she sidled around, trying to get a view of the deer's face. *Is that…*

ROSE chimed in, a little too eagerly.

[Yes, that's Grace!]

The chubby doe wore compression shorts, and a magenta sweatband against the pedicles of her graceful antlers kept her wavy, golden-brown tresses from falling into her face. Her modest breasts filled out a black tank top emblazoned with a giant K-LAW insignia. From her vaguely distracted expression, Maddy guessed that the lawyer was probably watching or listening to something through her cateye-framed RCGs as she pedaled.

They hadn't seen the deer in the few weeks since properly joining the Korps and moving into their quarters. When Maddy first inquired, ROSE had helpfully explained that Grace was temporarily residing at VCS, attending a trial in Vancouver; they'd hesitated to send a message when the AI offered, however. Maddy could do this on their own, could become acclimatized to their… career change, and make some friends on their own; they didn't *need* anyone holding their hand. *Play it cool,* the sheep-bear had thought to themself, an urge slightly undermined by remembering how comfortably they'd fallen asleep on the sweetly matronly doe's soft thigh at the Halloween party.

In any event, Maddy was… she was more *confident,* now; she was no longer intimidated by the deer, and able to own that she did, in fact, like the idea of fucking the gorgeous older woman. *A lot,* she pondered, flushing. The doe might have once good-naturedly teased her about her age in the context of a flirtatious joke, but it didn't seem like that was *necessarily* a dealbreaker? At the party Grace had seemed receptive to an advance from a woman only a few years older than the sheep-bear, after all…

Confident, slightly turned on, and still just the *tiniest* bit self-conscious, Maddy stepped in front of Grace's bike and gave her a hesitant wave.

The deer perked up, her attention definitively caught, when she recognized the face of the erstwhile Hero before her. "Maddy! Hello! It's so good to see you, dear!" Her hooves slowed the pedals until they stopped, and she took a long swig from a stainless-steel water bottle, breathing heavily. After a few seconds of catching her breath, Grace leaned over the cardio machine's control panel to warmly smile at the sheep-bear. "I hear you're settling in comfortably?"

"I, uh, yes! Yes, I am!" The sheep-bear realized they must have seemed a bit manic, but plowed ahead, reflecting that sometimes the only way out was *through*. "So! I was wondering! Would you like to, um, get lunch again some time? Or — or dinner, maybe? I'd love to tell you all about what happened after Halloween! Or just hang out, even...?"

Grace's eyes dropped to the panel of the exercise machine, and she chuckled. "I've still got a half-hour of workout left, and then I have some things to do at the office, but how about NAME in the mess hall sector at seven? Best sushi I've had on-base, anywhere but VCS. Unless you'd like to go topside?"

Maddy inhaled sharply. "Nonono, no, NAME sounds good! I'll see you then! Enjoy your workout!" The sheep-bear waved goodbye and hustled away, leaving the mildly confused doe to resume pedaling with a shrug.

A few hours later, Grace Dunlop, Barrister & Solicitor, sat behind her desk, and peered down at the traffic twenty-odd floors below. As Chief Counsel of the Korps front company Helical BioSpectra, Inc., her office came with an enviable view of University Avenue. She gazed out towards the weather beacon tower of the Canada Life Building; the flashing white signal, with lights running down the structure, signaled that snow and colder temperatures were on the way for the afternoon. Of course, she mused, she could just put on her RCGs and ask ROSE for a forecast any time, and a likely more accurate one at that. It was nice to have the quietly respectable antique on hand as part of the scenery, regardless.

The deer sighed. She spun around in her chair when she heard a polite cough in a familiar, reedy voice from the door.

It was Rin Gorgoni: her friend, colleague, nominal superior in the K-LAW hierarchy, and official CEO of the front company besides. The slinky blue anole was wearing a kicky jumper dress under a flowing turquoise parka, leaning feyly against the doorframe; they removed their faux-fur ushanka as they spoke. "Morning, hon. Press conference at the Sheraton went well. How's that brief for the Bloomberg thing going?"

The doe shrugged. "Done; I already flipped it to you while you were out," she said distantly.

Rin sniffed, eyeing Grace with concern. "I know *that* look," they murmured, closing the door behind them as they sat down in the chief counsel's guest chair, throwing their coat and hat atop her small side table. "What's up?"

The doe sighed. "Maddy."

"Oh, how are they? Still settling in?"

"It seems so! But my immediate concern is that, uh… she asked me to dinner tonight," she grimaced.

Rin beamed. "Sounds lovely! A nice chance to catch up, then?"

"Okay, though, I wasn't sure at first, but I think it might be a date…?"

The anole peered quizzically at Grace, tenting their long fingers. "… And? *I* was the one who had to get over a personal issue with Maddy, but you seemed very keen on her all along."

The doe grew increasingly exasperated as she tried to explain. "Well, *sure*, they're well-meaning and clever and kind, and I'm so very, very glad to have helped them get away from the Hero game, but that doesn't mean I wanted to — it's not — I'm not like — *I hadn't planned on fucking them, Rin!*"

Rin cocked one ridged, pierced eyebrow at the deer. "You're not like *me?* Was that what you were going to say?"

Grace's hand flew to her muzzle. "Oh, no, I'm sorry, I didn't mean—"

The androgynous anole brushed her off with a sly smile. "Hon, I am a *slut.* I'm a *proud* slut. I've had… let's see… at least a dozen partners in the last week? I'm still famous in field ops for my ability to horn up any mission, I know; if there was a 'Lifetime Achievements in Sexpionage' award, I'd expect to at least be *nominated.* That's just *me,* I like it fine, and in my fifty-five years on this planet I've never felt the need to apologize for that," they shrugged. "I know you're not a prude, but is it possible you're a little self-conscious about feeling like you're somehow not *allowed* to be that sexual as you get older? Like you 'ought' to be some kind of respectable surrogate mother figure in the background, for someone Maddy's age?"

"…Maybe," the deer said, slightly embarrassed.

"And further," Rin said patiently, "you're *clearly* into her. She's bigger, stronger, and butcher than you, and I happen to know that's exactly what you like in a domme. Tell the truth: you've thought about it, haven't you?"

Grace winced and rubbed at her neck, but nodded, silently.

"Anyway, if memory serves, both Marcy and I are more than a *bit* older than you, and that's never stopped you from playing with either of us. Or from freezing up around her like a little lost fawn whenever the doctor gets... *persuasive,*" the anole smirked kindly.

"Um. Twenty-two and fourteen years older," the deer mumbled shyly, looking away.

"Just like that, yes, exactly," Rin said, as they petted Grace's arm to soothe the doe. "So, if *you* can enthusiastically consent to sex with the two of us, with a respective twenty-two and thirteen—"

"—Fourteen—"

"—*fourteen*-year age gap, why can't our young sheep-bear friend do the same with you? I haven't heard you object on *material* grounds, just procedural ones."

"They're — they're a brand-new recruit...? And Maddy's just... they've grown up a bit sheltered, being pressured into a PHL career since childhood, is what I mean. I had a bit more, uh, life experience?"

"Grace Elizabeth Dunlop. *Darling.* As your friend, *never mind* the chain of command, I'm calling bullshit on that particular rationalization. You've told me how little you actually *lived*, pre-transition. Maddy's situation is a bit different, but it's not that far from a green young articling law student of a doe who first walked into this office in 2009, back when it was mine."

The deer huffed deeply, gently scowling. "Fine. *Fine.* I just... Rin, I'm *nervous*, okay? I'm afraid of hurting her. Even if most of her life's been sheltered, she's been through a *lot*, breaking free from the PHL. I don't want her to feel obligated to me somehow, just because I helped her in a crisis." Grace then looked up, thoughtfully. "...I hope ROSE has been suggesting therapy to her," she muttered.

"Did you ever feel obligated to Marcy for recruiting you? And more importantly, do you think she was wrong to fuck you?"

"No?! She was just, I mean, you know, super fucking *hot*, and I wanted... I was hoping some of that confidence would rub off on me, I guess."

"*Rub off*, heh," Rin snickered, with a waggle of their eyebrows. Grace hucked a wadded-up piece of paper at her nominal superior's sleek blue head; the anole dodged it easily, and gave the deer a huge, shit-eating grin.

"*Anyway.* Marcy was *goals* for me from the moment I woke up in that medbay at SHS. She was just so... powerful, so put-together, so unapologetically, defiantly terrifying and commanding and beautiful. How could I not get turned on by all that, as a dumbass egg who was just finally figuring out that I was attracted to girls *as a girl?*"

Rin lounged back in the chair, draping their long, bare limbs across it in a languorously blue-scaled tangle. "Those sound like valid reasons to be into Marcy to me," they said with a good-natured shrug. "When I first met her... well, to be fair, neither of us quite had a handle on the whole gender thing yet, but that was still the energy she had *en femme*. And it was and is indeed, I will grant, *super* fucking hot."

"Okay...?"

The anole nodded their long neck towards the back wall of the office. "And if Marcy walked through that door *right this second* and told you to get on your knees for her, wouldn't you?"

Grace's eyes turned to the doorway and grew wide as if caught in headlights, and her breath hitched momentarily in her throat before she faintly squeaked out a tiny "Uh-huh...?" Refocusing on Rin, she composed herself enough to ask, "But she's, um, in Ottawa right now? Right...?"

Rin snorted, bemused, and waved off the question. "*Anyway,* the point is that I'm positive you're just as jaw-droppingly attractive an older woman to them as Marcy was — and *is* — to you. And back then you were an adult, sound of mind and all that, even if a little inexperienced in matters of the *moister* bodily functions. So, it sounds to me darling, like you're not trusting Maddy with the same autonomy and competence to make decisions that you allowed for yourself, when you were in your twenties." Limp-wristedly propping their pale, pierced dewlap up with the back of one lanky hand as they leaned forward, Rin arched one heavily pierced brow. "Is that fair, do you think?"

Grace winced, and half-heartedly gestured in exhaustion before returning to staring out the window to University Avenue. "Yes. I mean, *yes, okay,* that's what I'm doing, I guess. And no, it's not fair."

"So, you're going to..."

The doe grinned weakly as she covered her face with hoof-nailed hands, rubbing at her graceful cervine muzzle. "…I'm going to go on a date with Maddy Gillespie," she chuckled nervously.

Maddy looked around as they approached the entrance of the sushi restaurant from the wide KDS corridor, just *slightly* anxious. The sheep-bear huffed to themself, straightening their back and standing in what they hoped was a cool, nonchalant pose as they examined the slogan banner hanging from the wall sign: *"IT'S PRONOUNCED 'NA-MEH.'"*

She'd visited the quartermasters' again that afternoon after the gym, following a long, cool shower — one in which she'd still had to *take care* of the excess nervous energy engendered by thinking about going to dinner with the older woman, her pre-Korps lack of libido *long* past — and had decided to consult a professional. Monty, the tiny old wallaby craftsman who'd made Maddy's Halloween costume in a matter of minutes, was pleased as punch to work with her on a newly tailored ensemble for her date; the sheep-bear had picked it up from his shop just a few hours later.

As a result, the sheep-bear had arrived clad in pinstriped navy blue trousers and a handsomely futch fuchsia vest that accentuated *just* the right amount of curves. The roguishly rolled-up sleeves and open collar of their lavender shirt were carefully calculated to impress upon the doe that they were fully casual about this whole thing, and *certainly* hadn't been second-guessing themself in the mirror up until the very moment of leaving their quarters. Maddy was about to don the RCGs folded up in their belt loop, and ask ROSE if Grace was on her way… and then she saw the deer, and flushed.

Grace wore a dark dress with one of her customary square-shouldered pink jackets, and it looked very much like her matching, opalescent hoof polish had been touched up since the morning. She smiled warmly and gave a tiny wave as she walked up. "Hi, Maddy! Shall we?"

"Grace! Hello, yes, of course," the sheep-bear said with an eager nod, trying furiously to tamp down the panic in her heart, and the two approached the hostess, a thin otter femme. "I've, heh, been looking forward to this all day…? Thank you. I mean, just, um… thank you. It's great to see you again…!" *Stupid, stupid, stupid,* the sheep-bear thought to herself, as the otter showed them to a booth with a glossy black-lacquered table.

They'd thought they were ready, but once the deer was right there, right in *front* of them with that lovely, soft, squeezable-looking body and charmingly sardonic wit, and she was with Maddy, on a *date*, and it was *happening*… the sheep-bear shuddered, as the hostess quickly hustled back to bring the two some water and green tea. They sipped at the glass, hoping Grace wouldn't notice the faint rattling of the ice as their hand shook.

The booth was separated from the others by drawable paper screens, and a conveyor belt of various dishes slowly crawled past along the far wall of the banquette seats. The deer wasted no time in getting started, and plucked a bowl of steamed edamame and several plates of rolls from the line, gesturing for Maddy to do the same before digging in.

"So! I know the broad strokes of what went down after Halloween — and I *certainly* heard about what you did to that twerp who knocked over our garbage cans, well done! — but I'm all ears," the doe said with a playful twitch of the same. "How was your road trip?"

"Well," the sheep-bear said thoughtfully as she reached for a hefty slab of fatty salmon sashimi with her chopsticks, "I found out some things about my family." She dipped it in soy sauce before depositing the delicious umami bomb directly onto her heavy tongue and shivered in pleasure momentarily as she chewed; Grace had been right about the quality of the fish. Swallowing and reaching for a piece of dynamite roll, she continued. "Dad was always a bastard, and they all knew. Fuckin'… toxic nerd who suddenly got powers and decided that actually, being an asshole bully was fine, as long as *he* got to do it. Granddad probably did think the lie was for my sake, on some level, but what he really wanted was a do-over on raising his sociopathic dead superhero son. Especially since Dad beat *him* up, too. It was… it was *sad,* honestly."

Grace nodded sympathetically as she tapped an order of hot, fresh vegetable tempura into the ROSE-based menu tablet mounted on the counter. "I can imagine, and I'm so sorry."

"Learning that was — it was the shock I needed, to push me all the way into your corner. Well, *our* corner, now, I guess." The sheep-bear chuckled as they perused the rest of the sashimi platter. "Even, uh, went and blew up the Heartwood statue in Grand Prairie, on my way out of town, and that was more satisfying than I expected. Fuck that guy, fuck him so *much*, I can't believe I'm even related to that monster."

"Oh, I saw that! Or, well, the 'mysterious disappearance' the local media was running with. Well *done*, dear," the doe said warmly, before diving eagerly into the conveyor-belt plate of tempura that had just arrived.

Maddy eventually relaxed enough to be warm, and funny, and candid for the older woman; they swapped stories of terrible relatives, expressed mutual admiration for one another's appearance and personality, and cackled together over Slider's extremely well-deserved comeuppance. After some time and many delicious sushi rolls, the sheep-bear looked at the menu tablet's screen to realize: they'd been in the beautiful, captivating, endearingly soft woman's presence for over three hours, and not the moments it felt like. They couldn't hold this back any longer and took a deep breath before speaking.

"Grace. I wanted to thank you, so much, for all of your help. And — and for seeing that I *needed* it, even while I was trying to do the 'Champion' thing. But that's... that's not why I asked you to dinner, and I feel like you know that...?" The sheep-bear cleared her throat, gulping down the last of her delicate white porcelain cup of tea. "I'm... I'm into you, and I was wondering if you felt the same. Nothing, um, nothing serious, necessarily, I mean, but, you're very pretty and I felt like you were being a little flirty that one time, and... oh, fuck, this was a bad idea, wasn't it," Maddy groaned lightly. Averting her gaze from meeting the eyes of the older woman across the table of empty sushi plates, she folded her burly bare arms in front of her bosom defensively, and almost-imperceptibly hunched down into herself.

The deer giggled shyly and seemed genuinely touched. "Maddy, no, it's *okay*, I promise. Of *course* you're attractive, and I like you very much. But when you get to be my age — especially after transitioning a bit later in life, like I did, and with all the baggage that gave me about 'male socialization' and what have you — you get extremely cautious about potential power imbalances in sex or romance with younger people. I'd never want to make you uncomfortable around here."

The mention of age reminded the sheep-bear of why they'd gamed this out as a possibility in the first place, and suddenly, they felt like they were on solid ground again. "You know, I have been with older women before…? On the way back from out west, I met this cool trucker-slash-recon agent at SCS, an older butch, and—"

"Oh! How *is* Lou?" Grace wiggled her soft eyebrows salaciously, clearly recalling some happy memories. "Does she still do that thing, you know, with her *tail*, and—"

Maddy snorted, trying and failing to keep herself from giggling. "— And, on your nipples, and… yeah, heh."

Grace nodded along, evidently delighted. After a moment, she looked down to the table with a sad smile, and idly nudged around the puddled drops of soy sauce on her last plate with chopsticks. "Anyway… it was fine to ask, I promise! All good! But I'm not sure it's a good idea. I'm just… being cautious. To… to protect you."

Maddy took a deep breath, puffed up their chest, steeled their jaw, and reached across the table to place one beefy hand atop the smaller, softer digits of the doe. "*I can protect myself,*" the sheep-bear said with an intensity — and a low, desirous, domineering *growl* to their voice — they hadn't realized they could summon. They stared into Grace's glistening violet eyes, wide with amazement, and realized that the deer's mouth was also hanging open in apparent shock. They quickly withdrew their hand, chuckling awkwardly and looking away. "Fuck, I'm sorry, I don't know where that came from…"

The deer blinked repeatedly and briefly shook her head, until she seemed to have thrown off the surprise. She silently pulled open the paper screen, and shimmied out of the booth, standing up with a blank expression. Maddy cringed and braced herself for the worst.

"Maddy," Grace said calmly.

The sheep-bear winced and dragged one meaty hand across her ursine face, chagrined. "I'm — I'm sorry. You said no, you have your reasons, and I can respect that. I hope… I hope we still be friends, at least?"

This time, the deer reached out and took *their* hand and leaned over to bring her face closer to the sheep-bear's. They realized that Grace wasn't upset; rather, she was biting her lip, trying to suppress a grin, and very faintly panting. "*Maddy,*" she whispered. "Would you like to see my quarters…?"

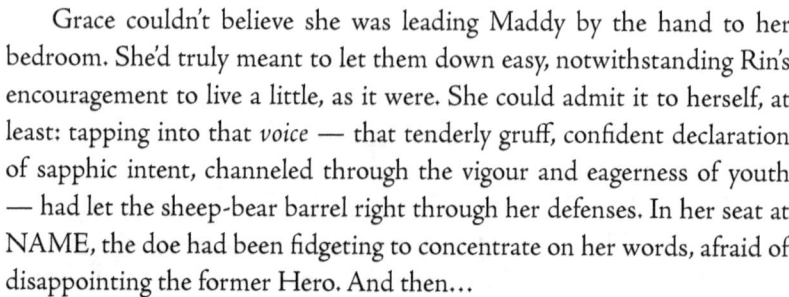

Grace couldn't believe she was leading Maddy by the hand to her bedroom. She'd truly meant to let them down easy, notwithstanding Rin's encouragement to live a little, as it were. She could admit it to herself, at least: tapping into that *voice* — that tenderly gruff, confident declaration of sapphic intent, channeled through the vigour and eagerness of youth — had let the sheep-bear barrel right through her defenses. In her seat at NAME, the doe had been fidgeting to concentrate on her words, afraid of disappointing the former Hero. And then…

In her mind, a ludicrous scene had flashed by in that instant — herself and Maddy, illustrated in muted oils as if for the cover of a vintage gothic romance, she as the delicately Rubenesque dowager countess overwhelmed by the bawdy swagger of the mysterious young sheep-bear rogue lately come o'er the moors — and it viscerally hit her, finally internalizing what she knew intellectually. She was allowed to be *desired*, just like she had desired Marcy, when she herself was new to this life. And desire, and clear-eyed honesty and good faith about what they might (or might not) be to one another, had left her weak. She could feel herself grow wet, even as she was fumbling to strip and throw her clothes to the floor.

The doe planted her wide bottom on the sheets and began to wiggle inwards towards the middle of the bed, eyes heavy and stammering. "Y-You can just — please, put your things anywhere—"

Maddy nodded as she stood at the foot of the bed, and made another low, pleased growl while carefully unbuttoning her vest and shirt. When each article was removed, the sheep-bear flourished a wrist; it floated telekinetically from her other hand to fold itself neatly in mid-air, before hovering to fall gently across the mauve pleather Barcelona chair in the corner of the deer's bedroom. After a moment she stood topless in her high-waisted trousers and angled one beefy arm to an equally beefy hip. She *loomed*, and Grace couldn't help but observe her broad, brown-furred musclegut, imagining nuzzling down the length of that slight shag of a treasure trail.

"You're beautiful," the sheep-bear rumbled, as they mounted the foot of the bed and slowly crawled forward with a cocky sneer, licking their dark lips. "Can I fuck you, Grace?"

The deer stared half-stunned up into steel-blue eyes and the saliva-shiny incisors of Maddy's open maw, nodding eagerly, and felt absurdly grateful for the younger woman's attention.

Maddy couldn't believe Grace had led her by the hand to her bedroom. The lawyer's quarters were only slightly larger than her own, but more clearly lived-in and personalized. As the two stumbled inwards past the foyer, dim pot lights illuminated automatically — *Thanks, ROSE*, the sheep-bear thought in passing — to reveal clean-lined modernist decor in gentle pinks and lavenders. Handsomely framed and inlaid vintage movie posters for "*La Fiancée de Frankenstein*'" and "*Il fantasma dell'Opera*'" lined one wall, the sunken, piercing equine eyes of the Monster and masked vulpine leer of the Phantom seeming to observe the entire scene. She suppressed a giggle as the deer, already nude and reclining sensually, meekly exhorted her to drop her clothes anywhere.

This was *happening*, and Grace seemed to have become instantly receptive once they took charge of the moment. Maddy wasn't *surprised*, exactly, that the soft doe was so responsive to being dominated by a big butch; she'd mentioned having similar fun with Lou Cartier in the past, as the sheep-bear had experienced themself not that long ago. Still, it excited them to have an opportunity to try out their skills with another transfem, hopefully free of any societally-induced self-consciousness about the dynamic. *You can do this,* they thought. It might have been easier with ROSE's voice in their head for moral support, but they *could* domme this deer and do it with flair besides.

Grace repositioned her body slightly on the bed, shifting her hips to reveal a peek of damp thighs and glistening labia. Maddy inhaled sharply, restraining herself from diving in muzzle-first before even stripping, and resolved: if she was going to do this, she was going to practice her *style*. The sheep-bear briefly pondered how to best assert dominance over the deer, before settling on the very personalized flex of carefully, intentionally using her telekinesis to neatly remove and fold each doffed piece of clothing. Once topless, she flexed a muscular arm in what she again hoped was a femme-baiting pose of suave swagger. It seemed to work, as the older woman gazed up at her wide-eyed and speechless, just as in their booth at dinner.

Summoning the doe-melting tone of voice once more, consciously speaking from their diaphragm, Maddy began advancing their bulky body onto the bed. "You're beautiful," the sheep-bear said confidently, despite the nervousness in their heart. "Can I fuck you, Grace?" The deer fervently nodded assent and spread her legs even wider, still evidently too overloaded to speak; Maddy rumbled appreciatively with each lumbering movement forward.

The sheep-bear pulled the deer's lower body closer and upwards, luxuriating in the plush softness of Grace's thighs and belly before bringing their muzzle lower, taking a deep, lusty whiff of the older woman's already-wet cunt. Maddy spread their broad jaws wide and let their long, meaty ursine tongue unfurl wetly along the deer's puffy labia, slowly lapping up and down. The doe huffed with tiny *meep*-like squeals at each deep, luscious lick inside her, and covered her muzzle with one hand; the other rested lightly at the crest of her belly.

Sensing an opportunity, the sheep-bear raised her mouth slightly, drooling a trail of the deer's prolific juices up her pudenda to gently (but firmly) nibble on those hoof-nailed fingers; feeling Grace push the hand further past her teeth, Maddy made a low chuckle and *tasted* the doe's fine hide and slightly sagging flesh. She was rewarded with a nervously joyous babble of submissive gibberish and squeezed appreciatively at the older woman's pillowy sides with her questing hands.

The sheep-bear reached down to unbutton their slacks before telekinetically shuffling them off of their hips to slump to the carpeted floor at the foot of the bed. (Grace was a little too preoccupied to notice another slick flourish of their powers, and their concentration for finesse with fine telekinesis work, like buttons, might be... *compromised*, admittedly.) Now clad only in practical, hip-hugging boxers, they removed the doe's hand from their mouth to take it in their own meaty paw, and kiss it gently and suavely, locking eyes with its owner.

"Ma-a-addddy," the deer panted through a giggly grin, "is there, ahh, anything you'd like me to do...?" She shrank into herself submissively, flushing, delicate pale tan ears turning bright red.

The sheep-bear growled, just a little louder than she'd dared before; the rough edge was clearly working for her partner, to her slightly anxious glee. She crawled up further atop Grace's soft body before bringing her muzzle close to the deer's, and throatily *rasping* into her face: "*Get on your knees, Ms. Dunlop.*"

The words rang in the doe's ears, and her limbs complied before she was consciously aware of their meaning. She wiggled her soft body off the bed and down to the floor (dimly grateful for having selected the soft high pile from the carpeting section of the Facilities catalogue) and knelt, facing her bed. Maddy was still sprawled out on the high mattress, apparently surprised at how energetically she'd obeyed, but looked all the smugger for it.

"Very good," the sheep-bear rumbled, and scooched up to plant her wide ass on the edge. Her boxer shorts were tented in her lap, and she smoothly undid a button to withdraw her cock; once freed, it sprung out as if it were a firing piston.

Grace gazed at it hungrily, licking her lips. She looked up; Maddy needed only to bare those fierce teeth in a lustful grin, and growl possessively, to make the deer dive forward. Her hands quested inside Maddy's trunks, caressing the sheep-bear's sack and angling the tip of their cock towards her waiting mouth. She nuzzled in and around the engorged flesh, gliding her lips across it, huffing its feminine ursine musk. Licking and lapping in helpless abandon, the desperately turned-on doe felt foolish that she had wanted to turn down this experience.

Allowing herself to drop into an almost mesmerized state, Grace drew her tongue carefully up and down each side, finally squeezing a few thin drops of precum into her mouth with an appreciative murmur. Maddy grasped her head by the antlers as if they were handlebars, gently (but firmly) steering the doe back towards taking the entire length. After a moment of enthused deep-throating, she tilted the deer's head off her sex, and asked, kindly and almost hesitantly: "Is this good? Am I doing okay?"

The deer nodded. "All good, dear. *Green.* V-very green," she mumbled happily as she continued to massage and knead at Maddy's cock. "And if, um, you're comfortable with penetration, you're welcome to, uh…"

"*Ah,*" Maddy said in a smug tone, taking a deep breath and releasing it into Grace's ears as an ominous rumble. She grasped the doe's wrists in her strong hands and led the older woman to stand up before sitting her back down on the bed and gently but firmly laying Grace down. Maddy carefully arranged the doe's limbs such that she was splayed out, her moist vulva spread wide and welcoming; apparently satisfied, she removed her trunks and climbed atop the bed.

Grace had no desire to object and tittered lightly as she allowed herself to be repositioned.

$$\equiv$$

Holy fuck, holy fuck, she really wants me to top…? The sheep-bear tried to centre themself by inhaling deeply, before positioning a willing (*very* willing!) Grace on the covers. Their heart pounded. Maddy had never really experienced bottom dysphoria *per se*; they liked their modest-but-chunky, mostly-ursine parts just fine. However, they'd also never had the opportunity to do… *this,* and flushed.

More of Maddy's sexual history flashed through her head; she realized that on some level she was surprised to have gotten this far with the deer, and suddenly felt unprepared, sure that the anxiety and false bravado beneath her domme act must now have been glaringly obvious. She'd only ever done hand stuff with her brief high school girlfriend, and in her few hookups since, the sheep-bear had either bottomed for a girl with a dick (strapless or not) or engaged in mutual oral. Once she was in fact presented with an opportunity for precisely the scenario she'd dreamed of for years — herself, a suave butch domme, just *plowing* a big soft subby femme in the pussy — she felt vaguely… *inhibited,* somehow. She gulped, silently grimacing as she tried to clear her mind and focus on the moment.

Some degree of respite came in the realization that the plump, shapely doe was again making the most *adorable* noises, pleasurable moans interspersed with tiny, needy whines. She scooched her pelvis forward towards Maddy, clearly eager to be mounted. They took a deep breath, screwing up the resolve to proceed; their nethers throbbed in anticipation as they shuffled their knees between the doe's legs, and then *heaved* up those big soft thighs with both hands. "Just relax," the sheep-bear said in a warmly imperious growl, with confidence that belied their internal agitation.

She lined herself up, dripping tip kissing at the deer's similarly-slick lower lips, and then *lunged* into Grace. The doe yelped and huffed to be so filled; Maddy, for her part, slowly withdrew and then thrust again, and again, and again, building up steam. *This is… this is pretty fucking great*, she considered. Her powerful hips pumped in time with Grace's squeaks and moans.

"I'm, 'm, uh, nearly, uhhhhh," Grace wheezed, as Maddy picked up her hands and removed them from where they'd crept to rub at her clit.

The sheep-bear *roared* to the ceiling before slowing down abruptly and chiding the deer. "You're going to cum when I *say so*," they intoned smugly. "And no touching. *I* get to make it happen. Do I make myself clear?"

The doe bit her lip and nodded eagerly. "Uh-huh…?"

"*Good girl.*" Maddy resumed the pace of her thrusts, huffing and growling with each motion, and tightly squeezed the deer's thighs; Grace was also thrusting *back* now, humping needily into Maddy's member. Grace was into it (holy *fuck* did she ever seem to be into it) and the sheep-bear was *topping* and *domming*, despite a nagging feeling of insecurity. *This is pretty fucking great, still*, she told herself. This was… this was exactly what she'd wanted, and it was *perfect*, and…

It was… it was…

It was *too much*, Maddy realized with a suddenly gut-wrenching rush of anxiety. Their muscles went slack, and they stopped fucking the older woman. Heaving with a sharp intake of breath, they quickly pulled out and clambered over her elegant cervine haunches, collapsing on their back.

"I'm — I'm sorry, I can't," the sheep-bear choked, stumbling on their words. "I want to domme, I *want* to top, but I just got all — all *up in my head* and started feeling weird about it, and then I was afraid to disappoint you because you liked the cool suave butch swagger thing so much…"

Grace's dark lips pursed into a concerned moue; she drew an arm around the bulk of Maddy's thickly brown-furred body and embraced them against her own. "Shh, shh, honey, it's okay, I promise."

The sheep-bear turned her head to the side, and looked again into those big violet eyes, now apparently holding back tears; she cringed. "Oh, no, oh no, no, *no*, I'm sorry, please don't cry, I'll — I'll go, *I'm sorry*—" She moved to debark the large bed, but the deer grabbed her arm with both hands.

"Maddy," Grace said calmly, and with an abrupt, surprising tone of authority. "It's *okay.*"

They sniffed. "Are you sure? You're crying! I just… it seemed like you wanted… like you were only into this if I kept domming you. And I do *want* to, but this was, um, actually my first time doing…" At this, they gestured weakly but meaningfully towards first their own genitals, and then the deer's.

The doe smiled warmly and affectionately and drew her muzzle closer to kiss Maddy on the nose. "Dear, please don't feel like you need to *perform* for me. I'm enjoying your company, believe me. If I'm tearing up, it's because I care about you, and don't want you to feel like you've failed me somehow with… 'insufficient swagger'?"

"But back at dinner, it sounded like you were trying to let me down easy! What changed your mind, then, if it wasn't me, uh, workshopping my domme persona?"

"Well… the voice, admittedly, hah," the deer giggled to herself lightly. "I'll cop to that. But it wasn't *just* that? It's a bit of a long story. Anyway, you don't have to try quite so hard to play out what you think I want in a domme, especially if it's making things more difficult for you. I'm into cuddly, affectionate fucking too, you know," Grace beamed.

Maddy smiled at hearing that, feeling remarkably comforted. "I wouldn't mind giving it a try…?"

Repositioning herself, she pumped her semi-deflated length until she was again hard enough to penetrate the deer, but this time, she entered *slowly.* Affected bravado gone, she luxuriated in the sensation of embracing

Grace's soft body while gently, pleasurably grinding into her pussy. The deer resumed her own pelvic thrusts back, at a similarly leisurely tempo.

*This is… this is **also** pretty fucking great*, the sheep-bear concluded, and she and Grace grinned at one another, delightedly flushed. Feeling bold, she craned down her neck to kiss the deer. She was rewarded by a cervine tongue affectionately probing into her mouth, feeling her sharp canines, and made a low chuckle when each of them withdrew from the kiss.

The pressure in their nethers was building, and their movements became erratic, needy, even desperate. Maddy came inside the deer with one last herky-jerky thrust and rumbled in ecstasy from deep inside their chest; Grace, meanwhile, still stuffed by the sheep-bear, reached down and pawed frenetically at herself until a moment later she also bleated with pleasure and spasmed rhythmically, slack-jawed.

Collapsing her legs down to the sheets as Maddy pulled out once again — this time, both of them sticky with her copious seed — Grace tilted her head towards the sheep-bear and kissed her again, slowly and happily. "That was *lovely*, dear," the doe panted happily. They laid entwined for some time.

After a while relaxing in the afterglow, the deer pointed vaguely towards a dresser on the other side of the bed, made of tubular steel and warmly-toned cherrywood laminate. "Maddy, would you mind grabbing me a towel from the top drawer? I don't want to be, ah, *dripping*, to stand up and get a glass of water," she chuckled.

They smirked again and rested a broad hand gently (but firmly) atop Grace's arm. "Wait, hold on…" Craning their neck to look more clearly towards the other room, Maddy spied a mug on the kitchenette counter emblazoned with the K-LAW division insignia. (*Naturally*, they observed, suppressing a snort.) With a moment of concentration and a few flexes of their hand, it was rinsed out and filled with cool, clear Lake Ontario water from the faucet, then telekinetically floated smoothly into the bedroom.

Grace gave her a brief, gentle round of applause, and giggled with bemusement anticipating the mug (as well as her requested towel from the dresser, traveling a much shorter distance) being delivered to her waiting hands. "And you don't think you have natural swagger, eh?"

Maddy flushed, biting their lip until their composure broke, and they joined in the older woman's laughter.

After the deer had set the emptied mug on her glass bedside table and wiped away some of the fluids on top, inside and underneath her, she resumed snuggling up to the sheep-bear. "So, I guess I *kind of* promised you a long story, didn't I."

"I'm all ears…?"

"Okay, well… let me tell you about someone I know. So, it was 2009, I was nearly finished with law school, and after this one evening class, I'm just a *complete* dumbass and accidentally get myself locked in the lecture hall…"

REACH OUT

Chapter 1

March 18, 2023

The Interstate flew by endlessly for the second day in a row as dusk fell over West Texas. Maddy Gillespie was tagging along once again in the passenger compartment of a familiar truck cab; in the driver's seat was Lou Cartier, the Korps transport operator and recon agent who the erstwhile Hero had first met in Saskatoon, back in the fall. In her peregrinations across North America, the broad pine marten was thrilled to have a travel buddy — especially one who, after a long day of driving, *also* enjoyed sharing the bed in the back of the sleeper cab. The young sheep-bear smirked to themself, thinking about how much they'd learned at the feet (so to speak) of the elder butch each evening they'd spent with her.

Indeed, Maddy's confidence carrying herself as a butch and a domme had skyrocketed these past several months. To her gleeful amazement, it had turned out that so many of the pretty femmes and enbies of KDS were just as thirsty for someone like the sheep-bear as she was for them, and had enthusiastically given her a surprising (but satisfyingly validating!) number of opportunities to practice her sexual technique — especially Grace. She'd accompanied a handful of other soft, subby new friends to their quarters since then for casual fun, but the deer had become a fairly regular friend-with-benefits, always happy to let Maddy experiment without judgment.

On the flip side, Maddy had also enjoyed broadening their horizons by playing with a few butch dommes, like Lou; or the theatrically haughty Jessica, a burly duck from Facilities; or the warm-but-exacting Ilse, a rangy Doberman and medical researcher who'd opened their eyes to pet play. The sheep-bear wasn't a natural submissive, exactly, but had figured out they were switch enough to appreciate a good *educational experience* on that count. One particular highlight was the slyly fiery Mabel, an arcane cat burglar of a supervillain who they'd met at the Dominion Club on New

Year's Eve; the catamount had given Maddy a newfound appreciation for the aesthetics of cigars... and, of course, the sapphics who enjoyed them.

Lou's destination was RIV, and her trailer held a load of machinery that was apparently too pressure-sensitive for transport via aircraft or teleportation. Between two massive, strapped-down cargo pods, Maddy had also been able to stash her beloved Yamaha V-Max; she was thankful she hadn't had to leave it behind in Denver, where she'd spent a day exploring the NORAD-adjacent Korps site AVA before meeting up with Lou. Of course, RIV was also where Mabel typically resided... and, truthfully, Maddy hoped that she might get to spend some more time with the mountain lion, alongside taking a tour of the facilities.

Lou yawned, twitching her whiskers about as she smacked her lips, and then glanced at the route directions in her ROSE-based dashboard display. She'd been telling her passenger old war stories, alternating with tales of her wild youth in Northern Ontario, but had been trailing off for a little while. "Whoooof, girl, I am *bushed*. Glad we're not too much further from Austin."

Maddy turned to her with a look of mild concern. "Are you okay to drive? I don't mind another pit stop if you're tired..."

"Yeah, nah, I'm good. Least until I need to piss again from all this coffee," Lou smirked, reaching out to shake the stainless-steel thermos in her cup holder, rattling the ice inside. "Feel like I've been running my mouth this whole time, though; you've hardly gotten a word in edgewise. Tell me, what's been up withya since Downsview? Out punching any PHL pricks yet?" The older woman raised an eyebrow, snickering at the sheep-bear with a playful leer.

"Heh, well..." Maddy took a deep breath, looking down at their hoof-nailed paws. They flexed them experimentally, telekinetically feeling the texture of the airflow through the cab, before peering out the window to gaze at the damply scrubby fields. "They *are* pricks, and I won't lie and say I didn't, uh, *really enjoy* beating the shit out of Slider when I got back to Toronto. I wouldn't mind dropping a bridge on Hagen, either, if I ever got the chance. But it's just... I don't know. I know what field agents *do*, and I feel like that's a line I'm afraid to cross, you know? I'm so grateful the Korps helped me out of the self-loathing little box I'd let myself be put in, but..."

"But there's a difference between *realizing* how fucked things have all got, and storming the Bastille yourself, eh?"

The sheep-bear snorted bemusedly. "Yeah. Yeah, exactly. But I still want to help out! I want to contribute somehow! I just have this mental block about, like, going topside to Be Gay and Do Crimes on the same streets where I was *technically* a peace officer, six months ago."

The elder butch nodded, as she carefully signaled and checked her mirrors to pass a slow-moving reefer truck. "There's plenty you can do for the cause without fighting, though! I've got this cousin, say; they're a farmer, their co-op supplies SHS—"

"Oh, I know! And I've been trying out some things, actually. That's why I've been doing this touring around, checking out other bases, too; figuring out where in the Korps I *fit*. Like, I spent a couple days with the Facilities team at VCS and CAS, helping out with excavating a new tunnel for the train connection. They had me shadowing a geomancer, this badger named Sierra — they go by 'Stalwart Sapper' when they're out in the field — and between their magic and my telekinesis we'd clear out the gravel from blasting."

Lou glanced over, nodding. "Oh, yeah? How'd you find that?"

"*Boring*," Maddy admitted with a good-natured smirk. "Mx. Collins was nice to work with for a couple days, but they're happy being underground in the dark; I'm... well, I just kept moving on." They sucked in air through their teeth. "Had a good time afterwards with this real handsome butch duck I met there, though..."

"Ah, gotcha. Good on ya, girl!"

"And then before that, I took a few days at KATS and helped with prepping air cargo. That didn't move me much either, hah. Although I did meet an interesting synth there; I thought she was a pilot, but actually, she's a plane? Or like, before *that*, Grace — Grace Dunlop, I mentioned her last time I was riding along? And from what she told me, it sounded like she knows *you* pretty well too? — offered that I could try out being a clerk for K-LAW."

"Ah, how *is* that fine doe?" Lou perked one heavy eyebrow salaciously, clearly recalling some happy memories. "So just how well have you gotten to know her now that you're on our side, eh? Does she still do that thing, it's cute, where when she's *real* hot and bothered she freezes like she's caught in headlights, and—"

Maddy sighed, trying and failing to keep herself from remembering that expression with too much yearning. "Yeah. Yeah, she does…"

The elder dyke's expression was so smug as to be positively *villainous*, even between nominal villains. "Knew it! I knew you were sweet on her, from the way you were talking last time. Well *done*, hah."

Maddy flushed and waved off Lou's snickering. "But *anyway*, yes, I was helping out with office work. Filing, making copies, binding their… what were those big coil-bound books called? 'Factums,' I think? And… it turns out that when K-LAW is, like, suing people and going to court, it's actually more or less the same as when normal lawyers do it. So that was, uh, not very exciting."

"For certain," the marten agreed. "I'm not one for fighting, leastways not as a *career*, but I'm also not one for *paperwork*. I need the open road to feel my oats; don't think I could stand to just sit at a desk like that, even for the Korps."

The sheep-bear rubbed the back of their neck. "I'm not opposed in theory, I guess? Like, I decided it wasn't really for me — I'm not creative enough — but I had a pretty good time when I was hanging out with the Propaganda Division at KDS."

"Huh!" Lou said, intrigued. "Okay, right, *now* I'm curious. How'd that happen, eh?"

"Well, I was at lunch with Grace one day, and we were talking more about that video of Dad that she showed me back before I left Toronto. I asked who made the decisions about keeping and using the embarrassing shit like that, the things Heroes want buried, and she introduced me to someone at Propaganda…"

January 3, 2023

"Hey, 'sup," the heavily pierced Canada goose on the high work stool said mildly, as he set down his tablet and extended a hand to shake

Maddy's. "I'm Kai. Maddy, right? New recruit, interested in seeing what we do around here?"

His RCGs were set in thick, hipster horn-rimmed frames, and he wore only board shorts and mesh arm-warmers, with heavy cork sandals on his webbed black feet. Through greyish-brown chest feathers Maddy could see faint, ragged lateral scars, and instantly understood why Kai "Propagander" Warren might habitually go shirtless at work.

"Well, we've got several different modalities of messaging," the goose sniffed. "Sometimes — and this is both good policy and good politics, gives us credibility and sympathy from the sectors of the public whose support we want — we're flat-out combating official disinformation with the truth. Maybe that's leaking documents obtained through fieldwork or electronic incursions, to contradict a CEO or politician; maybe that's signal-jamming to show our cameras' full-context angle on news footage; maybe that's subtly editing publications on their way to be printed. We're crowding out bad info with good, but it's not about us; the Korps doesn't even always claim responsibility."

Maddy nodded eagerly. "Got it. Drown out the lies with truth, let people think the leaks were Anonymous, or Russian spies, or something?"

"Exactly. The second main type is more what you'd think of as classical propaganda; direct or indirect messaging. Advocating for things the Korps thinks are good, denouncing things the Korps thinks are bad. That has aspects of the standard PR and communications department of any corporation, or organization, or government agency," Kai intoned rhythmically, and was perked up; he clearly enjoyed getting to give this little speech to a curious newbie. He motioned for Maddy to follow him down a corridor lined with some kind of framed artwork, tastefully lit in shallow alcoves. "Like your old friends at Ontario's Heroes, for instance. With us, though, the difference is that we might put word out to the targeted population directly and plastered with helices, or covertly through allies and cut-outs. You've seen some of our poster design work, I'm sure? The ones just straight-up riffing on mid-twentieth century war propaganda, corny as fuck, zero subtlety; *gods*, I love that shit. That's under this category too — mostly internal comms, more under the heading of sustaining morale and *esprit de Korps* than changing any minds."

The sheep-bear nodded as she scanned down the line of mounted posters. "I know they bothered the OH brass, anyway? Once I was with Caleb Hagen for a press conference at City Hall; on the way out, he saw one of those plastered over the side of a bus shelter, and his staff had to restrain him from punching the glass in…"

Kai laughed, a rough, honking cackle. "Fuck yeah. What a focus group…" The two shortly arrived at a huge flatscreen-lined lounge area, every display showing a stylized Rose emblem against a black and magenta background. "And then we've got my favourite part of the job: straight-up chaos. *Culture jamming.* ROSE, hit it."

The screens blinked away from their idle state; each started playing a different television commercial. Maddy recognized several from major corporate interests — banks, telecom companies, cable networks, fast food chains — but they were *wrong*, with varying degrees of subtlety. A goat in the background of a restaurant ad took a huge bite of his cheeseburger, then made an expression of disgust and spat it out on the floor, coughing. A movie trailer's dialogue had been smoothly recut, such that the leering, rubber-faced comic lead casually spoiled the big (and wildly transphobic) third-act twist. Children in a toy car commercial lamented that their brand-new, elaborate playset lacked walkable spaces and a public transit system. A prescription medication ad illustrated its legal caveats with vividly explosive depictions of possible side effects, rather than merely narrating a rushed warning over stock footage of active seniors playing golf.

The sheep-bear was dumbfounded and peered from screen to screen. "I'm… I'm not sure now if I've seen the original versions of all of these — I know how they're *supposed* to go, at least, from advertising tropes — or the Korps-tweaked ones." With that, she had a sudden epiphany. "…Oh! That's the point, isn't it? To undermine public confidence. Consumers and shareholders and whatever, they don't know what's going on."

The goose smirked. "Circle gets the square."

"…What?"

"Sorry, just a bit of cultural ephemera from before your time. Or mine, for that matter. *Yeah*, exactly, that's how it works; reputation's a fragile thing — people get nervous to buy shit and capital gets spooked, big corps lose billions in market cap. Remember back when Twitter started collapsing, the thing with faking statements from Big Pharma about, like, the price of insulin? That wasn't us, but *like* that: flooding the zone with bad info to crowd out the 'good,' really. These are just examples in the consumer marketing context, but we do the same things with enemies like Heroes, or the kinds of organized crime and supervillains who hurt the wrong people."

"Ah! Cool," Maddy murmured as they continued gazing at the displays. They were fairly confident that the premier hadn't been *winking* when making campaign promises in his ads for the previous year's election but couldn't be certain. They scratched the back of their broad neck as they turned to Propagander. "What I'm really curious about, though, is like… well, back when I first met her, Grace showed me this archive footage of my dad. Heartwood, I mean. Roger Oakes. He was a Hero with the Prairie League twenty years ago, and…"

"Oh. *Oh*," the goose said as his eyes rapidly scanned something in the view of his RCGs, and then looked up and down over Maddy's mostly-ursine form with chagrin. "Sorry, I hadn't made the connection…"

The sheep-bear gently grimaced. "Don't worry about it; he was a real fuckin' asshole, and I'm trying *not* to be associated with him. *It's kind of my whole deal now.* Anyway, I was just wondering who makes the decisions about saving and using content like that, when the media tries to bury it?"

"Well, we just do the creative piece here; it's KARD, the Archives and Records Division, that gathers the information, like raw satellite feeds right from mobile news crews. They collect so much more than we could ever use, though; they're *archivists*, and incredibly serious about saving information from being memory-holed. And look, I mean *serious*, serious — I've seen Mx. Director use a dagger as a bookmark before."

"So, it's like… the biggest library you've ever seen, with a whole section about ending people's careers?"

Kai snickered at the sheep-bear's comment. "…And the Director is always happy to let us rifle through, yeah. So, then it's *our* analysts and artists and shit-posters, here, who trawl the metadata, and decide what to action for agitprop. We've got our own presses and a manufacturing wing for publishing physical media, and a hacking team for digital distribution."

Maddy nodded. "But what gets used for the, like, pushing truth over disinformation thing…"

"It's pretty much at our strategic discretion, unless we get orders from the Boss, or requests to help with other divisions' plans. Although…" Kai squinted and arched his fingers with a smirk. "Maddy, how'd you like to try out for us with a little project?"

March 18, 2023

The sheep-bear was now talking very rapidly to Lou and gesturing excitedly as they did so. "…So he teamed me up with one of their editors, Delia, and we came up with 'Heartwood's Greatest Hits' from the archive video; just the *worst* fucking shit Dad ever said on a hot mic. And there's a *lot* of it. According to her, apparently the Prairie League actually started making the media give an extra-long tape delay on covering press conferences live, just because of him?"

Lou chuckled. "I saw that! A couple months ago now? Took me a minute to remember where I'd heard the name, at first."

The sheep-bear strained to keep herself from giggling. *"January 26th.* I got Propaganda to put it out on his *birthday!* They swapped out the files on the Grande Prairie newspaper's server, so it'd get put up for the annual memorial social media posts." Maddy huffed, rolling her eyes. "Didn't get much uptake outside Alberta, though, with the premier plugging some new conspiracy theory every day. Still, it kneecapped Heartwood's reputation in the only place that still gave a shit about him. Big editorial in the paper about needing Heroes that represent Alberta's *diverse future,* hah. The city council voted to study 'alternative proposals' for redeveloping the park, instead of replacing the statue I blew up. And the private crowdfunding for it stalled out at about a thousand dollars, last time I looked."

"Right on, girl! Sounds like you had fun," Lou smirked before taking a big swig of her coffee, eyes still on the road.

"It was! But it didn't really help with my whole… needing to feel *useful,* really. I'm not an artist, and outside of fucking over my awful family about the 'Heartwood Legacy,' I didn't really have any ideas to pitch Propaganda. Anyway, I feel like I need something a bit more active, more physical, you know?"

"Hmm, getting that anxious energy out? And you don't want to be out punching Heroes, eh? What about being a trainer? They can always use folks for sparring, and whatnot."

"You know, I was talking about that with my own personal trainer, actually? It's a possibility; Tommy made it sound like a fulfilling thing—"

"Tommy Legris?"

Maddy groaned sardonically. "…Does *everybody* know everybody else in the Korps? Ten thousand people at KDS, and I keep running into the ones who've fucked before…"

Lou laughed, a short, pitched yap, before descending into giggles. "Hardly, girl; let me *tell* you about how I met that lad…"

July 20, 1989

The scruffy, bedraggled blue jay was hanging around the truck stop with *intent*, Lou realized. She couldn't have been older than sixteen and was dressed in shabby hand-me-downs — a torn plaid blouse, and if not her older brother's dungarees, then *someone's* older brother's dungarees, donated to some charity or friendship centre; they were just flared enough to suggest the last days of disco. The girl tried to look nonchalant, one feathered arm resting calm on the strap of her worn canvas duffel bag. In the tiny in-between moments when she forgot the grown-up act, she fidgeted as if she was scared. A runaway, the marten concluded as she sipped her coffee and sighed. She'd have to try to help.

It had been a stiflingly hot day on the road (thirty-five degrees at least, Lou figured, never mind the sweltering *humidity*) and the tiny hamlet of Whitewood, Saskatchewan still faintly sizzled into the night. The lazy rotation of the ceiling fan in the dimly-lit diner helped, but not much. She squeezed the crown of her Thorn RC-60 wristwatch, illuminating the pale magenta backlight of the LCD cell; it was just past 11:30.

The leanly muscled mustelid locked eyes with the waitress behind the diner's counter, a tired-looking palomino mare in a sweaty gingham dress and held up her ceramic mug. "Miss? Just heading outside for some air, I'll be back." The horse nodded and continued to marry the ketchup bottles with faint irritation. Satisfied nobody was about to accuse her of skipping out on the check, Lou rose from the booth. Ambling out the glass front door, she proceeded to lean against the brick wall of the entrance to sip her coffee, periodically gazing up at the bug zapper hanging from the eaves; it made minuscule *fzzt* noises with each fried midge and mosquito.

The blue jay girl carefully craned her neck just enough to peer suspiciously at Lou from the corner of one eye. Snapping it back to stare straight ahead, she gripped the strap of her bag tighter.

Lou took a deep breath, releasing it out through her teeth with a gentle huff. "Awful late for someone your age to be hanging around a truck stop all alone, ain't it?"

The rail-thin young corvid said nothing, but huddled into herself, feathers involuntarily fluffing out, and clearly nervous.

The pine marten gazed out at the Trans-Canada Highway. A single truck passed through, into the night, and then the road was once again lit only in the faint, sickly yellow of sodium arc lamps. She sipped her coffee again and turned her head slightly to the girl.

"It's not real safe, s'what I mean. Never know what kind of fellas might come through in the night. Can't say that I'd want to just be out here alone, myself, and I got me a reputation as the toughest gal in Kapuskasing, Ontario," Lou said, flamboyantly enunciating every one of the eight syllables. The blue jay cocked an eyebrow, at that. "So. I'm begging your pardon, I'm sure, but I just feel like I ought to ask — y'know, woman to woman — if you've got someone coming for to pick you up."

The girl shuddered at Lou's words and fidgeted a moment longer before opening her beak to speak in a soft croak. "I'm — I've — I mean, yeah. *Yeah.* My — my aunt. My aunt's coming. Aunt Sandy. I called her. She'll be here soon."

Lou nodded amiably. "Oh? Good, good. Good to hear. I'm glad. Why wait outside, though?"

There was no response from the blue jay for a long moment. She stared down at her black talons, clad only in battered plastic flip-flops.

"They kicked you out 'cause you've got no money, eh?"

An ashamed nod, and a wince.

"See, the reason why I ask, is that this place is a highway truck stop, and not a big one. And I've seen me one or two places like this before. But someone who hasn't might well think, looking at the '24-Hour' sign, and all the lights, that it'd be safe to wait outside 'til morning; there's some folks *around* here, eh?" At this, Lou pointed a thumb over her flannel-clad shoulder, towards the diner portion of the ramshackle building. "But Miss Waitress in there? She's probably off her shift at midnight. So, then it's just the cook in the back, changing the fryer oil and doing overnight prep and whatnot for when the morning crowd starts coming in at sunup. He's not looking out front. And the clerk in the store? He's watching for gas-and-gos, and he's responsible for the contents of the safe, but he's not responsible for watching out for *you*."

She hated to do it, hated to have to scare the girl, but the corvid's widening, worried eyes told Lou that it had been necessary. Runaways this young had to learn quick, or they often didn't get much older. This stretch of the Trans-Canada was hardly as frightening for young women like her to hitchhike as certain parts of BC, for certain, but it was still no place for the blue jay.

"There's no Aunt Sandy coming, is there," the marten said gently. "How long have you been on the road, kid?"

"A… a couple days," the girl said, turning to fully face Lou and running fingers through her pale azure crest with agitation. Tears were starting to form in the corners of her eyes.

"And I'm guessing there's something *real* bad back home, right, or you wouldn't even *be* on the road. And how old are you? Fifteen? Sixteen?"

The blue jay's breath hitched in her throat, and it was clear that she was trying to hold back sobs. "Fourteen," she said, in a very small voice. "Please don't make me go back…"

Lou knelt down and placed a hand gently on the girl's slender shoulder, looking her in her dark eyes. "I won't. I promise. Whatever it is, I believe you, and I'll get you somewhere safe that ain't *there*. Deal?"

The girl looked at her, a glimmer of hope in her wet eyes, and nodded rapidly.

The marten stood up, smiling. "Deal, then. I'm Louisa Cartier, but only my ma says 'Louisa,'" she snorted, giving the name an aggressive Franco-

Ontarian accent. "You can call me Lou; pleasure to meetya," the trucker said, extending a dark brown-furred hand.

"I'm Mari — um, M.T. Call me M.T.," the blue jay whispered, as she cautiously raised her own feathered limb to shake.

After that pleasantry was complete, Lou downed the last of her coffee and gazed across the parking lot at her rig. "M.T., if you've been on your own for a day or two and you're out of money, I'm guessing you're hungry. Why don't we go inside, and get you fed? It's on me. And then, we can talk about some friends I've got along my route in Thunder Bay, folks who might be able to help you out…"

March 18, 2023

"Oh. Oh *wow,*" murmured an amazed Maddy. "He's, uh… he's done *really well* for himself?"

"That he has, and I'm proud of him," the trucker said with satisfaction, before waggling an eyebrow. "I'm a *cool aunt,* he always tells me."

With that, both women broke out laughing for several moments.

Eventually, the conversation drifted towards their respective taste in music. The two asked ROSE to stream the relevant audio in a back-and-forth of sharing their favourite artists, with Lou trying to pitch Maddy on the merits of Shania Twain and k.d. lang, and Maddy likewise attempting to sell Lou on the power metal of Hammerfall and Sabaton.

Just past midnight, the pair were less than an hour from RIV. Suddenly, a driving chorus on the audio system was interrupted by a low alert tone, sounding from what seemed like *everywhere* inside the truck's cab, accompanied by magenta lights pulsating in a quick staccato from under the sleek display panel. ROSE chimed in through the speakers immediately afterwards, the AI's usually-calming tone replaced by a blank, steely urgency.

[RED ALERT // RED ALERT // IMMINENT THREAT // ALL FIELD OPERATIVES AND COMBAT-RATED RESERVE PERSONNEL WITHIN 100 KM OF AUSTIN METRO AREA,

REPORT TO ASSIGNED TACTICAL POSITIONS OR NEAREST COMMAND STAFF // ALL NONCOMBATANTS PROCEED TO ASSIGNED EVACUATION AREAS]

"…Shiiiiiit," Lou grimaced, checking her mirrors and scanning the horizon for danger. As she punched the switch that flipped her imaging and aerial drone control panel into view on the dashboard, she took a deep breath. "ROSE, talk to us, what's up?"

A small holographic figure materialized from a projector on the pine marten's wide console area. Maddy observed that unlike her own iteration, Lou's ROSE appeared as a burly, butch polar bear woman with close-cropped hair; if not for being preoccupied with the immediate danger, she might have flushed at the realization that she was, in fact, specifically the elder dyke's *type*.

[It's the TPA, with a major offensive operation, and they're out for blood. Your orders from Site Command are to complete your supply run to RIV. When you arrive and your cargo is offloaded, you'll be helping to evacuate noncombatants.]

"Copy that. What about li'l Miss Gillespie here?"

Maddy winced and took a deep breath. "If we're under attack by *Heroes*, I, uh, want to help…?"

The tiny holographic ROSE shifted to an idle animation loop for several seconds, evidently thinking. She eventually turned to the sheep-bear in the passenger seat.

[Maddy, we understand you've been hesitant to fight your former colleagues, but in this emergency, can we rely on you to help protect the shipment in case of contact with Teepa hostiles? This would be only temporary; an escort team should rendezvous with you in approximately twenty-five minutes.]

The sheep-bear nodded, with some reticence. She looked to Lou, who gave a hopeful smile. She looked to ROSE's holographic avatar, patiently waiting for her reply. She looked out the window at the sparse traffic around them, wondering if — *when* — the attack would come, and from what direction.

"I can do that," Maddy said quietly, as the truck sped on into the night.

Chapter 2

March 19 2023

Maddy donned their RCGs and growled, jaw set in a worried frown. They couldn't *not* help in a crisis, and anyway, if Texas' state Hero force was attacking the Korps, that meant *them too.*

The Texas Protectorate Assembly was more unsettlingly paramilitary to the sheep-bear than most of its domestic counterparts or Provincial Heroes' League cousins; the functional separation between "law enforcement officer" and "state-sanctioned Hero" was sometimes thin, but in Texas, it was nonexistent. They had a reputation for relying on overwhelming force, like riot cops with superpowers. One or two more thoughtful-seeming members notwithstanding, on the rare occasions Maddy had met TPA agents at professional functions during her brief career, they'd also been contemptuous *assholes* to the young Hero. It didn't take telepathy to grasp the transphobia behind their sneers.

The sheep-bear began carefully tightening the laces of their heavy motorcycle boots — as they always did just before expecting the possibility of action — and continued to ponder. How far could they go, if it came to that? Kicking the shit out of Slider had been cathartic as hell, but that was *personal.* Moreover, behind the snark and bluster, he was a coward; a few broken bones had, in fact, been enough motivation for him to leave Mom and Brianna alone these past few months. Teepa Heroes wouldn't be so easily cowed, and if this was a full-on offensive operation, they'd be arriving in *numbers,* too. At that point, ROSE chimed in through their visor.

[*Maddy, I know you're still uncomfortable with this, but we deeply appreciate your help. We wouldn't ask if it wasn't an emergency.*]

"Thank you, ROSE," the sheep-bear replied mentally. "*I'll... I'll do my best.*"

[*I know you will. But, also, I wanted to alert you that you've never actually accessed your RCG device's full tactical operations suite. Training with Tommy has been a controlled environment; if you have to engage with Teepa hostiles now, it'll be both a real combat situation, and one where you'll likely be experiencing stress over this uncertainty. May I have your consent to assist with focus, emotional regulation, and pain suppression, if and when necessary, until the current situation is resolved?*]

Maddy inhaled sharply. Of *course*, the AI could do those things via her RCGs' so-called "root-level access" to the brain, she knew that; she'd conscientiously read all the way through the user manual. At the time, ever needing that help in a real fight had seemed like a very distant and unlikely possibility. "*...Okay,*" she thought quietly.

The sound of a siren screamed from somewhere behind the truck, and both Lou and Maddy looked anxiously in their side mirrors. Flashing blue and white lights made the sheep-bear's heart sink. An angry, gruff voice blared on a loudspeaker clear enough to be heard in the cab.

"THIS IS THE TEXAS PROTECTORATE ASSEMBLY. PULL OVER IMMEDIATELY FOR INSPECTION."

"*...How,* though? I thought your civilian cover was solid," Maddy winced. "What — what should I do?"

Lou's eyes darted between the mirror and the road ahead, grim determination in her voice. "Maybe some state trooper just got mad about seeing a fat old dyke at the last truck stop and called it into Teepa when shit went sideways. Maybe the cargo's not as well shielded from scans as the lab folks said, and we pinged an aerial sweep or something like that. Couldn't tell ya, and it hardly matters right now; you're on." The marten tapped a panel of her dashboard display, which refreshed into a map; a marker for the promised escort squad from RIV was inbound, with an ETA of fourteen minutes. The two TPA vehicles — from the rendering, chunky armoured cars — followed close behind Lou's truck. "Think you can go shake them for me until the cavalry shows up?"

Maddy's eyes bugged out. "I'd — I'd have to get closer to like, barricade them or push them off the road..."

"Doesn't your telekinesis let you fly? Or hover, at least? I thought that was a thing!"

They shook their head worriedly. "Not for everyone? It's difficult, and… anyway, no, not an option right now, so I'd need my bike for that! But we can't stop for me to go around back…"

Lou raised an eyebrow bemusedly as she kept her eyes on the road. "*Stop?* Who said anything about stopping? Girl, this may look like a civilian truck, but it's Korps through and through; ain't the first time someone's needed to get into the trailer from the cab while doing eighty…" The marten reached under her console to toggle a hidden switch and hooked a thumb over her shoulder towards the sleeping compartment. "Just let me know when to open the rear for you. And good luck, eh?"

The sheep-bear undid their seatbelt and hurled their weight around the flipped-up armrest to look in surprise to the back of the sleeper cab. With faint whirring and grinding noises, the bed was retracting vertically into the ceiling on two wall-mounted tracks; the recessed panel behind it had folded down to cover and clamp tight the bedclothes as the mattress ascended on its slim platform. "Oh, *wow*," Maddy murmured as they stepped forward, and pulled a heavy lever bar to open the revealed hatch; it popped ajar with a low clunk, and they swung it open.

On the other side, past a half-metre gangway encased by shaking, accordion-folded rubber bellows, was the hatch's twin; she again activated the lever release, and pushed it outwards, to reveal… the interior of Lou's trailer, entirely accessible. It caught slightly against one of the strapped-down shipping pallets of stabilized cargo pods, however, no matter how hard Maddy pushed forward; the result was that the sheep-bear had to suck in her gut to squeeze through the tight passage, huffing with relief once she was fully inside. After closing the hatches, she ran a hand through her short black hair and sized up the situation.

Releasing the clamps and tie-downs that had been keeping their motorcycle in place was trivial. After a few seconds of awkward telekinesis-assisted shuffling of the Yamaha around the trailer decking, facing it towards the rear doors, Maddy straddled the seat. Tucking their long scarf into their maroon leather jacket and making one last check of the cramped space of the trailer, they turned the oblong, teardrop-shaped head of the key, pressing it in to activate the choke. The bike rumbled to life, idling rough for a moment as it warmed up, like usual.

"THIS IS THE TPA, SASKATCHEWAN PLATED SEMI TRUCK. PULL OVER NOW OR WE WILL USE ALL NECESSARY FORCE TO STOP YOUR VEHICLE," the loudspeaker blasted through Lou's rear doors.

Gulping, the sheep-bear realized she'd have to rev up and hit the asphalt with a rolling start, and grimaced. "Lou…?"

The trucker's voice returned Maddy's hail through the audio feed of her RCGs. "Maddy? Do you copy, girl?"

"Copy. Mounted up. How far away are they?"

"Still tailing close, but you'll have a good five metres or thereabouts to work with, if you're careful. Ready?"

Maddy took a deep breath. "…Open the pod bay doors, Lou."

The doors unlatched with another faint grinding noise, and hydraulic actuators smoothly swung them open; the rubber seals along the edges flapped slightly in the breeze. The sheep-bear saw two pairs of high beams amongst the strobing blue-and-whites, and winced with a snarl, prompting ROSE to automatically activate her RCGs' anti-glare filter. She hunched forward over the handlebars, shifted into gear, and gunned the accelerator. With a roar equal parts her own ursine bellow and the V-Max's powerful engine, the bike tore forward and spun off the edge of the trailer's deck into the air.

The wheels landed *hard* on the highway surface, wobbling and threatening to careen; steering hard, Maddy carefully aimed for the dead-centre of the four headlamps. Putting themself between the two armoured cars — each easily eight or nine tons, hardened as they must have been — allowed the sheep-bear to use the vehicles as anchors. Telekinetically reaching out on each side to push back against armoured door panels, they managed to quickly stabilize the bike's path and keep it upright; through open windows, they caught startled Teepa operatives rubbernecking at the maneuver. With a wide figure-eight turn across four lanes, briefly swiping by oncoming traffic from the other direction, Maddy swung into pursuit of the hostiles trailing Lou's truck.

She immediately had to duck, as a focused, narrow blast of… *something* cold… passed just over her head. Maddy didn't recognize any of these Heroes, including the wide-faced, muddy-green salamander who was leaning out the right passenger window of the left cruiser, clearly trying to aim and fire their (elemental?) force-projection powers at the sheep-bear once again. She pulled back and swerved off to one side, blocking the amphibian's line of sight with the other vehicle; as she did, another (much weaker) stream of frosty air clipped its roof. At that point, one of the TPA agents in the second car began leaning out *his* window, drawing a bead on Maddy with what appeared to be some kind of lance-shaped beam weapon. She dipped back once more, and the vehicle's driver swerved to accommodate, sending the grizzled canine's shot wild; a golden pulse tagged a roadside billboard in the distance, leaving a large scorch mark across the "WHATABURGER – 10 MI AHEAD" text.

Lou's voice buzzed in through the sheep-bear's RCGs. "Maddy? Status? I saw that fella nearly nail you with something!"

"I'm fine," she said through gritted teeth, weaving to keep out of the pursuing Heroes' reach. "ROSE, any thoughts?"

[*Visual recognition and power cross-reference matches identified. The hellbender is Davis "Cold Day" Buttram, TPA reservist, home territory Bowie County and the Texarkana metro area; minor enhanced agility and extremely limited cryokinesis. The coyote is Joseph "Desert Knight" Moreno, TPA reservist, home territory El Paso and the Trans-Pecos region; enhanced senses and limited flight powers via riding desert sandstorms, an ability he terms "Dustwalking."*]

Maddy frowned, a low growl burning in their throat. "...Reservists? Shit, this *is* a big operation."

[*It is. Intel throughout the Austin area suggests that Teepa has activated and locally deployed all powered agents available to them. That includes retirees, minor independent Heroes, and low-powered public safety personnel affiliated with their emergency auxiliary program, from all over the state. Desert Knight retired in 2008 with thirty-five years of service, and Cold Day is ordinarily a Bowie County Sheriff's Deputy. Incidentally, I calculate — given previous encounter data, and the sharply diminished power of his second attack — that it should take at least two minutes before he can recharge enough to cause you any harm.*]

"You hear that, girl? These are local yokels, county mounties, and a greymuzzle older than *me*," Lou snarked. "You've got this; go fuck 'em up, there."

The problem with the armoured cars being heavy enough for the sheep-bear to anchor themselves while riding — after that initial, reckless jump off the deck of Lou's trailer that could have been a hard rock album cover, if the role of the typical post-apocalyptic barbarian meathead biker were played by a beefy butch lesbian — was that their telekinesis had *limits*. They could easily toss around a passenger vehicle or two in a crisis; they'd done it before, to get a line of stalled traffic out of the way of a toppling construction crane. Similarly, from experience, they could also *very carefully* (and with a great deal of exertion) right an overturned, fully-laden tractor-trailer. The cruisers were surely somewhere closer in mass to the former than the latter, even with their rugged plating. But those vehicles and the sheep-bear had each been still, on those previous occasions; it was very different while both telekinetic and their targets were in motion at high speed.

Maddy concentrated, reaching out with her mind to probe whether she could possibly lift the closest vehicle off the asphalt, all the while continuing to steer the V-Max. She growled, frustrated; try as she might, she couldn't get a mental grip on the armoured car. It was too heavy and moving too quickly, with her attention divided as it was. She wouldn't be able to simply disable the vehicles as she'd hoped to, carefully overturning them on their roofs like helpless turtles. This was going to be *messy*. Someone was apt to get *hurt*. She gulped and forced down a faint twinge of anxious conscience at the idea of hurting Heroes. She didn't want to—

"Can't — can't get a solid grasp on the cars, though. Too fast, too heavy."

"What about the passengers? Pull Mister Freezie or Ol' Dusty out, leave 'em on the side of the road, now the driver has to decide whether to recover the men they're down?"

"It's not safe for me to telekinetically grab a person! Not at this speed, not when I'm so distracted like this. If I miscalculated the pressure I might crush them, and if I couldn't match the velocity of the vehicles while dragging them out the window, they might get cut in half! I'm not... I'm not a *murderer*," the sheep-bear mumbled.

"Easy, girl, you don't have to take it so hard," Lou responded mildly over comms. "I don't have powers, I don't always know these things. I ain't saying you ought to kill anyone. Necessarily."

[*Would you like me to—*]

"No, ROSE, not right now," Maddy grunted. "I can... I can figure something out here. Give me a sec."

A new voice abruptly dropped into the conversation, masculine-sounding, warm and clipped and Southern. It put the sheep-bear in mind of NASA radio chatter from the space mission documentaries she'd fervently watched as a cub, back when she was young enough to have the ridiculous dream of becoming an astronaut.

"Cargo carrier SCS-25, Mizzes Cart-yay and Gillespie, *Good Morning* to you, friends, and welcome to Austin. This is Swashplate with your escort team in Condor RIV-19, and folks call *us* the Moonlighters. Our ETA is approximately eight minutes; ROSE managed to bump our departure up a few slots, what with your current pre-*dic*-a-ment. We see your respective video feeds, and if you can keep moving at your current speed, we should be able to disable the Teepa pursuit when we rendezvous."

Maddy veered slightly to avoid another golden pulse from Desert Knight's carbine-lance; they could smell the hot asphalt where the shot had landed, ahead of the Yamaha's front wheel. Their RCGs' HUD helpfully informed them that it would, in fact, be very harmful to be tagged by the energy weapon. They growled in frustration, and silently thanked the universe for the good fortune that the only armed member of this detachment was apparently a shaky-handed senior citizen. Still, he *was* trying to seriously wound or kill the sheep-bear, and they weren't certain they could keep this up until the escort team arrived in their helicopter. They would have to *do* something.

She replied. "Copy that, Swashplate, but I just can't keep running interference that long, even if these are second-stringers. I'm guessing you're already at maximum speed?"

"That is *correct*, my apologies. If you've got a better plan, by all means, we're behind you."

"Drone cams show we're clear for near-two hundred metres on either side of these jackoffs," Lou interjected. "There's an exit a couple minutes ahead, with a fair-sized truck stop. If you can even slow 'em down enough for me to get out of their line of sight, we might be cooking with gas here."

The escort pilot chuckled lightly. "Got it, Miz Cart-yay; we'll monitor to intercept if you two can pull it off."

"...ROSE? *What the fuck? What's the plan? How does he know?*"

[Swashplate just checked the loadout of Lou's installed equipment, and she's on top of it, dear. Camouflage, of a sort. Can you slow down the armoured cars in the space of the next six kilometres?]

"I can do that," the sheep-bear huffed. With a sudden epiphany, she realized that was the pressure she needed to come up with a solution. Her eyes darted behind the pink visor, looking past the pursuit vehicles to Lou's truck, and then gazing at their movements in parallel. At the edge of her conscious mind, she'd *noticed* something about their rumbling movement. Experimentally, she pulled back again, and one after the other, tested both drivers with a near-miss along each of the armoured cars' rear flanks.

With two fingers of their left hand — all they could safely free from the bike's handlebars, in case they suddenly needed to engage the clutch — Maddy modeled the movements they needed to telekinetically probe the vehicles' transmission systems. (They could, technically, accomplish the same thing purely mentally, but had always found some degree of physical gesturing helpful to their focus.) Grinning once they had figured out their next move, the sheep-bear pulled alongside to overtake the left car... and then sharply veered in front of it, lining the Yamaha up in front of the gap between the two.

She slowed, dropping back through the gap, to the Teepa operatives' surprise and loud profanities. As she'd expected from watching the left-hand driver's motions, he veered, *hard*, to try and pin the motorcycle-riding sheep-bear; however, he clearly wasn't used to operating such an unwieldy vehicle, and considerably oversteered. With a deep breath, Maddy sharply dropped her speed again, shifted into neutral, and used her powers to slow her V-Max back further still; it made an unnerving noise, but the maneuver *worked*. At the same time, she managed to get the lightest of telekinetic grips on the left car, and using its own momentum, sling-shotted it further into the path of the right car.

Shifting back into gear and revving up, the sheep-bear smoothly circled the armoured vehicles now on a collision course. They caught a glance of the left-hand driver's shock as he looked out the window... while his vehicle tipped to the right and tumbled over twice before the two collided in a heavy, thumping *screech*.

Maddy sped ahead and bellowed in satisfaction at her handiwork before she realized exactly what she had done and felt a faint twinge of guilt. She peered anxiously into her angular, lozenge-shaped mirrors; there didn't *seem* to be any immediate, obvious injuries among their pursuers? Two of the TPA reservists had stepped out of the still-upright vehicle, and were running over to help another climb out of the overturned one. Gritting her teeth, the sheep-bear clamped down on her bike's throttle and pulled up alongside the truck.

Lou gave them a wave as she spoke over comms. "Now *that* was right well done, girl! I'm having ROSE send you a route; g'wan ahead, and I'll meet you there, eh?"

"On it, see you in a few!" The sheep-bear smiled at that as she passed and sped up to approach the highway exit. The praise was almost enough to force down her discomfort at... wait, no, why *was* she uncomfortable? She had just saved herself and her friend from being captured, or even killed.

Captured or killed for, you know, being members of a criminal organization that does things like get in superpowered fights with law enforcement, the thought in the back of her head nagged. *God, what kind of charges would those be back home — I bet it's a capital offence here...*

[*Maddy, I'm sorry that was upsetting, but you did a good thing. You've helped not just yourself and Lou, but the forty civilian personnel waiting to be evacuated from RIV in her truck once you arrive.*]

"ROSE, I... I know. Thank you. And those dipshits were just as much TPA as their frontline units, just as much trigger-happy reactionaries as the assholes I met when I was one of the 'good guys.' I'm not... I'm not sure I actually feel bad about whether or not they got hurt? Or, at least, I don't want to..."

[*The escort will rendezvous with you at the truck stop ahead, in approximately three minutes. If you need to tap out now — if you can't bear the idea of getting into another skirmish with the TPA — I promise that nobody will think any less of you. If you're up for it, once you arrive at RIV, you can help with the evacuation; that shouldn't involve any further combat.*]

"I want to help, ROSE! Put me in, Coach, wherever I'm most useful! Even if it's a little bit uncomfortable, I can do that..."

[*Thank you, Maddy. Duly noted, and again, it's very much appreciated. Now, I need to help you with your currently-elevated stress levels, because my readings show you're beginning to hyperventilate.*]

The sheep-bear was about to protest, but suddenly felt... *better*. Her heartbeat — pounding faster than she'd realized — slowed, and she was able to deeply exhale and inhale, interrupting the quick, shallow breaths ROSE had recognized. An ineffable, gentle *pressure* felt like a warm hug around both body and mind. The feedback loop of anxiety that had begun to build over taking out the TPA operatives melted away; she felt relieved. She felt *loved*, somehow. Without the fear and guilt clouding her thoughts, she could admit to herself that the AI was right; she *had* done a good thing.

[How are you feeling now?]

"...Thanks, ROSE."

With the off-ramp in sight, Maddy proceeded (still rapidly, but dropping down to just a hair over the speed limit) to take the slight turn and merged onto the adjoining service road. The truck stop was just another moment away, and once on the property, they cautiously steered between several parked tractor-trailers, idling and waiting for Lou to catch up. They flipped to their RCGs' HUD and watched the dots for the trucker (and the escort helicopter, moving somewhat more quickly in the air) draw closer. Finally, Lou's dot slowed and then stopped inside the parking lot, apparently just on the other side of the vehicular valley where they'd taken shelter. The sheep-bear gently accelerated to swing out from their hiding spot... and became deeply confused.

It wasn't Lou. Maddy didn't know much about trucks, but she could tell this was a different make, and not a sleeper cab. It had a longer trailer, and a wildly different appearance; rather than the nondescript livery of SCS front company Prince Albert Logistics — the plain black lettering encircled by a thick silver ring, on a white background — the trailer featured a photomontage of fruits and vegetables arranged in the shape of the state flag, proclaiming "A FRESHER PICK FOR TEXAS," and the logo of what the sheep-bear presumed to be a local supermarket chain.

Maddy gulped and spoke softly. "...Lou? Where are you? My RCGs say you should be right in front of me, but I only see this grocery truck." As soon as they said the words, the trailer's rear doors automatically swung open.

"Yeah, no, that's me! Engaged the holographic projectors once nobody was looking right at us, should throw off anyone tracking by visuals or automatic plate scanners. Hop in, girl," the marten chortled.

Still half-disbelieving her eyes, the sheep-bear puttered around to the truck's rear, and killed the bike's engine. Sure enough, the interior was the same half-full collection of cargo pods she'd had to squeeze through on the way off the trailer's deck. Looking carefully at the doors, close up, she could see now that there was a faint haziness to their exteriors; she touched one, and was now unsurprised to see her fingertips vanish from view before they reached solid metal, as if she was a video game character clipping through a wall. She whistled; the holographic camouflage was impressive, as long as you didn't get too close.

With a glance over their shoulder to make sure there were no curious eyes watching, Maddy telekinetically lifted their beloved V-Max up to the cargo area before clambering up themself, and hastily strapping it to the decking. They sucked in their gut once again to pass through the gangway and could hear the hydraulics of the rear doors pumping shut behind them as the vehicle started to move.

Scrambling past the sleeping area and hurling herself into the passenger's seat, the sheep-bear strapped back in; she and Lou nodded to each other with a smirk, and the elder dyke spun her steering wheel with a flourish to turn back towards the highway interchange.

Swashplate's soothing staccato resumed as the truck gained speed, resuming course to RIV. "SCS-25, this is your eye in the sky. That was some fancy footwork, friends, and I can *confirm* no bogeys in our vicinity. The long-range shows those fellas back on the highway are still picking themselves up, and if they've called in a crash, it must have been *direct* to Teepa; no sign anyone else has heard yet. Let's get home before they do, y'all."

Half an hour later, Maddy was in RIV's main vehicle bay, carefully unloading the cargo pods with their telekinesis. Deploying and evacuating personnel flitted around with speed and purpose; nobody was panicking, everyone knew where they were going, and despite the tense atmosphere the sheep-bear was reassured just how *well* the crisis was being managed. They certainly couldn't imagine things going this smoothly back at OH

Lakeview in a similar emergency; every fire drill there was an absolute disaster, with half the Heroes doing their own thing, and the civilian staff an unruly, whining mob rushing for the exits. That was what leadership — and the logistical organizing capacity of a seemingly all-knowing AI integrated into nearly room, vehicle, system and *person* — counted for, they supposed.

[I do my best, dear!]

Having placed the last pallet onto a Lab Sector utility trolley, Maddy grunted with satisfaction, and waved to Lou. The heavy pine marten was alongside a back wall, chatting with a jumpsuit wearing nurse shark her RCGs identified as "Soren Zhang (he/him), Fleet Operations." Lou waved back, nodded to the shark, and began trundling back towards the truck, to her gratitude; the civilians they'd be evacuating were patiently waiting to board, and she wanted to be sure there weren't any other hidden switches or moving parts to disengage in the trailer area before letting the visor-wearing crowd pile in.

At that moment, the sheep-bear felt a gentle double-pat on their arm, and spun around to see a weathered hyena of indeterminate age and significant augmentation — if not a synth, then definitely a cyborg — in lightweight composite black and magenta tactical gear, a worn leather bomber jacket, and aviator-framed RCGs. He was eyeing them slyly. When they saw the personnel identification caption pop up in their HUD, they gasped with delight and extended an open hand. "Swashplate! Hi!"

"Miz Gillespie," he said, grinning as he gave the sheep-bear a vigorous handshake. "Y'can call me Chester, if you like. Anyways, I meant it, that was some fine work out there. *Mighty* fine work." He coughed, clearing his throat, and turned his gaze across the vehicle bay, hands on slim hips. "Look, I'll cut to the chase here. The Moonlighters, my team, we are *re*deployed in five, and we're down an agent; xe got pulled in to help Engineering when we landed. I read your file, you're *good* at this, and we are *auth*-o-rized to activate qualified civilian reserves for emergency field ops. How 'bout it?"

The offer took her aback. Life just wouldn't stand still; she'd — she'd only just gotten out of the line of fire, and was already faintly unsettled by going up against even TPA bench-warmers, but she *did* want to help however she could, and *definitely* wanted to get over that hesitation, and—

*[Maddy, I apologize, but you need to decide **right now**.]*

"...*What? Why?*"

[Maddy! **Right! Now!**]

The sheep-bear opened their heavy ursine jaw and closed it again, fidgeting for several seconds, uncertain of their decision until they heard themself say "...Yes? Yes. *Yes!*"

"Welcome aboard," Swashplate nodded, as he genially slapped her on the back. "Come meet the team, now...!"

As the two hustled towards the adjoining hangar bay, KATS insignia emblazoned on the dividing archway, Maddy read the all-hands priority message scrolling across their HUD, and snorted:

[ALERT (RIV-LOCAL) // AS OF NOW, NO FURTHER RESERVE PERSONNEL ACTIVATION IS AUTHORIZED]

Chapter 3

March 19, 2023

Maddy took a deep breath, rolling her eyes as Swashplate (Chester, apparently?) escorted her to the hangar bay.

"*That was a cheap trick, ROSE.*"

[Whatever do you mean, Maddy?]

Had the AI been projecting herself in avatar mode, the sheep-bear was *sure* they'd have heard the theatrically wounded tone from behind a smug vulpine grin.

"*You knew that was coming, didn't you? That announcement about no further authorizations for drafting willing civilians to go fight off the TPA. The... revocation, or whatever. You knew that was coming, and pushed me to make a choice right away, to get under the wire.*"

[I could never undermine the will of the Overlord, dear. And you can still change your mind! Like I said back on the Interstate, no one will think any less of you. If you don't want to go out into a combat situation — if you **can't,** *if you think you might be a liability to your teammates — nobody will force you. Swashplate and his team actually did want to see you in action, so he might be a tiny bit disappointed, but he'd understand.]*

"Well, okay, but..."

[But you **want** *to do this. I know. If you'd had more time to think, you'd still have said yes in the end, right?]*

"...Yeah. Yeah, I would have. The urgency just... shortcut past all my hesitation and went right to the I Want to Help part of my brain."

[To be fair — and believe me, I would know! — that is a very big part of your brain.]

The sheep-bear gulped as the two approached a Condor, the Korps's standard VTOL tactical aircraft platform, the entire body painted a somehow eye-watering, faintly optically-shifting shade of matte black.

The huge ringed rotor housings were tilted nearly-flat, and the door facing them was open, slid out along the sleek fuselage. Several field agents in varied body armour and covert ops accoutrements were inside: three sprawled across the mounted seating, and one sitting down on the cabin deck, dangling lanky legs out the door. The latter, a maned wolf, had a lap full of some kind of powered harpoon-looking device.

As they arrived, Swashplate put a hand back on one of those lean, twinkish synthetic hips, and dashed off a casual salute to his team with the other. "Folks, give Maddy a warm welcome to the Moonlighters while Biscotti and I finish pre-flighting, would you? Wheels are *up* in three," the hyena enunciated in his rapid-fire cadence. The maned wolf (according to ROSE's helpful popup: she/her, an infiltrator and unpowered skirmisher specializing in nets, grappling hooks and similar means of encumbering enemies) nodded and stowed her weapon in a bracket by the door. She looked vaguely familiar, and the sheep-bear wondered if she might be related to that one K-LAW agent from the New Year's party at KDS…

"On it, Chez," Biscotti said. As she hopped down from the deck, she gave the sheep-bear an encouraging pat on the shoulder. "Welcome aboard! Just be sure to buckle up with this one," the maned wolf smirked, pointing a clawed thumb over her shoulder at Swashplate, already on the far side of the aircraft.

The hyena ducked his head under the tail to peer back around at them with a sardonic snort. "Now don't *frighten* Miz Gillespie, y'hear? There is *nothing* to worry about, I as*sure* you; I will have you know that I am wearing my *lucky* jacket this fine morning," he said, tugging at the scuffed and scratched leather. The two chuckled together, and Biscotti joined the pilot in their visual inspection, leaving Maddy to grab a handrail and hop up into the cabin.

The sheep-bear peered around at the other three. According to her HUD, the secretary bird, oryx and mongoose were respectively Hank "Fascination" Lutz (he/him), a telepath, hypnotist and combat medic; Miray "Breakneck" Osman (she/they), a heavy and minor speedster; and Julia "Breakpoint" Walker (she/her), another unpowered covert operator like Biscotti, her utility webbing brimming with knives of all shapes and sizes. ROSE *also* helpfully added that the latter two were married but always in search of a third, causing Maddy to flush briefly with a nervous chuckle.

"Uh... Hi, everyone," the sheep-bear said with an anxious smile across their muzzle, and a tentative wave of a chunky, hoof-nailed paw. "Happy to pitch in, I hope I can be useful? Not, um, having been in the field since I changed teams, I mean, and what I know about Korps combat tactics and procedures is mostly from the other side—"

"Hey, we all saw how you handled that Teepa patrol! Give yourself some credit," Breakneck said with a gentle titter that belied her muscular bulk.

The secretary bird nodded. "You know we want you here, right? All of us! This wasn't something Chester or anyone else *imposed*. It was Aster who suggested drafting you for xer replacement when xe got requisitioned by Engineering on the return flight, and the rest of us agreed. Anyway, if you're not used to VTOLs, Bisc is right; strap in!"

Maddy did so, pulling the jump seat's harness around her torso and fastening the buckle with a heavy click. "Thanks," the sheep-bear said, her shoulders untensing, as Biscotti hopped in the side and pulled the hatch closed.

[Deep breaths, Maddy. Fascination is right; you'll do fine.]

After a moment — Swashplate humming and faintly murmuring to himself as he toggled various switches and started the engines — the Condor's twin drives spun up to a deep thrum. The craft lifted just off the ground, tilting just enough to delicately buzz forward and reach the tall entry shaft past the hangar door, where it could sharply ascend. Maddy looked out the window, watching the parkland west of downtown Austin grow smaller in the distance as they climbed.

Swashplate's rhythmic patter called back from the aircraft's cockpit, echoing through the sheep-bear's RCGs. "All right, friends and neighbours, we are now at cruising altitude, so listen up: this one's an extra*ction*. Safe house in a closed the-ay-ter up in the hills, one agent and one civilian on site, our job is clearing *out* and sealing it *up*. ROSE, if you'd be so kind?"

Information flashed through Maddy's HUD. The site was in a suburban strip mall; the theatre, apparently locally appreciated for its repertory and indie screenings, had been shuttered in corporate restructurings back in the fall. A few months later, having confirmed the building was effectively abandoned, RIV's Facilities team moved in.

A construction team had blitzed through in one night (there was, helpfully, an animated diagram of the design and installation process, in the multimedia mission brief that ran past the sheep-bear's eyes) and built a spartan but functional hidden apartment, in what had been a walled-off old storage area. The entrance was hidden on the projection booth level; it was unlikely to be discovered unless conducting a dedicated search with relevant tools or powers, or in the event of total demolition.

However, with the TPA on a rampage throughout Austin, it would be safer to extract and evacuate the current occupants, rather than count on them continuing to lay low. That was the Moonlighters' mission.

It took only a few minutes to reach their destination, near an elevated highway — US-183, according to the overlay in Maddy's RCGs. The Condor soon descended into a tight triangular service alley area, behind a cluster of white-roofed commercial buildings. Biscotti hoisted her harpoon gun and threw the cabin door open as they touched down.

Quietly, smoothly, each of the agents stepped down to the asphalt and positioned themselves in a tactical formation: Breakneck in front, flanked by her wife and the maned wolf, with Fascination gesturing for Maddy to join him bringing up the rear. Keeping watch on their surroundings, the team proceeded up a short flight of stairs to the defunct theatre's fire exit; Breakpoint produced a key and, holding the unlocked door open, hustled each one inside before pulling it shut behind her. It put the group in some kind of utility corridor with evenly-spaced steel fire doors — clearly the emergency exits for each individual auditorium — and another short flight of stairs up, at the end of the hall.

"Something's wrong," the mongoose whispered suspiciously. "There's a *breeze* in here. Hold up." Breakneck nodded grimly, and Breakpoint took the proffered ring of keys from her wife. She opened one of the doors and slunk inside; despite being shuttered for several months, the faint smell of artificial butter flavouring and spilled fountain drinks still wafted out.

A moment later, Julia's voice came directly through Maddy's auditory cortex. "Confirmed. Pretty sure we've got Teepa in here; one of the lobby glass doors has been smashed in, and if the fuck-huge SUV on the far side of the parking lot isn't an unmarked car, I'd be shocked."

"Copy that, Breakpoint, I will have wheels off the ground in *one* for a stealth fly-by *confirmation*," Swashplate chimed in, in his Southern staccato.

Biscotti sighed. "It fuckin' *figures*," she said, attempting to hail their comrades over RCG comms. "Safe house complement, do you copy?"

There was no response. Without a word, the team moved just a little bit faster up to the second-floor landing, joined after another few seconds by the returning mongoose. The door was closed, but its lock mechanism lay shattered on the floor. Shrugging, Breakneck glanced back at the rest of the field agents. The oryx grunted, kicked in the door with one massive cloven hoof, and barreled through with a bellow; the others followed.

Maddy gazed down the long, dim room. There were scars on the linoleum floor from where now-removed projectors had been mounted, in front of each glass window looking into a darkened auditorium. More importantly, in front of an open section of sliding wall leading to a warmly-lit area beyond, there was a group of five TPA Heroes (in their paramilitary-looking uniforms, ridiculous tiny cowboy hat on their heavy to make him seem "approachable" and all) who'd clearly been kicking two other prone figures on the ground in front of them. The noise of the team's entrance had caused them to turn around in surprise. Her nostrils flared in anger at hearing the faint sobs of pain emanating from the floor.

"That 'pears to be a positive on un*marked* Teepa vehicle, friends—"

"*Thanks, Chez, we copy*," Biscotti rasped through bared teeth, snap-firing her weapon from the hip. With a muted *thoom* sound, it instantly launched a spear-tipped shaft across the twenty metres or more between the two sides; almost too quickly to see, the projectile split apart to form a fine mesh net with a dart-lined edge, slamming a lanky Boerbok goat TPA agent against the sliding wall segment and pinning him there. Half a second later, the net buzzed with crackling sparks, and he went limp. Maddy's RCG HUD indicated that the Hero known as "Integris" had been tased into unconsciousness.

Gazing over Breakpoint's shoulder, the sheep-bear realized that one of the other Teepa Heroes — a meaty wall of bobcat her RCGs captioned as "Screaming Halt" — was bringing one shaggy, clawed hand above his shoulders. She recognized what activating a compact communicator earpiece looked like; Ontario's Heroes had used a similar model. She darted under the mongoose's raised right arm, in the process of drawing a slim spade-tipped throwing knife to hurl at the man. Lunging forward into a half-kneel, Maddy fixed searching eyes on each of the still-conscious Heroes' heads.

Without even having to ask, ROSE sensed Maddy's intention and highlighted each of the TPA communicators; the devices lit up with a bright yellow glow and warning symbol in the sheep-bear's vision. They mentally *pulled*. All four came telekinetically flying towards an open hoof-nailed hand, halting in mid-air. The sheep-bear snapped their grasp closed, instantly crushing the earpieces into fine shards of plastic and wiring. At the same time, Breakpoint's throwing knife buried itself in the bobcat's forearm, and it appeared to take him another second to realize what had happened.

"GET THOSE KORPS BITCHES," Screaming Halt yowled in rage, as he withdrew the knife and tossed it aside. With a wince, screaming per his moniker, and trailing blood, he bounded towards the supervillains of the Moonlighters. Suddenly, his eyes went glassy; he pivoted on one ankle with a sharp turn, careening into one of the sides of the room. The bobcat's shoulder crashed through one of the projection windows, and he took a tumble into some wall-mounted electrical boxes.

At the rear of the villains, Fascination cackled gutturally at his handiwork. "How are those psi-blockers working for you, kitten?" he taunted. Maddy was perplexed as she maneuvered around Breakpoint and Breakneck, who were tag-teaming a sneering dolphin ("Blackwater," apparently) firing off blasts of dark purplish energy from both hands. The heavy was drawing her fire, dodging around too quickly to be caught at this short range. The Hero was joined by another, a slim gecko in mirror-shades ("Twilight Cowboy") who sinuously darted around the melee, trying to land a blow on the wife-and-wife team. Neither of the Teepa agents were able to touch them; between their speed and reach, they seemed to effortlessly spin their opponents in circles, even finding the time mid-melee to steal a kiss before swapping their dance partners.

"ROSE, how…"

[I assure you that Breakneck and Breakpoint are just like that, dear. Or did you mean Fascination's banter? Neurochemical psi-blockers like the ones used by Heroes tend to focus on influences on the prefrontal cortex of the brain,

to prevent their will from being pressured or even puppeteered by a powerful telepath. However, those are less useful against his favourite trick — skewing the processing pathways in an opponent's occipital lobe, such that their visual cortex suddenly sees the world at a ninety-degree angle for a moment, causing them to overcompensate. Also, watch out!]

With the AI's warning, the sheep-bear dived into a roll forward. She winced and growled as Screaming Halt narrowly caught her flank despite flying wild, raking sharp claws into her flesh until she could kick him away. When the bobcat got to his feet again (more enraged than ever) he barreled not towards her, but instead towards the avian telepath who'd made him trip over his own feet. Then, Fascination did it *again*, clearly — his opponent's path ran wide, and the bobcat hurtled head-first towards the other wall.

If not for Biscotti using the butt of her harpoon gun to smash out another one of the projection booth windows just a second prior, Screaming Halt's face would have collided with the glass. Instead, he toppled through into one of the darkened auditoriums. Maddy sucked in her breath sharply, seeing the Teepa heavy's momentum carry him out of the fight, and hearing the faintly cushioned, clattering *thud* of his landing in the rows of theatre seats below.

Reflexively, Maddy whipped their head around just in time to see the last TPA operative appear behind them. They'd recalled the mallard drake from one of those professional Hero conferences, as an illusionist and martial artist. They *also* recalled him sneering and declining to shake their offered hand at the morning mixer... and loudly snickering with his fellow Texans, in the back row of the closing plenary session, about how stomach-turning it was for Canadian Hero teams to recruit *trannies*.

She grinned with as much villainous menace as she could muster, stared at the duck, and *growled* from deep in her chest. The deep cuts to her leg *stung* with the full-body vibration. "Hey, Marshlight! *REMEMBER ME...?*" Without taking her sight off the man, Maddy raised an arm to her side and telekinetically *yanked* the gecko out of the melee with Breakneck and Breakpoint, bringing him flying across the room. He hovered in midair, uselessly kicking his long legs.

Marshlight's bill hung open, and his eyes boggled. "Wait, who—"

They didn't let him finish. Miming the motion with their right hand, Maddy slammed Twilight Cowboy's face into the duck's, over and over and over again, until they felt him go limp in their mental grasp; with a gleefully enraged bellow, the sheep-bear hurled him to the floor behind them.

For his part, Marshlight staggered about, his face bloody, evidently trying (and failing) to blink out of visibility to get away. "*Pathetic*," Maddy sneered, looking down her snout at the man. She made a flicking motion with two fingers, and knocked him flat on his back, where he quacked out a distressed groan. The duck didn't try to get up again, and with a smug nod, she let him be. "Come *get* some, you fucking *dicks*," the sheep-bear laughed to herself with satisfaction.

That was when they realized that, in fact, most of the Teepa force was already down; Biscotti and Fascination had proceeded to the far end of the room and were already rendering first aid to the Korps personnel on the floor.

"Miray? Julia? C'mon, let's wrap it up," Biscotti said with a snort and a glance at the happy couple, as she looked up from tending to the wounded.

Breakneck and Breakpoint turned to the maned wolf upon being called and nodded in unison. Breakneck took a wide step back, her wife shoulder-checked Blackwater forward, and with another fierce kick from the oryx — right in the solar plexus, with a wet *crunch* that sounded like several broken ribs — the dolphin was sent flying into the far wall.

The entire melee had taken only minutes, Maddy realized, panting with exertion… and she was still *fired up*, despite the jagged pain in each breath. She jogged over to the rest of the team, who were helping the extractees to their feet.

Ten minutes later, the entire team — plus the two personnel who'd been on-site, Alvi and Kepler — were back aboard Condor RIV-19, and strapping in. The burro and jerboa recounted, as they were gently (but quickly) helped down the stairs and out the fire exit, how the TPA strike team had stormed in just moments before.

"No clue how they knew," Alvi groaned, rubbing a bruised cheek, "but we'd called for extraction, we were hunkered down in the hidden room, and suddenly that dolphin comes in blasting, and Screaming Halt manages to dislodge the entire sliding wall mechanism. They were on top of us too quickly to even alert ROSE." They sighed, looking down through the window as the aircraft quietly climbed above the mall parking lot. "And that was some of my best work, too."

The Moonlighters had, of course, needed to demolish the installation on their way out; it couldn't be a useful safe house again after the Heroes had rumbled it. Between their brawn and telekinesis, Miray and Maddy had made quick work of wrecking the furniture and stripping the electronics, such that no useful evidence of the Korps's weeks-long presence in the abandoned theatre would remain.

While they laboured, Maddy had flushed with pride to hear the team's compliments of how well she'd acquitted herself in the fight. They then all departed, leaving the TPA operatives still groaning on the floor. Maddy, still faintly anxious on that count, had quickly looked each one over with her RCGs as she exited (including poking her head through the broken window marked "#4," gazing down into the auditorium at the bobcat sprawled over several seats) to confirm each was still breathing. They were, although several would certainly be on the injured reserve list for a while.

Swashplate called out from the cockpit. "Friends, I've reported that we are *five* by *five*, and lucky us, RIV has *dis*patched us for another extraction up in the Canyonlands. Our ETA is eighteen minutes, so kick back and *enjoy* the downtime, y'all." There was a brief pause before the hyena continued. "But *first*, well… Bisc, would you kindly do the honours?"

The maned wolf's eyes lit up behind her visor, and she scrambled up past the fore of the cabin into the co-pilot's seat. "Wouldn't turn it down, Chez," she grinned.

Maddy rose from her seat and looked through the short corridor into the cockpit. Biscotti was operating a small set of handlebars that she popped out from an under-console panel. The fuck-huge SUV Breakpoint had noted alone in the near-empty parking lot earlier, a dark blue Hummer, appeared on a small targeting display. Licking her lips, the maned wolf activated twin triggers. The constant thrum of the Condor's engines was accompanied for a few seconds by the *chukka-chukka-chukka* of its autocannon, and the Hummer *exploded* in a blaze.

"Hell fucking *yeah*. Let's get to the Canyonlands, Skip," Biscotti said as she shoved the gunner's controls away and cracked her knuckles.

Maddy smirked and returned to the cabin, buckling up, before opening the next mission brief in her RCGs.

Several more hours (and a dozen more passengers from all points around the Austin area, several also requiring first aid from the secretary bird medic) later, into the mid-morning, the Condor was finally on its way back to RIV. Per updates from ROSE and a message from what appeared to be a giant snake woman streamed through the cabin's holoprojector, the Teepa offensive had largely collapsed. Isolated clashes were apparently continuing, though, with Heroes who hadn't noticed yet (or didn't care) that their master plan — some kind of high-powered signal jammer to incapacitate the RCG network? — had failed.

The melee in the theatre wasn't the only fight the sheep-bear had seen that night. Even as dawn broke over Texas, Maddy and the others had been slugging it out in the streets with a group of Teepa operatives deployed from Houston; given the opportunity to run wild, the Heroes had marauded through the diverse neighbourhoods of East Austin, storming bohemian storefronts and local community spaces with the outlandish claim to be "rooting out Korps sympathizers." They had *definitely* enjoyed telekinetically hurling one of them, a raving, spittle-flecked Rottweiler strapped with multiple firearms, far into the Colorado River. Another, later fracas saw the team clearing a joint APD-TPA roadblock in the way of the RIV evacuees' return to base; the local cops had scattered and ran, on seeing Breakneck kick Captain Lubbock so hard into a SWAT assault vehicle that the engine block caved in. After all that, the sheep-bear was sore, and reaching the limit of their powers as well; they hadn't exerted themself so hard since their training trials to graduate from the PHL Junior Development Program. They nonetheless felt strangely *satisfied*.

Maddy looked around the packed aircraft cabin at the regular members of the Moonlighters, and the various agents, civilians and allies extracted from danger. Her heartstrings caught at the team's camaraderie, joking and commending one another, and she felt a warm glow. It was… well, she'd never felt like she was part of something worthwhile, with Ontario's Heroes. The sheep-bear had effectively been on her own, never trusting that any of her teammates had her back, never convinced any of them cared as much about *helping* people as "getting the bad guys." The best thing she'd been able to accomplish as an officially licensed Hero was to hold herself to a higher standard than her colleagues, carefully refraining from their cruel or reckless excesses. But here…

*I want this. I want to be on a team again; a real one, this time. I want to protect everyone. I don't want anyone else to be hurt by the whole Hero machine, like I was… and I want to hurt bullies bad enough that they leave queers alone. That they leave **everyone** alone. I want to **help**.*

"ROSE? I think I want to be a field agent. I want to be a field agent **here**, in Texas, where the Heroes might as well be wearing jackboots and armbands. How do I do that?"

*[We have a process! It'll involve some training, for one, but there'll be more than that before you're cleared for field work. However, the **first** thing you'll need to do is get approval from RIV's commander. I can arrange for you to meet with Mistress Celia, if you like? It may be days or weeks before she can spare a moment, though; she's had an even busier night than you, actually.]*

"Thank you, ROSE. Yes, I'd like that."

The sheep-bear sighed, relieved. After finally making up their mind to take such a big step, it was a comfort to have some time to psych themself up again before meeting someone in *authority* at RIV… although the night had brought other concerns to mind.

"Also, I feel like maybe I should talk to someone about, uh… my trauma…?"

[Of course, Maddy. I was going to strongly suggest that anyway, after tonight, especially if you were planning to settle in at RIV for a while — and if I hadn't, Celia would have. I've made an appointment for you with a therapist.]

Maddy sighed under her breath and smiled again, faintly, as she sat back to relax for the last few minutes of the Condor's return to base. She was already daydreaming about checking out the cafeteria for a pizza, and then (once she found her assigned quarters) sleeping for the next day or so.

Then, one last thing came to mind, if indeed they would be planning to stay in Austin for the foreseeable future. The sheep-bear flushed with a different kind of warmth, as they recalled one of the reasons they'd decided to take in RIV on their tour in the first place. Their ursine smile grew broader.

"*Um, ROSE?*"

[*Yes?*]

"*Can you message Mabel Greysmoke for me…?*"

Epilogue

March 21, 2023

Maddy stepped out of the elevator onto RIV's Command level. They hadn't expected to be summoned so *soon* after asking ROSE to submit their request for field agent qualification. The sheep-bear was a newcomer to the base underneath the sprawling urban parkland of central Austin; they also hadn't shown any previous interest in actually *being* a supervillain taking part in the Korps's illicit operations in the four months since defecting from Ontario's Heroes. In fact, they'd told anyone who would listen that the idea made them feel vaguely uncomfortable… but that had been before getting a taste of the real thing, in volunteering to help protect RIV during the recent Teepa offensive. With that in mind, Maddy was perplexed, and ever-so-slightly anxious.

[*There's nothing to worry about, dear; I promise. There was an opening in her schedule today, and she was able to squeeze you in.*]

"It still feels really fast, is all. I just hope I can make that lunch date…"

The AI responded with the abstract mental sensation of a friendly shrug as Maddy proceeded down the corridor. She soon came to a small atrium-like area; in the centre, on a small, rough plinth before a set of large double doors, was what appeared to be a granite statue of a male snake in a three-piece suit. One of the figure's arms was outstretched, and his expression seemed dramatically lifelike.

In the ascetic, shadowy quiet of the Command level, the effect was ominous. Or, at least, it would have been, were the statue not sporting an askew canvas snapback cap emblazoned with the phrase SNEOPLE PLEASER.

They weren't sure if they were supposed to know the man, but the sheep-bear circled around as they proceeded towards the site commander's office, craning their neck with curiosity at the statue's remarkable detail.

Shaking their beefy, horned head and trying to focus, Maddy took a deep breath before stepping close enough to trigger the *whoosh* of the automatic door mechanism and entering a cavernous space dimly lit in flickering magenta.

Behind a wide, altar-like desk stood — sat? — the massive woman herself, Celia. A lamia, her lower body was coiled in lazy loops as she rested one elbow on the desk and tapped at a similarly oversized tablet. She looked up at the supplicant, and set down her device, leaning forward with only *slightly*-villainously steepled fingers.

"Missss Gillessspie, good morning. May I call you Maddy?"

The sheep-bear nodded respectfully. "Please, Ma'am."

"Missstressss."

"I'm sorry…?"

The giant snake tilted her head cryptically before responding again. "Ssshould you ever feel the need to addresssss me with an honorific in thisss officce — and *pleassse*, you need not today — the appropriate one is 'Missstressss.'"

Maddy nodded again, some of the tension in their shoulders melting away. They saw, too, ROSE's silent prompt in the view of their RCGs, suggesting that they could in fact address the commander by name. "Thank you. Uh, Celia."

"Getting to busssinessss: there are three topicsss I wisssh to discussss with you today," the woman hissed sinuously. "Firssst of all, your requessst to be a field agent. You come before me with *admirable* referenccccesss on that count, little ssssheep-bear. The Moonlightersss, Agentsss Backchannel and Bassstet, and of courssse, Missss Cartier; all sssspeak highly of you."

Notwithstanding that she had no *clue* who Agent Bastet might be — possibly someone she'd met recently in her travels — Maddy glowed a little at the praise.

"I have alsssso reviewed your work myssself, asss recorded by ROSSSE. It isss clear to me that you fought bravely for the Korps when asssked, dessspite previousssly professsssed… *reticccenccce*. I merely have one query before I make my decccisssion."

An entire wall lit up, and Celia turned to it; it appeared to be a giant display screen. After the familiar, near-instant ROSE bootup sequence, a video began playing. It was a recording of Maddy's RCG view during the fight at the shuttered movie theatre. They followed their perspective of the melee, somehow slightly different from their own first-person memories of the scene. In the aftermath of the fight, once the entire TPA squad was unconscious or faintly groaning on the floor, they saw the HUD toggled to the biosign vitals-scanning mode, with the fallen Heroes highlighted in various shades of green, yellow and deep orange. The view hesitated slightly, as the sheep-bear of two days prior had turned their gaze to each foe, and then briefly dipped their head out of the broken projection booth window to look down at the bobcat who went by the name of Screaming Halt.

The giant snake woman turned to Maddy — or rather, turned only her *neck* to Maddy, the rest of her upper body still facing the large display — and raised one scaled brow inquisitively. "Exxxplain," she hissed.

Maddy grimaced. "I wanted to make sure they weren't dead."

The larger woman said nothing but maintained her curiously blank expression. In the dim room, Maddy could feel the silence stretching out like a thread on the brink of snapping, until finally, the commander spoke again.

"You have a conssscienccce," Celia said.

It felt like… judgment, of a sort. Not unkind, exactly, but merely a summation of the fact at hand — possibly a disappointing one. "I—"

The lamia held up a flattened reptilian palm, and silenced Maddy. "Good."

"We do not kill… indissscriminately, nor recklesssssly. There isss alwaysss a *cossst*. Perhapsss a ssstrategic one, ssshould it provoke our opponentsss beyond our capacccity to combat… and alwaysss, *alwaysss* a persssonal one. Thossse Heroesss had to be dealt with *sssomehow* to exxxtract our people, and you and the Moonlightersss did sso, quickly and ssskillfully. Likewissse, on the highway, with your clever motorcycle tricksss. It wasss not necccessssary in either sssittuatttion to kill, there and then," Celia nodded. She proceeded to turn all the way around to Maddy, elegantly shifting her coils about, and tented her fingers again. The woman's tongue flicked out, tasting the air. "*But*. Asss grave a weight on one'sss conssscienccce asss the taking of sssentient livesss may be, all field agentsss mussst be *prepared* to kill when called upon, or cccircumsssstancesss require it to protect the Korps and fellow agentsss... isss that sssomething your sssoul will permit, little sssheep-bear...?"

"I — I think so. If it's *necessary.*"

"You may not alwaysss *think* it necccesssary, in your own opinion. Could your colleaguesss — your friendsss, your *family* — rely on you ssstill?"

Maddy opened her mouth but found herself unable to articulate the conflicting motivations within her.

"I add thisss complicatttion to the query," Celia sniffed. "You *enjoyed* harming thossse Heroesss. Ssseeing them in *pain.*"

The sheep-bear gritted their teeth, wincing, as they looked away from the commander's gaze. They couldn't deny it, even as the faint echoes of shame and guilt flared through the heart of the erstwhile Hero. "...Did ROSE tell you that?"

"No. If you have dissscussssed the matter with our multiplicccitiousss friend, ssshe hasss not betrayed your confidenccce, I promissse you; ssshe would not, unlessss livesss hung in the balanccce, or you would endanger the Korps. But I have *eyesss,* Maddy. And alssso your vissssor's footage of the variousss encountersss with Heroesss in whiccch you've found yourssself sssinccce joining usss — including your firssst, with the unfortunate Missster *Ssslider.* You wisssh the pain you inflict to be a *lessson* to thessse hateful foolsss; an incccentive, if you will, to ccceassse their predationsss upon the innocccent and downtrodden."

"I've never—" Maddy paused and rubbed a thick hoof-nailed paw against the back of her neck diffidently. "When... when I was a Hero, I mean. I tried to draw a line. I wouldn't be *cruel,* like some of my teammates. I wouldn't hurt people just because I was a Hero, and I *could,* and would get away with it, because society thinks villains and criminals deserve it. I held back, no matter how much 'killer instinct' the trainers encouraged; I promised myself that I wouldn't treat anyone like an inferior, or a monster. But some people, people like the thugs that call themselves Heroes in this state..."

"Embracccing the monssstrousss — ssstragically playing upon foesss' fear and contempt for onesss' very *exxxisssstenccce* — can be both very perssssonally empowering, and a particularly usssseful tool in our variousss ssschemesss. Asss I sssuspect you have gathered for yourssself in recccent monthsss, *frightening* our enemiesss keepsss them in our power, in a way that sssimple death doesss not."

The sheep-bear nodded, hesitantly. It had, admittedly, felt good as *hell* to slowly frighten their former teammate while choking the air out of his lungs. The look on his face as he'd realized that Maddy was serious, and no longer taking his *shit*, was worth the price of admission to supervillainy alone. The look in Slider's wet, terrified eyes as they'd snapped his leg and made him genuinely afraid, on the other hand... that was *euphoric*, somehow. On some level, haunted by memories of inculcated Heroic self-righteousness past, it was mildly disconcerting. On another, they realized that they wanted *more* of that dark thrill.

Celia slithered forward and coiled loosely around the centre of the room, encircling the sheep-bear, and crossed her arms before her impressive breasts, tightly covered in an industrial-looking black latex bustier. She raised a finger to her scaled lips enigmatically. "And henccce I have a ssseeming contradictttion before me. You are eager to help, and that much isss... uncomplicated; you are *earnessst* in how driven you are to contribute, even understanding that it isss not a requirement or a compulsssion. It wasss a common theme, in fact, in each of your acquaintancccessss' endorsssementssss."

Maddy perked up, grateful, but still uncertain.

The lamia continued as the screen blanked out and faded to black, leaving the room once again only faintly lit in low pink-purple. "But in ssso doing, you both fear to kill thossse who would dessstroy you, and long to *hurt* them. Ssshould you become a field agent, could you alssso be relied upon to *not* indulge those needsss — valid and sssusssstaining asss they may be, I well know — when appropriate? In sssum, can you ssseparate busssinessss from pleasssure, and viccce versssa, for the good of the Korps?"

"Yes," the sheep-bear said, firmly. "I can."

"We ssshall sssee," Celia said, her alien face impassive, but her tone seeming to suggest wry anticipation. "Maddy, you are approved for field agent training and provisssional qualificatttion. ROSSSE will draw up a ssschedule for you. I note too that you have already taken ssssstepsss to ssseek out counsssel from one of the Medical Divisssion'sss contingent of therapisssstsss; *exxxcellent*. I would have insssisssted upon that asss well, and that you have already done ssso isss a point in your favour, in assssessssing your sssuitability for field work."

Maddy gulped. "Thank you, Mistress."

"Sssecond, I mussst confessss that I had another motive in prioritizzzing *you*, little sssheep-bear, in my busssy ssschedule. And that reassson—"

Celia nodded towards the screen, and it flared to life again; a new profile loaded into the RCG minicam playback interface. It was the site commander's own, Maddy quickly realized. It showed the lamia's view of a scene on a roof, focused on a brawny horse in the ragged remains of a TPA uniform; the video froze on the Hero's close-up face.

"—isss that we brought home a *guessst* from thisss week'sss unpleasssantnessss. Sssomeone I believe you may have met, in the courssse of your brief PHL career."

Maddy squinted at the equine's profile until it hit her. "That's, um — yes! He wasn't *purple* then, but we were both at this training conference thing in New Hampshire; there was a big Teepa contingent, and most of them were just out-and-out phobic to my face. Including that duck I kicked the shit out of, and *yeah, okay*, I enjoyed that. But — I want to say, Slate? Slate, right? — wasn't. He wasn't gross at all about me being this diversity mascot trans girl, or being, like, so young and inexperienced. He was respectful. He was *kind*, even; called me 'ma'am.' And as much as I'm glad I'm not a Hero anymore, that was the kind of thing that used to *sustain* me." She paused, as realization hit her. "Wait, so you took him prisoner?"

Celia shook her head solemnly. "No. I *made her an offer.*"

"Oh. *Ohhhh.* And so—"

"—Ssso, we have asss our guessst, a horssse with no name, who appearsss to have very recccently realizzzed a great many important thingsss about herssself and her placcce in the world," the lamia nodded gently. "It would be *apprecccciated* if you were to help usss in thisss matter, asss a very recccent recruit yourssself. A ressssourcccce, a *sssupport*, ssshould ssshe wisssh it. The persssspective of another former Hero peer, one ssshe hasss at leassst *met* before, could be usssseful to her."

"Of course! I'm so glad she… I mean, I remember when *my* egg cracked. I could have used a friend."

"Asss do I, though in a lessss metaphorical sssensssse. In any event, thank you, Maddy. And ssso we come to my *third* point." The snake woman's posture changed again, and her loose coils suddenly constricted, until they were only a half-metre away from the sheep-bear's boots. She *loomed* and sneered down her snout. "One of my resssponsssibilitiesss, here at RIV, isss training dommesss."

Maddy's eyes snapped wide open; she hadn't expected the conversation about field agent qualification to take this turn. "...Oh...?"

"You've changed your broadcasssted dating profile with ROSSSE ssseveral times sssincccce you began usssing the feature, each time sssuggesssting an increasssing *confidencccce*. Each day, ssshowing the kind of dominant butccch you wisssh to be; I can sssee with my own eyesss how you try to carry yourssself, too. And, of courssse, there isss the matter of pain, and the evident uncccertainty you feel about *enjoying* inflicting it." Celia's tongue slipped in and out of her pursed lips.

"Is, uh... would that be a condition of getting certified for field work too...?"

"No. Not at all. It isss merely... an optttion I am offering to one who might, perhapsss, be interesssted in exxxploring *additttional* avenuesss of educatttion, if planning to ssstay with usss here in Aussstin. Broadening your ssskill ssset in this manner would be an entirely ssseparate matter and would not influenccce any part of your evaluatttion for field agent training, I asssssure you. It could be desssirable to hone your practicccesss in that regard, and to dissscusssss, let usss sssay, a few important, underlying *precccceptsss*, as one aficccionado to another," the woman said with the hint of a smirk. "You might well find sssome of thessse to be *transssferable* ssskillsss, at that."

Maddy took a deep breath, flushing. As surprised as she'd been, the thought appealed to her. "I, um... I think I'd like to try that out. Thank you, Mistress."

"Exxxcellent," Celia hissed with a self-satisfied expression. "ROSSSE, you may ssshare my *private* training ssschedule to arrange for our young friend'sss sssesssssionsss. Pleassse make cccertain that Maddy isssn't *too* terribly tired out from sssparring, or what have you, when we meet."

[Confirmed, Mistress.]

Celia folded her arms as she slunk back over to a position behind her desk, all business again. "I regret that there are other pressssing mattersss to which I mussst attend." Her eye twinkled as she looked down her snout at the comparatively-tiny sheep-bear. "I look forward to our firssst... assssignation," the lamia grinned. "Be ssseeing you."

"Thank you! Thank you, Celia," Maddy replied, nervously rubbing her arm and biting her lip, expression neutral; turning on one motorcycle-booted heel, she trod out of the office to leave the commander to her tasks. The sheep-bear was thankful that she managed to at least get halfway down the hall before beginning to snort and snicker uncontrollably, beaming, delighted at her *luck*.

With a spring in their step, they proceeded to the elevator, enroute to the foodservices sector for their lunch date. When they told her, Mama Mabes would *definitely* get a kick out of this...

<hr>

March 22, 2023

The brown rat stood at attention in Caleb Hagen's grim, bunker-like office underneath the Mississauga waterfront and tried to keep his expression neutral. He despised the man (and that was fine, because the Director of Ontario's Heroes despised everyone else, too) but his position as a Hero demanded *some* propriety, even if both men knew it was the barest of put-ons.

He coughed, when the wolverine didn't acknowledge him upon entering the room. Hagen's secretary Lola had surely informed him Slider was here, hadn't she? "Reporting as ordered, sir," he said evenly, snapping off a flouncier salute than was probably wise.

Hagen took a deep breath, and looked up, scowling. "*Salton*," he said darkly. "Would you be so kind as to summarize your recent achievements as Oakes' handler on the... special project?"

Neal "Slider" Salton grimaced. In truth, he had none; Heartforce had fucked off and defected to the Korps *months* ago. Fearful that the sheep-bear might return to break his other leg, he'd weighed the risk of making a full report of how badly he'd fumbled the mission with his self-satisfied ego-tripping — he'd thought he could bait Oakes into doing something to get messily fired, or even criminally prosecuted — against the hope that that fucking *diversity hire* was serious in claiming to be quitting the super game entirely. (That was, as long as *he* didn't do anything to Oakes' dopey mother and slutty frosh sister.)

So... he'd lied, and then kept lying. He'd spun a story about how the sheep-bear had beat the shit out of him as some kind of twisted test of loyalty to the magenta-clad sex weirdos, all according to plan — but it had to look *good*, hence the multiple fractures, internal bleeding, and severe concussion. (Slider was *happy* to take one for the team, of course, as he'd repeatedly insisted to Hagen and team lead Lightbox in his medical ward debrief, several days later.) He'd continued expanding on the lies, submitting entirely-falsified progress reports, based as best he could on available intel... and catering whenever possible to the boss's wild-eyed, paranoid obsession with Korps perversions. Even *Slider* was pretty sure the queers didn't quite fuck as often, or as creatively, as Hagen breathlessly imagined.

Regardless, pressured to come up with some kind of *results* after several weeks of submitting nothing but increasingly lurid, entirely fictional accounts of Oakes' sexcapades, the rat did the only thing he could think of: he broke into Lightbox's office, found out what he needed to know about the really *good* OH slush funds, and began siphoning off just enough cash to begin (to his disgust) *paying* for intel. He'd been able to make several busts that way, painting the petty criminals with barely-observable powers he'd detained as key Korps agents, supposedly per the sheep-bear's tip-offs. Hagen had seemed faintly irritated but satisfied at the arrests.

Until now, apparently.

"Nothing new since my last filed report on Monday, sir. Our last contact was early in the morning of the 19th, at a vacant house in Brampton. We discussed potential missing persons leads we suspect were abducted, brainwashed and sex-trafficked by the Korps. As a new recruit, it's still taking some time to build enough trust to be let in on the *real* villainy. *Sir.*"

The wolverine nodded. He turned to his workstation and clicked around briefly, murmuring irritably to himself. After a moment, he turned his massive flatscreen display around on its crane-like mounting arm to show his subordinate. "Salton... *watch this*, would you?"

It was shaky bodycam footage, the rat could tell that much. The timestamp read 03:26 AM. It was clearly some kind of skirmish between a Hero team in mostly blue-and-white uniforms, and Korps agents; he recognized nobody, nor was he certain who the team might be, but the pink visors and body-hugging black leather and rubber on their opponents were obvious enough indicators. The melee continued for a moment — punches were thrown, some kind of energy discharge powers activated — but he couldn't see the relevance.

"Sir...?"

"Just keep watching," Hagen said with a growl, rage in his eyes.

That was when a burly figure in a maroon leather jacket, tactical cargo pants and heavy motorcycle boots slammed into the frame, facing away from the bodycam-wearer. They attempted to dodge a barreling heavy and rolled out of frame for a moment. When the figure popped up their head from out of a defensive crouch, Salton recognized the unhinged, bloodthirsty leer on the ursine face... and the short, curved horns... and the streaks of red dye in the close-cropped hair. *To say nothing of the pink visor.* It was Madison Oakes. Fucking *Heartforce.*

Slider was only semi-consciously aware of cringing involuntarily, and making a surprised, straining choking noise from somewhere deep in his throat. The sheep-bear roared and said something in the recording; he didn't register what it was, beyond a threat.

Oakes then proceeded to telekinetically pick up one of the Heroes, a slim gecko wearing mirror-shades, and *bash his face into the bodycam-wearer's* over and over and over again, until the gecko was rag dolled off to the side in a bloody, groaning heap. His teammate's feathered hands reached up past the device's field of view, and shakily moved back down (also covered in blood) before the avian fell onto his back with a pained quacking noise. The last few seconds of the footage had the camera aimed straight up at water-stained drop ceiling tiles, jarred only slightly by the rhythmic motion of the Hero's ragged breathing, which was uncomfortably audible on the soundtrack. By the time Hagen paused the video, the sheep-bear was laughing maniacally, off-screen, and daring the remaining upright Heroes to approach.

The wolverine stood, *looming*. He folded his still-bulky arms menacingly in front of his chest, every inch still the ex-RCMP heavy who had been Canadian Shield, despite the too-tight gray suit and cheap blue tie he wore. In a tense, seething growl, he began. "Salton, that footage came from the Texas Protectorate Assembly operations early this Sunday morning. *In Texas*, in case that wasn't clear. Seems like they tried to move against the Korps in the Austin area and made a soup sandwich of it. Bloody *amateurs*, thinking they can just go in like riot police." He fixed his eyes — nearly as unhinged as Oakes' — on Slider. "But what *I* would like to know, right here, right now, is how you might *care* to *explain* how in the God-damned Hell you met with Oakes in **Brampton** on Sunday *WHEN HE WAS IN FUCKING TEXAS?!!*"

That was the moment that Slider realized *just how badly* he had fucked up.

Tune-Up
by Bibi Heartsglow

May 2, 2023

Dawn really did do excellent work, Maddy mused, as they wiped an excess of grease off of their freshly-polished and shaped hoof-nails. Their V-Max hardly *needed* their close attention — the drones that looked over the hangars and garages of the Korps's RIV base could hardly be accused of being anything less than thorough — but the sheep-bear hybrid found a sort of quiet comfort in taking personal charge of their vehicle, all the same.

Unfortunately, her quiet comfort wasn't meant to last.

The door slid open with its usual trademark-infringing sound, and a leather-clad jackal drone strode inside accompanied by a short, top-heavy vulpine in a Canadian tuxedo and a plain white undershirt: Ellen Foxpaw, the Hero formerly known as Lawful Neutral. Whether she was formerly known as a *Hero* was something of a sticking point, Maddy had found during what had turned out to be an unforgettable luncheon.

And here she was, making her way toward the propped-open Maserati beside Maddy's V-Max, under the low ceiling of the Small Personal Vehicles Garage (referred to by some as the "SPVG," and by more than a few as the "Supervag"). Her hair was pulled back past her ears in a short, sporty red ponytail that only served to sharpen her easy, smiling features. The sheep-bear was only just trying to decide on an appropriate greeting when the fox noticed them in turn, perking up and breaking off from her jackal escort to make a beeline towards them.

"Maddy!" she hailed, striding right up to her and coming to an almost comically-abrupt halt.

"Hey, Ellen." They glanced dubiously at the sports car beside them, then back at the fox. "Wouldn't think she'd be within your price range, with how much Phillips wasn't paying you."

"If she's ever mine, then something has gone *horribly* wrong," Ellen said, chuckling with a bit of discomfort at the thought. "She's Carmen's, actually."

"She lets you stick your fingers in her?"

Ellen stared back at them like Maddy had just suggested she take up amateur chainsaw-swallowing, then doubled over as she broke into a coughing fit.

"The *car*, I mean."

"*Oh!*" Ellen wheezed. "Right." The fox had gone a very arctic shade of pale in an instant, and Maddy realized with dull surprise that the rumors about her crush on the tantalizing tabby were probably true. "Yeah. Well. Kind of — I'm trying to brush up on some old interests now that I'm, uh."

She trailed off, and Maddy, despite herself, couldn't help but wonder where that sentence had been ambling.

"All right, I'll bite. What's got Ellen Foxpaw: Everyone's Hero, angling for a job as Ellen Foxpaw: Carmen Rayne's Mechanic?"

Ellen squirmed on the spot; it was a strangely familiar motion, but Maddy couldn't quite place it. Finally, she spoke:

"I, uh. Decided to stay. For sure."

Maddy regarded the vixen with some surprise. Truthfully, they hadn't known that was in question — when they got right down to it, they weren't sure the Korps would *let* someone just… leave.

"For Carmen?"

"For me." Ellen cleared her throat. "Carmen helped."

"A-ha." Maddy eyed the fox, then the fox's Maserati-in-law. "Well, we'd better not keep the lady waiting. I'm all done here; do you know what's wrong with yours?"

"That *is* the mystery." The pair rejoined the jackal, who had apparently been standing silently at attention, waiting patiently for the pair to finish their conversation, xeir strappy leathers shining with a similar gloss as the cars and trucks and motorbikes under the many ceiling lights. "I've been looking over the manuals, but this is a modified car to begin with. They don't expect me to fix it… buuuuuuut I've been given clearance to look at it 'til my eyeballs dry up and see if I come to the same conclusion Abasi here did, and then maybe they'll let me watch someone certified do the work."

"That would be me as well," the drone chimed in.

"Right! Turns out xey're something of a jack-of-al-trades. So: care to join me?"

The headlights blinked and the doors swung up and open in distinctive style. Maddy found themself sinking into the luxurious passenger's seat as Ellen slipped the key into the ignition and gave it a turn.

"Engine turns over," Maddy noted, and Ellen nodded.

"I might need to run it around the garage a bit and see if I can figure out what xey found."

"Might just." Maddy leaned back and got comfortable, careful to lay their horns without poking the seat. Ellen adjusted hers, scooching closer to the wheel and lowering it to fit her shorter frame. To be honest, Maddy was a bit surprised she could see over the dashboard.

But the car didn't go, and Ellen didn't make any move to ask the jackal if she was allowed to drive it. An uncomfortable silence against the purr of the engine stretched between them until, just before Maddy was about to insist on breaking it, Ellen did for them.

"So, uh. Hey, do you... remember... last time we talked?"

Maddy did, in fact, remember. She'd been less than delighted to find that Ellen had about as much boot lingering on her breath as she herself had had, only a few months before. Still, sometimes it beggared belief that someone so naive could be sitting beside her, hundreds of metres beneath Austin, breaking bread with people whose view of Heroes hadn't the first sniff of charity.

"I think so," Maddy said, and meant "yes."

Ellen drew in a sharp breath through her teeth. "Thought you might." She leaned back as far as her pushed-forward seat would allow, folding her arms beneath her impractically heavyset chest. "So, I spent... a *while* being kind of... pissy about that, I guess."

"Pissy, huh?"

"'A championship-level pissbaby,' according to Volta. The, uh... thing is, you kind of did give me a lot to think about, actually. About me, I mean, and... *Heroes*, I guess, and what kind of Hero I wasn't *actually* allowed to be. And I thought about how, like... I *did* want to come out. At some point, it stopped being about what my parents would think, and became about what *Jack* would think. And I just kind of moved from hiding from one gaoler to another without thinking about whether or not it made *any* sense for Heroes to have to *hide*. Like... we were supposed to be the champions of the world, right? Fighting for what's good and all that? And yet... so many of us had to hide *from the other champions*."

"Interesting choice of word, there," Maddy replied sardonically.

"I mmmmight have given that article a re-read or two," Ellen admitted, nearly as sheepish as Maddy. "But still — I guess when you get right down to it, it's no wonder so many of us end up, y'know." She gestured. "Here."

Maddy raised an eyebrow and hoped that it outpaced the grin she couldn't quite hold back. "In Carmen's Maz?"

Ellen blanched. "H — I mean, I would have *seen*—"

It took a moment of sputtering for her to spy Maddy's wry smirk, and Ellen abruptly turned her pinkening face to the window.

"You know what I meant!"

"Yeah," Maddy snorted. "I mean, honestly, I *get it*. I get *you*. For the longest time, I just thought... I thought if I was good enough — *did* good enough — even the assholes would respect me, and then they'd respect people like *us* in turn."

"But it never really works, does it?"

"It never works! Because at the end of the day, no matter how much good you do, you did it under *their* thumb, and that's all they'll remember. The best you'll ever be is 'one of the good ones.' You'd be better off trying to do good *without them*—"

"...Except that the 'real' Heroes would show up to arrest you for... frick, what was it? It wouldn't be vigilantism if you're putting out a fire, but... obstructing emergency services, maybe?"

Maddy shrugged, their jacket creaking. "It really didn't matter what they said, just what they figured out made the most sense to put on the incident report a few days later... once they figured out the best story they could tell with the evidence."

Ellen grimaced. "We were private — mostly we just jotted down a few notes and handed over any evidence to the local PD and they did the incident reporting for us."

"And you never... *looked?*"

"Once in a while, when it seemed relevant. Nothing in them seemed... *too* far off, I guess?" She shrugged. "But I always figured the courts would filter out any problems, so I could just focus on, y'know." She raised a fist in a wavering mockery of a powerful stance. "*Saving the world!*"

"By making sure people who *really* needed help got three hots and a cot?"

Ellen clicked her teeth through her grimace. "Exactly. Everyone tells you that you're helping those people by getting them off the streets. And hell, maybe sometimes you *are*, but..."

"...But usually not," the sheep-bear finished for her, shaking her head.

"But usually not," Ellen agreed.

Maddy took a deep breath, arms folded over their chest. "You know, it's frustrating. There were parts of that job I *did* like. But even those parts had the same *stink* on them. I'd pull a car full of people out of the lake and I'd feel *good* about it, but at the end of the day that was only a part of my job so that it could legitimize the rest of it. Every good thing we did was to make people — *us included* — feel better about the Heroes who... I don't know, used their superspeed to disassemble a homeless camp in seconds."

Ellen groaned. "That was in New York, wasn't it? What's-his-nuts. Speed Trap."

"Would you believe that guy chose his name *specifically* so he could go around asking trans people if they were 'triggered'?"

The vulpine grimaced. "That's... ugh, he's still employed, even."

"*Extremely.* There's a bidding war for his next contract."

"Between New York and *who?*"

Maddy shot her a look.

"...You're screwing with me."

"Wish I was."

Ellen let her face flop against the window, cheek sliding down the glass as she gave a moan of frustration. Maddy let her stew in silence for a moment; there wasn't much to say, and it was better to simply let the fox cycle through the five stages of grief until she finally settled back into the backrest and rubbed the stiffness out of her cheeks.

"Nowadays I can't help but wonder what life would be like if folks like us were *actually* meant to help people and not just sweep the 'unsightlies' under the rug."

Maddy hummed her agreement. "I guess we'll just have to win and find out, then, right?"

"Right." Ellen snorted, shook off the lingering dread off her like a dog coming in from the rain, and buried an elbow in Maddy's shoulder. "Should be easy now that we've got *you* on our side."

"Hey, now," they chuckled. "You can't go around giving psychics swelled heads. Who knows what kind of power you'll unleash?"

The fox grinned and fell back against the driver's seat with a fancily-cushioned thump. "Well, hey, if there's anybody I trust with that kind of power…"

Maddy opened her mouth to speak, then fell back with a curious expression. "If I didn't know better, Foxpaw, I'd wonder if you were flirting with me."

August 16, 2023

"I'm starting to think you *were* flirting with me," huffed the sheep-bear, adjusting the towel beneath them to smooth a wrinkle that had been agitating their knee for the past few minutes of car sex.

"*I'm* starting to think you just like to see how flexible I am," grunted Ellen as her feet twitched on either side of her head. "Now *please* let me down — or stuff that handkerchief in me."

Ellen felt the sheep-bear cum *gush* out of her still-clenching cunt, soaking the rag as she let her legs fall back down and Maddy retreated from the Maz to make room.

"Fuck, that's as cramped as always," the sheep-bear groaned, cock twitching and dripping a spatter of cum onto the garage floor.

"I'll tell Carmen to get a bigger car."

"I meant *you*."

"Oh." Ellen stared back at them. "I don't have a car."

ACKNOWLEDGEMENTS

This collection was originally published online, with the title story originally separated into *Champion* (Chapters 1 – 4) and *Change of Heart* (Chapters 5 – Epilogue). The following characters appear by permission of their owners:

+ Caleb Hagen and Sunrise belong to Karen King
+ Carmen and Volta Rayne belong to Syntax Takes
+ Ellen and Vixie Foxpaw, Russell, and Rabble belong to Bibi Heartsglow
+ Dawn, Orion, and Celia belong to Runa Fjord
+ Mabel Greysmoke and Betty Kallist belong to Mabel Ramona
+ Liam, Martin and Swashplate belong to Lexi Reynolds

The *original* genesis of Maddy was, basically, that I wanted to have a "fifteen minutes into the future" contemporary OC, to interact with my friends' contemporary OCs. I've enjoyed writing in the "Historical Korpsverse" niche, but it ended up that the characters I'd spent a lot of time fleshing out before this story — and who were intimately tied to, e.g., the specific historical context of being a middle-aged closeted queer professional in the 1990s — didn't make much sense to write supervillain spy intrigue in this setting by the 2020s.

(See my short stories *It's All Yours* (set in 1987), *Disclosure* (set in 1992), *Chapter Break* (set in 1994) and *After Hours* (set in 2004/2010), the last of which also introduces Roger "Heartwood" Oakes in the course of Rin recounting their field career-ending injuries.)

On the other hand, I *had* once written about a raging asshole Hero named Heartwood, and I got to thinking… how did he treat his family? How would *they* have dealt with his untimely death in the line of duty?

And what if he had a kid, railroaded into upholding his Legacy when they manifested powers of their own... and they turned out to be queer?

From there, it was just a question of figuring out: so, what would come next for Maddy, after she learned the truth? She'd be free to pursue validation and fulfillment in response to the things she was denied in the course of being forced into a Hero career, right? It's always fascinating to come up with a character, and then work out how to figuratively mash their action figure together with all the others — accompanied by "pew pew" or making-out noises, of course, as the case may be.

As to Maddy's characterization, I wanted to work out some complicated feelings about career success in my old job, since coming out as trans in the late 2010s. In the end it was just too toxic; I quit in the early 2020s for a position where I didn't feel obligated to be the Diversity, Equity & Inclusion component of middle management. Relatedly, my fursona Grace Dunlop is very close to a pure self-insert character in my Korps works, and she's specifically spun out from a wish-fulfillment answer to the question: "What if I'd transitioned earlier, and didn't make certain life and career choices I regret?" What I realized in writing *Change of Heart*, though, is that Maddy (while not fundamentally *me* in the same way as Grace) is actually something of a rebuttal to that premise; even if I'd had the knowledge and self-awareness and necessary epiphanies to transition earlier than I did, I surely would still have made *other* bad choices. And so Maddy did!

Similarly: Slider. I was very happy to see how much readers enjoyed him as a moderate-threat-level antagonist, as this was published serially, and I was considering all kinds of directions for him as I wrote — including some I discarded foremost because I was the wrong person to do it. In the end, though, I think it was a good call to just write Slider as starting from the baseline of being a very ordinary, boring jerk of a coworker; That Fucking Guy who can't be written off solely as your usual hate-spewing maniac, like Caleb Hagen or Roger Oakes, but remains obnoxious to work with as a trans person. Neal Salton is smart and genuinely competent (if prone to the arrogant overconfidence that's his repeated undoing), and usually canny enough to keep his harassment plausibly deniable around others. That's a much more difficult kind of transphobe to deal with in some ways, because they better understand how to carry out their antagonism under the radar of "allies."

It's surreal, in some ways, revising these notes in 2024. *Change of Heart* isn't where I started writing fiction, nor even fiction in the Korps setting, but it's where a lot of things started coming together — especially the extensive collaborations with my dear friends in the MFBC. Maddy wouldn't exist as she does without all of their enthused feedback, and subsequent sheep-bear (or "beep," playfully) stories would only continue that thread. Look for the continued adventures of Maddy Gillespie soon, in the second book of the series, *Snowflake*...

Korps Universe Glossary

Common terms in the Korps Universe

The Korps — To the public, the Korps (pronounced "core") is known as a shadowy, secretive band of supervillains based in Canada, with a reputation for mind control and plans to take over the world; Korps operatives are believed to be easily identified by their trademark RCGs, scandalously revealing costumes, and the magenta helix insignia. Under the leadership of the mysterious "Overlord," by the early years of the 21st century, their brazen criminal schemes and growing reach throughout North America and Europe have authorities (and allied Hero groups) increasingly concerned. The truth is far more complicated than any of those authorities know, starting nearly seven thousand years ago with a warrior's exile to Earth by his conquering interdimensional empire... but that's another story.

RCGs — Rose-Colored Glasses are a powerful, versatile AR/VR visor headset that interfaces directly with the wearer's brain, created by the Korps. In addition to operating as standalone PDAs and communication devices, RCGs also have the ability to affect the wearer's mind and mental condition to a granular level. A civilian model exists, distributed by Korps front and consumer electronics manufacturer Thornetech (alias Thorntech, due to trademark registration conflicts in various international markets) in a plausibly-deniable manner. Models for the consumer market have comparable base functionality to Korps devices, but are severely underclocked and have many higher-level functions disabled at a hardware level in order to avoid suspicion.

ACGs — Amber-Colored Glasses have much the same functionality as RCGs, but are crafted with additional anti-magic and anti-memetic defenses for use by KDARC agents. They do not render the user immune to magical effects; however, they can be crucial in efforts against mystical and eldritch threats by adaptively blocking cognitohazards and helping to keep the wearer's sense of self intact should reality start to weaken.

Aurora Squadron — Aurora Squadron, Canada's federal-level Hero group, is part of the Canadian Armed Forces and based out of Department of National Defence HQ — popularly known as the War Tower — in Ottawa, ON. Closely overseen by Minister of National Defence Arthur Simonds, formerly the second Hero to be known as True North, Aurora Squadron fields a highly professional, dedicated and capable team of Heroes in the fight against superpowered threats to Canada, including the enigmatic Korps.

Bradley Group — The United States' federal-level Hero group is formally named the National Hero Administration, but rarely known as anything but "Bradley Group" due to its institutional history; during the WWII invasion of Normandy, a secret strategic reserve of supers were activated to join American forces under the command of Gen. Omar Bradley, with "Bradley Group" used as a code name for this classified unit.

After the war, the group was put under the jurisdiction of the FBI, until later becoming its own massive, independent federal agency. In the present day, Bradley's superpowered forces number in the hundreds, with Heroes based all over the United States; considered highly prestigious within the industry and known to be selective in recruitment, even Bradley's lesser-known operatives are perceived by the public to be more competent and professional than many of their state-level counterparts.

Candesca — Candesca (pronounced "can-dess-ah") is one name for the energy that practitioners of the mystic arts manipulate, in order to work their spells and enchantments on the material plane. While other terminology is used for this concept in various diverse cultures, candesca is the neutral, academic, non-appropriative term most commonly used within the Korps. While a renewable resource, the body can under normal circumstances hold only a small amount. To paraphrase Lao Tzu, like a bowl, the magic-user must be refilled after being drained; the bowl is still useful, but has nothing left to give.

Cape — Vernacular for "Hero." Neutral to derogatory.

Chișinău Protocols — Shorthand for a series of separate but inter-related 1969 agreements negotiated in the city of Chișinău, Moldova, as amendments, codicils or interpretive addenda to various existing international treaties, including the 1899 and 1907 *Hague Conventions*, the 1948 *Universal Declaration of Sentient Rights*, the 1948 *Genocide Convention*, and the 1951 *Convention Relating to the Status of Refugees*. A Second Chișinău Conference was convened in 2006 to rationalize these provisions with and prepare similar addenda to more recent international instruments, such as the 1979 *Convention on the Elimination of All Forms of Discrimination Against Women*, and the 1998 *Rome Statute*, but these too are colloquially referred to as merely part of the same *Protocols*.

Collectively, the *Protocols* specify the permissible use of superpowers and treatment of supers by parties to the agreements, in both peacetime and in armed conflict. These agreements also introduced into international law the still-contentious declaration that involuntary, long-term restriction or suppression of powers in a way that causes the subject "greater than *de minimis* physical, psychological or moral harms" is a form of torture, war crime, or crime against sentience.

Color Guard — Bradley Group's elite strike team, currently consisting of twelve active members; each Hero's callsign and uniform is color-coded and themed around their powers for marketing purposes. Considered the best of the best, as patriotic as the Fourth of July, national polling consistently indicates higher levels of confidence and support for the Color Guard among Americans than even the military. However, the team's seemingly-flawless reputation is only maintained by Bradley's ruthless PR department, which has covered up or prevented their innumerable scandals from reaching the public consciousness.

Empire Enhancements — A subdivision of Korps medical services dedicated to in-depth body modification, including transgender care.

Everyone's Hero Association — The Everyone's Hero Association is a private Hero group based in Milwaukee, WI. It was founded in the 2010s by serial venture capitalist Jack Phillips, who named it as a challenge to Bradley Group's official legal designation, the National Hero Administration; government elites might have their own pet Heroes in Bradley, but the EHA is for *everyone*, as he invariably recites in press releases. Its roster is made up of supers with weak or unwieldy powers, and the group was considered something of a joke until Phillips' gamble on (cost-effectively!) finding a diamond in the rough paid off with Ellen "Lawful Neutral" Foxpaw's rise to B-tier prominence.

Federal Meta-Registry — The Federal Meta-Registry is a massive database maintained by Bradley Group of all U.S. citizens and resident foreign nationals with classes of superpowers deemed potentially dangerous. Registration is mandatory for all such known supers present within the United States, even if only briefly transiting through sovereign American territory. Evading or refusing registration in any way (particularly by intentionally concealing powers) is a serious criminal offense under the U.S. Code, and may be prosecuted as acts of terrorism in some circumstances.

HCH — Home County Heroes was a Hero group operated by the British government in the southeastern counties surrounding London. It was fully privatized in the 1980s under the Thatcher government, with all licenses, assets and personnel contracts sold to a corporate Hero management firm.

The former group has been variously divided and subsumed by other organizations since the 1990s, and though no organization called HCH technically exists anymore, some of its former member supers are still regularly referred to as Home County Heroes in the press and by the public. One such member is the Hampshire-born Howard "Green Belt" Bride.

Heavy — A heavy is a cape whose powers and role revolve around tanking damage and being a physical threat, usually having a powerset revolving around super-strength and enhanced durability or resistance to injuries.

Hero — When capitalized, Hero usually refers to a professional (and professionally-licensed) career superhero, whether part of a government or privately-operated Hero group. While Hero licensing requirements vary from jurisdiction to jurisdiction, most require some form of accredited training, full disclosure of an applicant's name and other personal information to the jurisdictional licensing authority for security checks, and an oath to serve the public good or otherwise to be of "good character."

Most professional Heroes have superpowers, but a significant minority are unpowered gadgeteers, stealth operators, or even just heavily-armed mercenary types.

Informally, superheroes may be referred to interchangeably as "heroes" regardless of whether licensed and operating in a legal capacity. Unlicensed heroes may also be referred to as independent heroes, vigilantes or mercenaries in some contexts.

Hero group — A Hero group is any team or force of licensed Heroes. When directly operated or officially backed by some level of government, Hero groups are effectively a type of specialized law enforcement agency or military unit, with Hero members typically being granted similar legal powers to those of law enforcement officers in their jurisdiction. Private-sector Hero groups also exist, with their members typically having lesser legal powers similar to those of private investigators, security consultants, bodyguards and/or bounty hunters, depending on local laws and the political attitudes of authorities.

Significant Canadian Hero groups in these works include Aurora Squadron and the member Hero groups of the Provincial Heroes' League (PHL). Significant American Hero groups in these works include Bradley Group, the Everyone's Hero Association, and the Texas Protectorate Assembly.

KATS — Korps Aerial Tactical Support (KATS) is responsible for pilot training, air freight logistics, and fleet maintenance. Aircraft in the division's care include the Korps's signature gravwell-drive Condor VTOL gunship platform, as well as cargo planes, helicopters, and a small wing of rarely-deployed fighter jets.

KARD — The Korps Archives and Records Division (KARD), sometimes referred to simply as "Records," is a division of the Korps responsible for the acquisition, preservation, and circulation of various media. KARD acts as both a library of media resources collected over the decades, and a secure repository of sensitive information useful (and yet to be proven useful) to the organization's goals

Beginning as a loose collection of analysts recruited from dissatisfied members of the intelligence community in the years following WWII, it was not organized into an autonomous operational division for some time. KARD has branches across multiple bases, but is headquartered at and conducts the bulk of its operations from KDS. KARD regularly partners with other divisions and individual field agents, in order to help equip them with the most esoteric and obscure information required.

KDARC — The Korps Division for Arcane Research and Control (KDARC) is responsible for the study, safekeeping and strategic use of the strange and unusual. From ancient arcana to demonic incursions, memetic objects and more, if a problem for the Korps is outside the mundane — that is, outside the mundane in a world of supers — there's a better-than-zero chance that KDARC will be on the front lines.

KDARC was originally founded by the enigmatic Carlotta Davisson and several colleagues in 1935 as the Davisson Arcane Research Company (DARC) of Minneapolis, MN, and headquartered in the massive Madison Center. In the years following WWII, Carlotta came into contact with the Overlord, and DARC was fully integrated into the Korps in the early 1960s. In 1968, the Madison Center mysteriously vanished from the Minneapolis skyline; unbeknownst to the public, it had been magically moved to Toronto, ON, at the early lowest-excavated depths of KDS, to serve as the newly-minted division's secret headquarters.

Despite claiming to be a "civilian research division", KDARC maintains tactical operation teams (named TAROT) and a great deal of independence from the Korps. Some agents wonder why the Overlord overlooks the pseudo-corporate structure, and rumours abound of unionization attempts by KDARC's senior staff. Still, much of the division's motivations, intentions, and methods remain as enigmatic, incomprehensible, and dangerous as the bleeding edge of the arcane itself.

KDS — Korps Downsview Site is the headquarters of the Korps, located beneath the former Downsview Airport (previously Canadian Forces Base Toronto) in the industrial sprawl of Toronto, ON. With a footprint of over eight square kilometres and many subterranean sub-levels, futuristically eco-urbanist in aesthetics and centrally-planned design, it is a completely self-sufficient underground city. KDS was slowly built outward from a small excavation in the 1970s, becoming fully operational as a headquarters only in the 1980s-1990s.

In addition to the command, logistics and strategic functions required for the vast supervillain organization to operate, like all major Korps bases, KDS features apartment-like residential sectors, research and lab areas, an enormous medical complex, and a recreational sector that would translate to many city blocks' worth of restaurants and entertainment facilities — including a "red light district," the Dominion Club.

K-LAW — Sometimes a supervillain collective needs to engage with the legal system on its own terms; as a division, the Korps Legal Affairs Wing (K-LAW) operates covertly as the legal departments of various front companies, as well as through front law firms and other sympathetic individual lawyers in private practice.

Criminal defense of Korps members and allies on trial is only a small part of K-LAW agents' work. The majority of K-LAW's resources are directed towards litigation to gather intelligence on targets or tie them up in red tape, and street-level *pro bono* work helping marginalized people assert their rights without regard for the cost of legal fees.

KTAKES — The Korps Tactical Acquisitions and Kleptocratic Extirpation Squadron (KTAKES) is a now-disbanded division of the Korps that specialized in obtaining "lost" items and returning them to their rightful places — via. heists, capers, thefts, smash and grabs, and good old-fashioned burglary as appropriate. The group functioned as a kind of "thieves' guild" within the Korps, with their own projects, but also taking commissioned work from other divisions.

Pegasus Phalanx — A unit of the Texas Protectorate Assembly and Dallas' foremost Hero team, the Pegasus Phalanx handles the biggest threats the city faces — short of those requiring federal intervention from Bradley Group forces. While the team's roster has changed over the years, it most recently consisted of leader Kevin "Texas Trickshot" Romero, Susanne "Heavenly Dazzler" Geraldine-Walters, Chet "Macho Poleax" Huntyr, Rodrigo "Ethicoil" Alquitano III, and Slate "Slate" Johnson.

PHL — The Provincial Heroes' League (PHL) is a Canadian organization comprised of all Hero groups operated by the provincial and territorial governments, led by Director Lawrence Rockwell. The PHL aggressively advocates for 'law and order' Hero operations, and has had a great deal of friction with Aurora Squadron, accusing the federal Hero Group of being 'soft' on the Korps.

However, the PHL is not a Hero group itself, but instead a professional organization promoting the coordination and cooperation of affiliate members, as well as a powerful voice advocating for professional Heroes and the Hero industry. Heroes operating through one of its affiliates may nonetheless be indistinguishably referred to as "belonging" to the PHL, or being a "PHL Hero," and "fuck the PHL" is a popular sentiment among Korps agents operating in Canada.

Member Hero Groups include the Cascade Group or CG (British Columbia); the Prairie League or PL (Alberta, Saskatchewan and Manitoba); Ontario's Heroes or OH (Ontario); L'Association des Superheros Québécois or ASQ (Quebec, nicknamed the "Superté" by analogy to the provincial police force, the Sûreté du Québec); and the Territorial Superheroes' Association or TERSA (Nunavut, Yukon and Northwest Territories).

RIV or RIVER — RIVER is a Korps site located beneath downtown Austin, TX, secretly excavated deep below the parkland surrounding the Colorado River.

ROSE — ROSE, or the "RCG Operating System Experience," is the OS/Complex AI that runs on all networked RCGs and provides the conversational interface for wearers of RCGs. ROSE's default avatar when appearing as an augmented-reality overlay to wearers is a fox woman, but this can be customized to individual preference.

SHS — Sandy Hill Station is a Korps site located beneath downtown Ottawa, ON. Originally founded as a WWII-era safe house for the Overlord's consolidation of proto-Korps resources and personnel in Canada, it grew significantly in importance as a surveillance station during the Cold War, due to the local neighborhood's concentration of foreign embassies.

SHS was the testbed for many of the Korps' now-standard excavation and covert base-building practices, and was formerly the location of many research labs and high-level command functions, prior to Toronto's KDS becoming fully operational as a new headquarters in the 1980s-1990s.

Supers — Supers is generally vernacular for "those with superpowers," whether or not referring to superheroes generally, or whether or not licensed Heroes.

SIS — The Secret Intelligence Service, a.k.a. its wartime designation of MI6 (Military Intelligence, section 6) is an arm of the British state responsible for the gathering of foreign intelligence.

TPA — The Texas Protectorate Assembly — commonly shortened to "Teepa" by members of the Korps — is Texas' state Hero group, extremely well-funded both by the state Department of Public Safety budget, as well as substantial donations from wealthy individual benefactors and corporate partnerships.

The result is that the TPA has unusually-vast resources for a government-backed state-level Hero group, and platoons of Heroes, many trained in the TPA's own Academy facilities located throughout Texas. TPA Heroes are institutionally encouraged to approach their duties in the manner of militarized riot police or SWAT teams, exercising very little restraint or concern for civil rights.

About the Author

Grace Reed (she/her) is an actual professional deer, lives in the Toronto area, and is never, ever not tired. You can find her at www.deergrace.ca, and @deergrace on social media.

About the Publisher

FurPlanet Productions is a small press publisher serving the niche market that is furry fiction. They sell furry-themed books and comics published by themselves and most major publishers in the community. If you can't get to a furry convention where they are selling in the dealers room, visit their online stores:

FurPlanet.com for print books
BadDogBooks.com for eBooks